ELITE SQUAD

ELITE SQUAD

ELITE SQUAD

Luiz Eduardo Soares
Andre Batista
Rodrigo Pimentel

Translated by
Clifford E. Landers

WEINSTEIN
BOOKS

ISBN: 978-1-60286-080-3

First Edition
10   9   8   7   6   5   4   3   2   1

INTRODUCTION

In their daily exercises, the soldiers of the Battalion for Special Operations of the Military Police of the State of Rio de Janeiro (BOPE) learn to chant their songs of war:

"Man in black,
What is your mission?
To invade the favela
And leave bodies on the ground."

***

"Do you know who I am?
I'm the cursed dog of war.
I'm trained to kill.
Even if it costs my life,
The mission will be carried out,
Wherever it may be,
Spreading violence, death, and terror."

***

"I'm the combatant
With his face behind a mask;
The black and yellow patch
That I wear on my arms
Makes me a being unlike others:
A messenger of death.
I can prove that I am strong,
If you live to tell the tale.
I am a hero of the Nation."

***

"It's joy, it's joy
That I feel in my heart,
For a new day has dawned,
For me to carry out my mission.
I'm going to infiltrate a favela,
My rifle in my hand,
To fight against the enemy
And sow destruction."

***

"If you ask from where I come
And what my mission is:
I bear death and despair
And total destruction."

***

"The blood runs cold in my veins
And has frozen my heart.
We have neither feelings
Nor compassion.
We love our comrades
And hate the conventionals."[1]

***

"Commandos, commandos,
Just what are you?
We are only
Cursed dogs of war,
Only savage
Dogs of war."

Should the police be trained to hate and kill? Should they pride themselves on representing terror and death? Should they disdain their own colleagues who are members of different institutional units? Should they be taught to distrust the poor, the residents of favelas? Of course not. Just the opposite—they should be messengers of peace and safety, and guarantors of rights and freedom. This is what is expected of the police in a democratic state under the rule of law, a state such as Brazil. But the reality has been an even harder translation of the cruelest fiction. In the state of Rio de Janeiro in 2007 alone, 6,133 persons were murdered and another 1,330 were killed in confrontations with the police—many of the victims were executed (all of them were poor; the majority of them were young black men).

A segment of public opinion and the majority of administrators believe that the proliferation of serious crime in Brazil is due to the police's lack of freedom to employ sufficient force—that is, the degree of force they find convenient. They forget that a police corps placed above

---

[1]Conventionals, in the jargon of the BOPE, are military police who are not part of the select BOPE corps. –Ed.

the law constitutes a danger for both justice and freedom itself, and leads to the degradation of the institution: when the police acting in the favelas are given free rein to decide over the life and death of suspects, they are indirectly given the freedom to bargain with life, and this engenders an inexhaustible source of corruption, turning the police into an arm of crime and condemning it to impotence. This is the path that leads from the expectation of strength in the fight against crime to the reality of chronic ineffectiveness. It all begins with the toleration of police brutality.

Inequality in access to justice—which begins with the police's arrival and ends with the serving of a prison sentence—has perhaps been the most dramatic manifestation of Brazilian structural inequalities. There is, in practice, no citizen equality before the law. And the entire process that ends up criminalizing poverty begins on every street corner of the large cities, when policemen deal with suspects and submit the noble principles of legality to the filters of class and color. But are the police to blame? Should we condemn them, one by one, as individuals? No. They too are victims of this process. Originating, almost always, in the same communities from which the majority of their "enemies" come, they are subjected to training in which they learn that, by acting like savage dogs of war, devoting themselves to a fratricidal "war," they will be carrying out their patriotic mission and will deserve the gratitude, the affection, and the respect of society. Would, then, the responsibility not lie with the institutions that educate them for death and terror? With safety policies that stimulate police brutality? With the state, finally? A state manipulated by perverse and cynical political games? A state occupied by administrations that resign themselves to these inequalities and maneuver the police forces, submitting them to private interests?

This book, about police and politics, was written so that no more books like it will be necessary, or at least so that in the future they can be written merely as works of improbable fiction.

As Nelson Mandela taught us, to change and to ensure that one day forgiveness is possible, one must look truth in the eye and recognize it, without euphemisms or subterfuge, without hypocrisy or political rhetoric. Naked and raw. However painful and misshapen it may be. Even if we encounter it only through the mediation of fiction. "Truth and reconciliation," he said, when he overturned apartheid: reconciliation can be achieved only by passing through the hard moment of truth. Psychoanaly-

sis demonstrates that mourning is a necessary stage for overcoming suffering. Mourning presupposes the recognition of loss.

Elite Squad is dedicated to those who work inside and outside the
police forces in Brazil, in the United States, in all the world, toward less
inequality and more respect for human rights.

The accounts that make up this book are fictional until proven otherwise. Even so, any resemblance to reality is no mere coincidence. If our
imagination reflects what has actually happened, it comes from the fact that
this book stems from our experiences and our having lived, each in his own
way, the reality of public safety in Rio de Janeiro. We can attest, dear reader,
that when the narrative doesn't correspond to actual experiences it is because the latter exceed the former in violence and repulsiveness.

A powerful ally of this book and the motivation behind it is the film
of the same name, directed by José Padilha. Both the book and the film
were constructed through an exchange of ideas and, despite the difference in the two narratives, share the intention of laying bare, unabashedly,
the corruption of the police forces by bringing to the surface the subjec-
tivity and the voice of the police. Both the film and book focus, in raw fash-
ion, on a dehumanizing machinery. Our desire is to humanize victims and
executioners of the fratricidal "war," because both are pawns in a chess
game between political ambition and institutional irrationality.

—Luis Eduardo Soares, André Batista, and Rodrigo Pimentel

Contents

Part II. Two Years Later:
The City Kisses the Canvas

War Diary

Friendly Fire

The news about Amâncio took me by surprise. Maybe that's a dumb thing to say; of course it was a surprise. How can you be prepared to find out that one of your best friends has taken a bullet in the back and is hanging between life and death in the intensive care unit of a military hospital? It was more than a surprise: it was almost like catching a bullet myself. Amâncio was a policeman, too, a former BOPE sergeant. He'd left the force when his first child was born. His wife asked him to, and he felt her concern made sense. Funny. When you're in the BOPE you practically never think about danger. But danger is your constant companion. So much so that you should never be surprised by the news that a colleague is wounded and hovering between life and death in the ICU.

Amâncio's case was shocking precisely because he had already left the BOPE, and because of the reasons that had led him to get out. It was fucking ironic that he had survived

dozens of BOPE incursions into the most dangerous favelas*
to end up shot like that, on a Sunday afternoon, as he was getting ready to go home, eager to see his wife and kid after a
twenty-four-hour shift at the 2nd Battalion P2, the intelligence section. By law, P2 should limit itself exclusively to investigating improper conduct among fellow officers of the
2nd Battalion, also known as military police special operations, also known as the BOPE. But that's not what happens.
Since the civil police,† with rare exceptions, don't investigate
shit, it's P2 that campaigns‡ at the entrances to favelas, taps
traffickers' phones, and tails suspects around the city. That's
why P2 cops drive civilian cars with standard license plates.

There are several advantages to being a policeman of any
kind. One of them is that you know everybody at the military hospital. In urban warfare there's always something going on at the hospital. People come by carrying people,
visiting, telephoning to get the news. So you can understand
how it wasn't hard for me to get into the ICU, violating medical regulations. I sat down beside Amâncio, who was hooked
up to all kinds of apparatuses, and took his hand. He opened
his eyes, forced a half smile, closed his eyes, and whispered,
"It wasn't in the goddamn back. It was in the stomach. Shot
in the stomach." I felt the tremor that runs through my body
when I'm about to explode. That makes it sound like I'm

---

*Favelas are shantytowns, usually found on hillsides, in Rio de Janeiro.—Ed.

†In Brazil, the civil police (polícia civil) are separate from the military police
(polícia militar), of which the BOPE is a part.—Ed.

‡In police vocabulary, "to campaign" means to keep a watch on, to observe without being seen.

some kind of weapon, a grenade maybe. There are situations when I feel like a grenade. In this case, the metaphor is very appropriate.

Amâncio squeezed my hand and joked, "Remember the grenade?"

"Shit yes, of course I do, how could anyone forget?" I said. "The lives of the entire team were in your hand. Literally."

A clearing in the Serra do Mar range, winter, 3 A.M., some years earlier

So you don't lose the thread of the story, it's important to know the tale of the grenade. But for me to tell it, we have to leave the hospital for a moment and go back in time, to the qualifying tests for the BOPE.

After riding a horse bareback for sixty miles without resting, dying of hunger and thirst, totally devastated from physical exhaustion, our thighs and asses chafed raw, we had the option of sitting in a basin of brine. The experience showed that it was worth it to sit, despite the shooting pain. Some of us fainted from it. Even so, it was better. Whoever spared himself was unable to even move the next day: inflamed sores covered with pus; swollen thighs, balls, and ass. The result? Immobilized, the nonsitters were washed up. And the worst part was the ritual of humiliation that went with their dismissal: they had to dig a grave and simulate their own death by lying in the bottom of the hole.

Let's move on from the brine, because what comes later is better—or worse, depending on your point of view. While

some of the horses dropped dead from fatigue—I'm not exaggerating, they actually died—the meal was served. But if
you're thinking of a bountiful and tasty meal on a tray, you're
mistaken. The food was thrown onto a canvas spread on the
ground—we were out in the open and it was a winter night.
We had two minutes to eat. I did say two minutes. With our
hands. Eat what you can, however you can—that's the motto.
Anything goes. At times like this you see that, reduced to our
lowest common physiological denominator, all of us humans
are alike and resemble the lower mammals. The fight for survival is ugly to see and even worse to experience.

But after the storm came the calm, just as after extreme
physical challenge comes contemplation, abstraction, and intellectual instruction. Now, try to imagine this: a band of
dirty, mud-caked guys, stinking of horses, with their balls
rubbed raw, their asses and thighs burning, drained of their
last drop of energy, still famished and thirsty, their fingernails
black with vestiges of food, their hands greasy, forced to listen to a long and boring lecture about the theory of antiguer-
rilla tactics, a lecture in which there's no reference to action,
just the fundamental concepts.

Add to that the following ingredient: the lecture was read
in a deliberately hypnotic monotone. We were a bunch of
sick, sleepwalking specters. We forced our eyes wide open,
knowing that dozing would cost very dearly.

Amâncio couldn't resist and began to nod, overcome by
sleep. The instructor rose slowly and addressed him. He ordered him to squat over a tree trunk, took a grenade from his
belt, pulled the pin, and placed the grenade in the wayward

student's hand. One slipup would have meant the end of our fine and brave pack of trainees. From then on, no one took his eyes off Amâncio—watching our colleague's watchfulness. Fear kept us awake better than the best hot, bitter coffee could have done.

Back in the ICU

"You held us all in your hand," I repeated. Amâncio maintained his half smile, taut as a tent in the troop's camp. Now the combat was his alone, just his. He was by himself, with the grenade tied to his hand. I squeezed his hand so he'd know I was still at his side. "You know what happened? What really happened?" he asked in a faint voice. I told him it was better not to talk, he needed all his strength to win that battle. I didn't mean to be all dramatic and talk like that, with fight-for-life images and stuff that sounds pretty in a book but does a godawful lot of damage when spoken at the deathbed of somebody who knows there is no fucking battle, just a pitiless massacre.

But he insisted. That's how I learned what had happened that Sunday afternoon.

Santa Teresa, an artists' neighborhood near the center of Rio, Sunday, 4 P.M.

This is the faithful account of what Amâncio told me.

"Me and my partner were heading back to the 2nd Battalion in the plain-wrapper Volkswagen that we used for certain

missions. We were on Rua Almirante Alexandrino, in Santa
Teresa, because we'd been following a guy who was the link
between the traffickers in the Santa Marta favela and the
lowlifes of Tabajara. But we lost him, and since we'd already
been on duty for over twenty-four hours, we decided to go
back. Up there, near the Balé favela, there's a fork in the road.
We wanted to head down to Cosme Velho and Laranjeiras,
but my partner, who was driving, took the wrong road. When
we realized it, we were on a very steep incline that was taking us straight to the heart of the favela. There wasn't any way
to back up, or to put on the brakes, get out of the car, and
run away on foot. We were practically sliding right into the
middle of the favela. Our car was like a neon sign. Shit, two
men in a Volkswagen like that, we had to be either outlaws
or cops. Either way, we were gonna get shot at. The car moved
ahead slowly, down the slope, and I could already see the traffickers gathered in the middle of the street. They were handing out the guns and ammo. It hit me that we had only one
way out: accelerating.

"I shouted 'Step on it, push it to the floor and keep your
head down!' It was like bowling a strike. The car shot forward
down the hill and we got three or four of them. It was a shit-
storm; guys were thrown everywhere; the car rolled over several times. I managed to escape, in a hail of bullets. I ran,
firing and looking for cover. I don't know what happened to
Amílcar. I couldn't look back. All I could do was run down
alleyways in the direction opposite the entrance. You must remember the favela. It's in a valley, between the incline coming down from Santa Teresa and the steps that go up, at the

other end. I ran up the steps. They didn't follow me. They must've been seeing to the wounded. Probably their leader was one of those we ran over. I gave it all I had and took the steps three at a time. When I was about halfway up, some guys from the 1st Battalion showed up at the head of the steps. I signaled to them and thought I'd been saved by the bell.

"Suddenly they pointed a rifle at me from up there and all I felt was that kick in the stomach. Everything went black. I woke up here, after surgery. It was friendly fire, amigo. Friendly fire. What I wanna know is, why? Sure, I'm black and I was armed and out of uniform, but fuck, why shoot at me before identifying a fellow officer?"

Amâncio didn't live beyond that day. At the funeral, when they fired the salute, I felt like telling them to stop the farce, the charade. But I thought about his widow, his son, pondered it a bit and decided the best thing would be to put a rock over the affair. Better to have a father who was a hero, killed by enemies, than the victim of a misunderstanding. I say misunderstanding in order to maintain a certain level of moderation, out of respect for the memory of a dear friend, a courageous man. What I really felt was like crying and vomiting out the truth about all that shit.

A Thousand and One Nights

The Special Operations Battalion, BOPE to insiders, arrived at the war grounds. We had got a real hard-on to invade the favela, fucking A. Excuse me for talking like that, but am I supposed to tell the truth or not? Soon you're going to discover that I'm a well-educated guy, with schooling that few in Brazil have. You may even be surprised to learn that I'm a student at the Catholic University, speak English, and have read Foucault. But that comes later. I'm going to take the liberty of speaking with total frankness, and, you know how it is—when you're sincere and speak freely, your words aren't always the most sober and elegant.

If you're expecting a nice, polite testimony, forget it. Better put the book away right now. Sorry, but I get irritated at people who want the truth and a refined account at the same time. Truth has to be coaxed out, or sometimes it descends from the foulmouthed type who refuses to filter the voice coming from his heart. The truth follows rough street language rather than

the bowing and scraping of court. I'm going to deliver this testimony as if I were sitting around at my house. It's going to
be beautiful, sublime, and horrendous, just like me, just the
way my life has been. And the way yours probably is too.
Come on in, make yourself at home. The place is yours. At
first you'll find a few things strange, but you'll soon get used
to it. I found them odd at the beginning too. When I joined
the force, I found a lot of things odd. But I soon got used to
them. People adapt. Therefore, my dear friend—may I call
you that?—fasten your seat belt and let's go.

The first story takes place in the Jacaré favela.

It was more or less this way. We were arriving at Jacaré over-
flowing with love to give—if you understand me—and with
a shitload of willingness. As soon as we got out of the wagon,
two junkies came toward us—because we had stopped just
beyond the curve of the main incline. I was a lieutenant at the
time and commanded the patrol. The junkies didn't even have
time to pretend to be straight or try to flee. I grabbed the taller
one by the arm and shook him, so the son of a bitch would
wake up and understand he'd been caught in the rattrap. He
wasn't armed but had some envelopes of coke in his pocket.

"So the cocksucker's here to score some blow, eh? I'll bet
you this fag also gets a kick out of marching around all dressed
in white and demonstrating for peace, huh? Say something,
asshole."

"No, sir."

"No, sir what, you piece of shit? You didn't buy powder or
you don't like parading for peace?"

"I don't deal, sir. I just came to get some for my own use."

"Ah! Just for your personal use, so that's it."

I grabbed a fire extinguisher from one of our wagons and discharged it in the guy's nostrils. He looked like a meringue pie.

"You want powder? You want white? Then have some white, you animal."

Well, at that point I must admit that I'd gotten hot under the collar and lost it. But I just knocked him around a little, because I had a brilliant idea. I ordered Rocha to stop beating on the other junkie.

"C'mere, you two. Stand up and look at me. That's right, at my cell phone. You've got three options: phone your daddy and ask him to come get you, that's the first; eat a dozen boiled eggs, each of you, without water, that's the second; get the shit beat out of you is the third. Your call."

They both chose the eggs. I knew they would. The last thing a junkie wants is for his father to find out. What they didn't know was that the eggs had been in the transport since the night before because of an occupation the BOPE was executing. In that delicious summer heat in Rio, the eggs were the equivalent of a good working over. God writes straight with crooked lines. The junkies' free will was honored; even so, the divine plan was carried out. Careful, don't think I'm a born-again. That's pure prejudice on your part. Not every cop or crook who mentions God is a born-again. So, you see? It's not just cops who are prejudiced, after all. Speaking of prejudice, write down in your notebook that I'm black. Black in the politically correct sense of the word, because from the merely physical point of view I'm mulatto, dark-skinned, in reality. But let me make myself clear—no pun intended—I'm black and prefer you to think of me as black, okay?

The problem was that there were only a dozen eggs, which forced me to improvise. But, all modesty aside, I'm quite creative. The solution I found was ingenious. While the shorter junkie was swallowing the eggs, to the rollicking applause of my men, the other was burying himself up to the neck in a Dumpster. Be honest—isn't that an interesting punishment? If at this moment you're recoiling in horror and invoking human rights, maybe you'd better close this book right now, man, because you're risking a heart attack in a little while.

Well, actually I don't want you to close the book, and I wouldn't like you to get a bad impression of me. Don't take what I say all that seriously. Sometimes I say whatever comes into my head and end up giving people the wrong idea, as if I were inhuman, perverse, that kind of thing. But it's not like that at all. When you get to know me better, you'll see. I just wanted to tell this story because it has a very funny ending. Here's what happened: I was coming down later on from the favela worn out; it had been a rough night. Over three hours of chasing junkies, without result. Two soldiers from my unit were already waiting in the vehicle. I could hear their laughter from a long way off. When I approached, they pointed the searchlight at the Dumpster, from which the junkie's head was sticking out, still buried in that shit up to his neck.

"What're you doing there, man?" I asked.

"You told me to stay here."

"You can go now, dickhead."

I swear to God that I'd forgotten. If it wasn't for the sound of the rats, the boys wouldn't have seen him. And if they hadn't seen him, he might still be there, even now.

Black Box and Blue Ribbon

I'm not generally a joker, I want you to know that. The case of Tuiuti is interesting. I mean, it's useful for you to get to know me a little better, and my BOPE team. The preceding story could be misinterpreted. Especially because, nowadays, when you mention the police everybody automatically thinks about all hell breaking loose, busting heads, and corruption. The episode with the Dumpster sounds kind of ambiguous, and you might have gotten the impression that if the junkies' parents showed up, my colleagues and I would've set a price to let them go. Let me make one thing clear right now: there's none of that in the BOPE and there never has been. Actually, there was a case or two, but their own comrades found a way to expel those responsible, before our honor could be sullied.

Beating up lowlifes, executing criminals, that's what we do. But there's no business involved. With us, there's no such thing as looking the other way. It's funny—funny and sad at the same time—that even the language of outlaws and dirty cops is becoming more and more alike. In the end, if you take a close look at it, the money is the same, the motivation's the same, and everything ends up as a single package: the police sell weapons to the traffickers, then hit the favelas for the show-and-tell of political exhibitions for the media. The next day, they return the weapons and charge the traffickers a fee. Those same guns are used against the police, but the dirty-cops are nowhere around to face the consequences.

From one day to the next, if the BOPE doesn't act, the guys on the take in the battalions negotiate a percentage of drug sales and make a daily pickup. Now and then, somebody welshes and it turns into a shooting gallery. For that very reason, it's important for me to be completely transparent so you can separate the wheat from the chaff. With the BOPE there's no deals, no doing business. And I'm not bragging when I say we're the best urban warfare troop in the world, the most technologically savvy, the best prepared, the strongest. I'm not the one saying that; the Israelis come here to learn from us; the Americans too. Our level of quality comes from many factors, one of which is this: nowhere else in the world can you practice every day.

There are 150 of us, approximately. Every time they've tried to increase that number, it's turned to shit. It's not easy to get into the BOPE. That I guarantee. It's not for just anyone. We take fucking pride in our black uniform and in our symbol: a knife piercing a skull. Criminals tremble before us. I'm not going to bullshit you: criminals get no mercy from us. At night, for example, we don't take prisoners. On nighttime raids, if we run into a lowlife, it's lights out. That didn't used to be the policy, but now, there's no alternative. It's kill or be killed. Before this policy was implemented, years ago, the criminals would surrender when they were outnumbered. The shoot-to-kill order, eliminating any chance of surrender, produced a paradoxical effect: it increased their resistance and antipolice violence. The guy knows there's no point in giving up, so he fights to the death. That way, he at least postpones dying and takes somebody with him.

So there has been a significant increase in "incidents of resistance followed by death," which is what we call civilian deaths in confrontations with the police. And revenge killings of policemen have also soared. The sickest kind of revenge, directed against an entire corps. A reflection of the violence that we ourselves practiced, sometimes against an entire favela. Blood is a poison. The more you spill, the more you fertilize hatred. And the wheel keeps on turning. In the end, we all pay the price, the whole society. Shoot-to-kill was an insane policy. And now? We're the heirs of that insanity. The only thing to do is shoot first so you don't get killed. Let the politicians and the academics debate the sex of angels.

Tuiuti, August, 7 A.M.

This case occurred some years ago. We were coming down from the Salseiro favela, in Tijuca, where we had spent a rough night. Across from the old América Stadium, on Campos Sales, an automobile was stopped in the middle of the street, with the driver's door open, next to an armored car. A distraught older woman flagged us down. We stopped behind the car. There were five of us. We found the body of a woman, slumped over the steering wheel with a rifle bullet in her head. You can just imagine the scene. I'm not going to go into the shocking details. You can understand why the older lady, the victim's mother, refused to accept that she was dead and insisted on the corpse being removed for medical attention, despite the obvious. If I told you the condition of the dashboard and the windshield, you'd understand.

The criminals had attacked the armored car and gotten away with six million reais.* The young woman, frightened by the scramble ahead, had tried to keep the car immobile, following the order from one of the outlaws, but she took her foot off the clutch, out of nervousness, provoking the lurch that startled the criminal. He fired, a sharp and accurate shot from behind. For you to have an idea of the destruction, a rifle bullet penetrating the human body damages an area fifty times the diameter of the projectile. Corporal Ronaldo honored the mother's state of denial while he took her statement. Maternal desperation manifests itself in strange ways. He stood at her side as sentinel of her pain and, little by little, bridged the gap between madness and reality. The dead woman's mother slowly crossed the abyss. Even today, at the end of every year, she remembers us, phoning, sending cards. Gratitude that comes forth in extreme situations isn't forgotten.

---

*The Brazilian currency is the *real*, plural *reais*. In early 2008 it was worth approximately 1.76 to the dollar.—Ed.

We left Ronaldo there and set out. Half a mile away, in Bandeira Square, there was a crowd. We opened a passage through the mass of people. A fat sergeant, on the ground, his eyes bugged out, lay dead in a pool of blood. A rifle bullet in the neck. After a night of tension, that was too much for us. The blood rushed to our heads and two of our men yelled at the people crowding around to see the corpse. "You complain about the police, you talk about us . . . that man had a family, his wife is waiting for him at home, his children too, he was working," Private Castro said. Corporal Álvaro continued: "You want us to catch the sons of bitches who did this? So they can go back out on the streets, laughing in our faces? The sons of bitches killed a girl, robbed an armored car, killed a working man. Now what do you say? Is some son of a bitch gonna talk about human rights? What about the rights of this man who bled to death like a pig in a slaughterhouse?" Castro added: "Do you want the killers' blood? You want us to go after them? What then? What then, for chrissake? Are you gonna testify for us to the judge? Are you gonna rip out the bars of the cage where we'll be rotting?"

I doubt anybody heard those cries in the midst of all the confusion. The death of the street cop tied up traffic, and I had to leave another of our men behind to handle removal of the body and impose order on the chaos. The city had to go on with its journey into the smoke, the haze shattering against the sides of buses, the smell of blood and gasoline. Just one more day like any other. After all, in the state of Rio de Janeiro, eighteen people are murdered every day. And that's been going on like clockwork for over twenty years. We've learned to live with the curse. Especially us, the police, who are more exposed to the risks and the poverty in which outlaws sprout like weeds. We're the wild animals of the jungle. Wild animals by profession.

We went back to the transport. There were two possibilities: either the criminals had gone to the right, heading to Rio Comprido by Avenida Paulo de Frontin, or back to the left, toward the train station, São Cristóvão y Maracanã. I opted for the left. When we passed below Tuiuti, pedestrians pointed up toward the favela. I suspect the kingpins of Tuiuti weren't happy with the awkward visit by the armored-car robbers, who had gone up the hillside facing first-degree murder charges, to share responsibilities and risks. We started up the incline. It wasn't hard to locate the house where they were hiding out. The residents cooperated openly, a sign the bad guys didn't belong there. Otherwise they wouldn't have dared violate the law of silence imposed by the drug trade.

There were three of us. We readied our weapons, announced that the house was surrounded, and ordered the criminals to come out one at a time with their hands on the backs of their necks. Nothing. We fired into the house, prepared to raze it. Some four hundred rounds were fired. The house was still standing, riddled into a toothpick holder. One of the lowlifes announced he was coming out. He took the first steps outside. Delgado took aim and squeezed the trigger. The cartridge was empty. He had time to reload, while the outlaw stood there, hands behind his head, trembling and pale. Then Delgado's shot exploded into his chest. No sign of life from inside the house. It was time to storm it.

We found two bodies in the rubble and one survivor. The guy was disfigured but alive. The scene would stay with us for a long time, turning our stomachs and haunting our sleep. Each man in the troop dealt with it in his own way. Two of us ended up with the nickname Black Box because of it— that's the nickname given to someone who takes prescription medicine with that type of warning label. Even for someone who sees death on a daily basis, it's not easy to face a life ending that way. The poor devil had lost his jaw. Don't try to imagine it; you won't be able to. It's better not to.

"She's dead, she's dead"—an old black man was carrying a little girl in his arms, bathed in blood. He came from the rear of the house. "The outlaws killed my granddaughter," he said, showing us the child. "It was the shots from the outlaws," he repeated. Private Délio took the girl from her grandfather's arms and ran to the transport, saying, "We're going to save the child, we're going to save the child." I ran alongside him, grabbed him by the arm, looked him in the eye, and said, "Délio, the child is dead. You hear me? She's dead." He stood there motionless, looking in front of him, the child in his arms. After a few minutes he came up to me: "Captain, it was us who killed the little girl. She was in the rear. The criminals had their back to her, shooting at us. It was impossible for them to hit the girl. We shot forward, toward the house. The bullet came from us." I looked into his eyes again, deeply: "Forget that." "We killed the little girl, Lieutenant," he insisted. "Forget it, goddammit. Forget it," I said. "Her grandfather is convinced it was the outlaws, so it *was* the fucking outlaws. Forget it. It's over."

The lowlife without a jaw died on the way to the hospital.

When it was all over I went to check the events at the morgue. I counted six bodies side by side in the refrigerated room. It felt like I was in some gloomy grotto, some secret estuary of rivers that flow beneath the city—even when you're underground the city goes on making its noises. Délio was just one cog in the wheel; I was another. We barely knew the workings of the machinery that was in motion. Besides that, at that hour, we were overcome with profound exhaustion.

Vidal stayed at Tuiuti, protecting the bags of money. The birds of prey in the civil police have an excellent sense of smell. They arrived with a team and ordered the military police away. They would handle the case. Vidal climbed onto the bags of money and swiveled 360 degrees, pointing his rifle in all directions: "Anybody who touches the dough will eat lead. I'm not joking. I'll shoot. I'm going to shoot. I'm warning you. I'm going to shoot." Our civil counterparts preferred not to play with fire. After twenty-four hours on duty and the battles we'd been through during that period, Vidal would have been quite capable of shooting.

The relationship of men in the BOPE with the BOPE commander varies a lot. If the guy has been through everything we've gone through, in terms of training and selection, and if he has the balls to defend our honor with the scumbag politicians, fine and good. He has our loyalty. But if the guy's an opportunist and sacrifices everything to keep his superior, and the governor happy, he's fucked. Pardon my putting it that way, but he's fucked. That's what happened in the final chapter of the Tuiuti case.

The commander was sought out by the bank whose money we'd rescued. The insurance company would pay five percent to the cops involved in recovering the six million. That is, three hundred thousand would make its way from the insurance company's multibillion-reais holdings to my savings account and those of my modest comrades in uniform. Not a huge fortune, but nothing to sneeze at: divided by five—or eight, if we wanted to honor all the personnel in the unit under my command, whether or not they'd participated in the operation (in fact, if it had been planned, all eight would have been present)—the dough would funnel either 60,000 or 37,500 reais into each of our accounts. The commander decided to submit a, shall we say, more generous list, practicing charity with someone else's money: he included himself and five or six more of his closest buddies. We decided to rain on the parade. We talked to the insurance company, explained the difficulties, and suggested a Solomonic solution: the money should go for equipment for the unit, earmarked for bulletproof vests. Ours were old, heavy, and fragile. It turned out to be very useful. And the commander's outrage was the icing on the cake. It did our souls good.

Speaking of souls, the day for commendations arrived. Many months had gone by, but the wound was still open. Délio hadn't gotten over the death of the little girl, and the specter of the disfigured robber still haunted some of us. We lost sleep and peace of mind for a long time. The ritual of awarding commendations would force us to relive the experience, because the account of the occurrence, in all its details, would be read at the ceremony. To have that past stirred up again was the last thing any of us wanted. If they wished to reward us, they should have left us in peace, forgot about us and let us forget. Memory, at times, is like a vault in which we're buried alive.

There was no way around it. They pinned the fact on our chests, all wrapped up with a blue ribbon.

Emergency

Not everyone who arrives wounded at the military police hospital assembly line leaves feet first. Some are saved. At times, even those who think they're really clever are saved. Even if their shrewdness costs them dearly. That's what happened to Lieutenant Ricardo, a young man who liked to validate his own pass. Before the story, a few technical notes. They would have been of great use to the lieutenant.

Doctors who specialize in treating gunshot wounds in Rio de Janeiro have become international points of reference— just like the boys in the BOPE. The doctors count on the contributions of the police and the underworld, whose lethal output has become reliable over the years. There's been no shortage of fractured bones, shattered muscle, shredded organs, and mutilated limbs on an industrial scale. From plastic surgery to orthopedics, Brazilian doctors are among the best in the world. When it comes to dealing with repairing war injuries, especially those related to firearms, as I've said, they're second to none. At first, our specialists would visit American surgeons who had worked in Vietnam. Now it's the gringos who come to us.

One lesson we learned from our surgeons saved several lives: when the projectile is large-caliber, it's better to sacrifice tissue and organs, as far as possible, than to try to save them. Experience has shown that preservation ends up being counterproductive. In sum: if the bullet is from a rifle, you open the victim from top to bottom and remove anything that's not vital. For instance, Sergeant Romero took a lateral rifle shot in the ass that went in one buttock and out the other. Apparently, there were only two holes, one entry and one exit, with a straight intramuscular trajectory. Nothing that time wouldn't cure, or at least that's what the nonspecialist who did the initial treatment thought. He didn't even make a suture, just gave Romero two bandages and an anti-inflammatory. But as soon as Romero sat down in the wagon to be taken home, he started bleeding to death. The hemorrhage was drained through the anus. He went into shock and almost died. He was quickly returned to the emergency room, to undergo surgery that removed I don't know how many yards of intestine and saved his life.

Too bad Lieutenant Ricardo didn't know this when he arrived at the emergency room, playing the tough guy. He'd caught a bullet from a friendly pistol, in the police wagon. He wasn't the only one this had ever happened to, as a matter of fact. Lots of people have the same bad luck. Some don't survive. Ricardo was sitting in front and his colleague, seated inattentively in back, didn't take the necessary precautions.

The pistol, with its safety off, accidentally fired, hitting the lieutenant in the back of the shoulder. To avoid paperwork and impress the nurses, Ricardo came in saying, "It was nothing. Just a scratch. A bunch of traffickers set up an ambush for me, but I took care of them. It's just a rifle wound in the shoulder." Before he could relate his next feat, they stuck a needle in his vein, intubated him, and called in the surgical specialists, who opened him from navel to neck, following the standard procedure. The lieutenant survived, but he learned that it's not always a good idea to play the macho by exaggerating the caliber of your heroism.

Miami Dolphins

My wife, who has a thing for psychoanalysis, often says that when we transmit a certain impression it's because it expresses at least one side of us. If my wife is right, your perception isn't totally wrong. But, in any case, it's partially wrong. In plain English: I'm not entirely what you're thinking. Even if I'm also not fully what I myself would like to be. I say I prefer plain talk to psychobabble, and that I get straight to the point. I say that I'm direct, and I call my wife's critical view nonsense, but I end up beating around the bush, pussyfooting around the matter I want to talk about. It's because the subject is thorny, hairy.

The subject is the violence that we, the BOPE, commit. Some call it torture. I don't like the word, because it has a diabolical connotation. I feel there are cases and there are cases, and that not all torture is torture, in the usual sense of the word. Do you understand? No? Okay, the thing is complicated. I don't even know if I understand it myself.

What I mean is that I'm not ashamed of not being ashamed of having smacked around a lot of lowlifes. First, because I only bash lowlifes, I only kill lowlifes. I can state that with total confidence. My soul is clear and my conscience clean because I've only executed outlaws. And, to me, an outlaw's an outlaw, whether he's a street kid or a grown man. A lowlife's a lowlife. And there's something else—it's not a BOPE rule, it's my own, but I follow it to the letter: I don't beat or kill women. Except in self-defense. Then there's no way around it, it's kill or be killed. Apart from that, I respect women. Because there's no reason not to. Women panic right away and will hand over even their mothers. There's no need to hit them. But not men. There's some guys so slimy that they'll take a beating all night long without giving anybody up. Maybe it's because they know their partners' revenge would be even worse than the punishment from the BOPE.

Well, it's a really sticky question, and if I could I'd just as soon skip this part, but I feel obliged to talk about a few things, since we agreed I would hide nothing. Later you can evaluate, draw up your own balance sheet and tell me whether I'm a coward or whether I did the right thing—or at least what you'd have done in my place. Are you going to tell me you wouldn't make a kidnapper talk, even if you had to use force? If your daughter was kidnapped, her life at risk, in the hands of sickos, you're telling me you wouldn't beat the bastard to death to get the information out of him? Okay then; the only difference is you wouldn't know how to go about it the right way and would waste energy striking the less sensitive points and using hate and desperation more than technique. We're pure technique.

Today, looking back, I feel kind of inhibited about narrating the facts, but in the heat of the moment I admit I didn't have any problem with it. Here's the truth: my colleagues and I had a lot of fun. So, that business about "pure technique" isn't really true. We're technique, fun, and art . . . as the popular song says.

I remember, for example, one criminal we picked up almost by accident, as soon as we got to the Providência favela. It was March. We had a complete team, eight of us. First, we gave him a routine working over to get him to give up the pieces—that's what Rio traffickers call guns. He was carrying a cheap revolver and swore it was the only one he had and that he was just a holdup man and had nothing to do with the drug trade. Just then, his girlfriend came by, saw the commotion, came up and addressed him by name: Juninho. That's when it hit us. We realized that the guy was the head honcho there. You ever see such luck? Suddenly, without our really trying, the boss, the big gun, had fallen into our net. It was everything we could ask of our heavenly daddy. From that point on, we intensified our work.

The verb is *work*. When a subordinate radios his commander and asks, "Chief, can I work the perp?" he's requesting permission to make him sing. The same way the state governor authorizes the secretary of public safety to authorize the military police commander when he says, "Do whatever it takes to solve the problem." The governor sleeps the sleep of the just; the secretary retires to his splendid cradle;

the commander slumbers like a good Christian; and the soldier, on the front line, gets his hands dirty with blood. If it turns to shit, everything explodes at the weakest link, and the one left holding the bag is the soldier. The one who faces indictment is the soldier. The one named on the lists of international human rights organizations is the soldier. The governor equivocates and sleeps soundly; the secretary is subtle and salves his conscience; the commander uses euphemisms and slanted syntax to protect his honor and his job. It comes down to the soldier, who busts his ass out of duty to his office. It's odd: ambiguity can be cultivated only in the solemn confines of the Palace of Government, where fraud and violence are sweetened by the elegant choreography of politics.

When the arena is the favela, the rituals are different, less sophisticated. On the battlefield there's no room or time for solemnity or ambivalence. What was sweet turns bitter and sour; it rots and falls. We, the ones who must act at the leading edge of decisions, pick the rotten fruit and do what we can to digest it. Because of that, maybe it's mistaken to say that ambivalence is found only in courtrooms. It's everywhere. It's here among us, and inside us, in me and in you.

One way to adapt ambiguity to the field of combat is to find amusement in the pain of others. I'm suspicious of our laughter. Even today I can hear our guffaws, and they sound kind of strange. I don't know anymore if we enjoyed it and really found it so funny. But we laughed; what else were we going to do? And we tried to enjoy the practical tasks with a maximum of creativity. For example, I took pride in coming up with new approaches. There would be a premiere night, with a party and everything. The coolest show was one I called Miami Dolphins. The premiere took place that night with Juninho. We took advantage of his resistance to test the efficacy and beauty of the new spectacle. The idea was to soften his machismo with water.

Water is an excellent conductor of electricity. The idea was a more or less natural outgrowth of traditional tortures using plastic bags and water: suffocation and drowning. Every BOPE policeman leaves the barracks with a small plastic bag, which has become part of the basic kit. The bag is placed over the criminal's head, tightened at the bottom, and tied at his neck. The guy suffocates, vomits, and passes out. That's when we loosen it. It's kind of disgusting but effective. We worked Juninho for hours on end. First, a beating, the good old reliable beating, which is usually enough. Nothing. Then we stuck wooden slivers under his fingernails. The bastard howled but didn't open his trap. That was when it came to me to debut the Dolphins. We went to a nearby cistern. We removed two wires from the light pole. We ordered Juninho into the cistern and stuck the ends of the wires into the water, on either side of him. Beautiful! You should've seen it. He leaped around with lightness and grace. All that was missing was a sound track and a light show. Even so, the son of a bitch wouldn't crack. I stuck the wires in the water several times. I think he came close to having his obituary written, as we say. I was getting nervous and irritated. You see what I mean; it had been hours and still nothing. The blood rushed to my head and I fired at the cistern, until my colleagues stopped me. I was beside myself. Fortunately for that lowlife, the bullet's trajectory was diverted by the water. If not for that, he'd have been fucked. He barely escaped. When I shoot I don't miss.

I got on the radio to the commander. I told him we'd been working the perp for some time, without result. I wanted to eliminate the scumbag, but I had to listen to my superior, given the special circumstances of the case. He ordered us to take the guy to the Precinct for the Protection of Children and Adolescents, which handles minors. There was nothing for it but to take him. The guy was white as a sheet. Mangy. In front of the precinct chief he whined, "The BOPE police-men tortured me" and showed his bruised fingers with their raised nails. The chief, a woman, was an experienced profes-sional and didn't let us down. She looked at the guy and cut him off at the knees: "Oh, is that right? Poor little thing . . . Do you have a boo-boo? Want me to call your mommy, you son of a bitch?"

If it weren't for cooperation among police professionals it would be impossible to carry out our duties with even a min-imum of efficiency. People complain about us because they think it's easy to maintain order in the city. They don't know that, while they're enjoying dinner with their family in front of the TV in the comfort of their home, outside, in the un-derworld, a lot of blood is flowing, ours and the criminals'.

An Eye for an Eye

Maximum force: quick, devastating, and efficient. That's the BOPE motto. If you were the governor of the state of Rio, would you forego our services or, even if you never made use of our squad wouldn't you like to have it available for rapid deployment, ready to act at any moment, in case of some critical emergency? Actually, I'm not interested in your answer. Because I have no way of knowing what you're thinking at this exact moment, but I'll bet, sight unseen, that deep down, way down deep, you'd like to be able to count on the strong right hand of the BOPE to crush all the vandals and vermin.

Speaking of sight unseen, I just remembered a story that has to do with that, both in tactics and consequences. It was another of those nights. In fact, one like all the squad's nights. Captain Ângelo was commanding the team. This time, Private Marques was point man—the point man is the one who goes at the front of the assault group, opening the way, indicating the path and passing along information through signals. The commander is always third. The Turano favela was quiet. It was already late. The plan was to take Fabinho's group by surprise, on the Limão hillside. We had a map of the place. Thanks to previous incursions and some supplementary information obtained in the interrogation of a trafficker, we knew just where the weapons were and where the outlaws normally met to organize the raids that would descend into Tijuca and raise hell.

The favela was bordered by a long, high wall. Our intention was to make our way down in absolute silence, clinging to the outside face of the wall, and penetrate the favela through the lower part, the one most closely watched by the traffickers' lookouts and therefore the least auspicious for a police raid. But that's precisely why we chose it: being the least auspicious, it would be the least likely option, which meant that, paradoxically, it could be the most vulnerable. We descended in the pitch blackness, treading carefully, hardly breathing. That type of single-file formation is very risky. The slightest mistake and we'd be fucked. If they tossed a grenade over the wall, nothing would be left on this side. Our movements were controlled by Marques's signals: stand still, go forward, step up the pace, stop. In such situations, the point man acts as a bloodhound. His hearing also has to be extremely acute. The eight men move according to a rigorous score, as disciplined as an orchestra. With one difference: the tiniest slip doesn't mean a wrong note, it means death.

When you're in that kind of procession, one comrade behind the other, mutual confidence is as important as self-confidence. None of that was missing, thank God. I was proud of the group's skill and had faith in myself and my weapon. It wasn't until much later that I discovered what it was to be afraid of dying, when my first son was born. The fear printed on the face of the enemy was our fuel. Actually, it was more than that; it was our drug. The black uniform with the skull pierced by a knife was the privilege of few. It wasn't easy to stand up to the tests to get into the BOPE, the same way it wasn't easy, after passing and being admitted to the Special Operations Battalion, to take the bus every day like a common citizen, arrive at the barracks like an ordinary mortal, put on the black uniform that was our source of pride—but which also signified one huge fucking responsibility—and transport yourself to another dimension where the citizenry of Rio de Janeiro disappears from the scene and is replaced by the hell of war. It might as well have been the Gaza Strip; it might as well have been Baghdad: eighteen deaths a day for twenty years.

The city only touched its other dimension tangentially, when a stray bullet crossed the borders. Otherwise, it carried its shadow the way a pilgrim carries the cross on his shoulder, feeling its weight and gauging its size without looking at it directly to know its shape and understand its nature.

You must have noticed that I said "arrive at the barracks like an ordinary mortal." You must have found that weird, maybe even comical: "Shit, does that madman think he's some kind of immortal god?" Rereading what I wrote, I confess I found it strange too, but I decided to leave it the way it is, because it came out so spontaneously and expresses my feelings so well. And because the goal is for you to get to know me better, I decided to keep it. No, I don't think I'm immortal, and my BOPE comrades aren't crazy. But the fact is that when you live alongside death every day, every night, when you know it's kill or be killed, while you survive, you feel your victory over death, a kind of skimming flight over the precipice. If you want to call that delusional, fine. I'd like to see you go through the same experience. It'd be interesting to find out whether your concepts change just a bit. But, hey, you can think anything you like. It won't make any difference. Let's get back to the story of the wall.

We moved on, step by step, avoiding the noise of dry branches and the high brush, fearful of running into a stray dog outside the route. When police go into the favelas, there are typically three sounds: gunshots, fireworks from the traffickers' lookouts, and the barking of dogs. That's the sound track of police incursions. In general, as we go up we silence the animals. When the shot is accurate they don't suffer. That night we couldn't silence the dogs because we didn't want to give away our presence. But that meant their barking could set off one hell of an alarm. It was a fucking dilemma. So, all we could do was count on luck. Obviously, we had thought about that risk when we planned the operation. We're not as shortsighted as you may be imagining. We were betting there wouldn't be any dogs around there. We'd never seen them on that side. And, in fact, none showed up.

When you're concentrating on a war operation, everything changes, every sense is altered. You hardly hear anything and only see what your attention is focused on. It's what's called tunnel vision. The name is quite accurate. It's as if you're in a tunnel, with a single point of light at the end. Time revolves around that point and seems to freeze, perhaps because it gets mixed up with space—I mean, with the image. I don't know. All I can say is that you leave this world and roam. The universe retreats in slow motion. It's as if all the velocity in the world has been absorbed by your muscles and the synapses that keep your brain alert. The result is that at the end of a firefight, you have the impression that half an hour has gone by. But you look at your watch and it's been two, three, five minutes.

Some extraordinary things can happen at a moment like that. Once, for example, I was leading the invasion of a favela in Copacabana. The point man got separated from the rest of the team and I decided we'd wait. We were heading up a narrow slope. There wasn't a soul around. Ahead, the alley turned to the left. That silence wasn't normal. Not even the barking of dogs. No fireworks were going off. I was determined to proceed. Cautiously, but to proceed. Just as my brain was sending the command to my legs, an old woman came around the corner and down toward us. She was carrying one of those cloth bags used for shopping at outdoor markets. She walked with a firm step despite her age and showed no sign of surprise when she saw us huddled against the wall. As she passed by, without looking at me, she whispered, "Don't go up there, son. If you do, they'll kill you." I didn't answer. I've learned to respect that kind of communication in the favelas. You have to take the greatest care not to show any reaction, so the bastards won't see it and take revenge against the person trying to help us. So I counted to twenty and, instead of advancing, threw a grenade into the entrance to the alleyway, just to get a response from the traffickers and identify their location and amount of firepower. The immediate, intense gunfire showed they were prepared, waiting for us.

I told Sergeant Aguinaldo, beside me, "That old woman saved our lives. It was an ambush." "What old woman?" he asked. "Whaddya mean, what old woman?" I said. "That old lady, for God's sake. The one who passed by and whispered the message to me." "Lieutenant," he said, "Lieutenant, there wasn't any old woman here, no old lady at all. Nobody's been by here since we arrived. Do you think that a little old lady would walk between two lines of fire, just like that? And even if she did, that we wouldn't see her?" A chill ran down my body. Even today, I get goose bumps when I tell that story.

With tunnel vision, anything is possible: close encounters of the third kind with unreal characters or total delirium—I might have gone temporarily insane or have been in perfect mental condition; in that case, it wasn't my imagination that was fantastic, it was reality. And there's also the hypothesis that my colleague may have gone momentarily blind from the tension. Blind and deaf. But the matter is beyond my understanding. Better to go back to the Turano favela and the great wall.

So, there we were, focused, riveted to the mission by adrenaline, step by step, down the wall, gripping our rifles, holding our breath. It was a long trek. I prefer open confrontation to waiting. Sometimes I root for the bomb to explode and be done with it. I feel that slow anticipation congealing my blood and suffocating me. The outbreak of confrontation rarefies the body and the mind. The blood lifts the spirit. One more step, then another, one more, in silence, down the hillside, inching along the wall. Private Marques raised his right arm. We stopped. He'd come to the lowest point of the wall. It was time to start the climb on the other side, where we'd be much more exposed. When Marques jumped to the other side, he ran into a group of traffickers on their way down, also edging along the wall. They were relaxed and distracted, although armed to the teeth. They weren't expecting that encounter. All our point man had to do was pull the trigger. We ran to back him up while the enemy scattered frantically, fleeing up the hill to escape the line of fire. They'd had no time to react. We must have hit someone. It wasn't possible they'd all survived. We went up after the criminals, shooting.

We had in fact hit one of them: we discovered a trail of blood and followed it. Way up, in the upper part of the wall, on a plateau, a lowlife was dragging himself. He had run that far, but his strength had given out. One of us fired to finish the job. The bullet went through his brow in a straight line and took out both eyeballs, which dropped on the ground like billiard balls. I remembered a famous scene from *King Lear*, which I had to read in college. That business of viscous jelly gushing from the eye sockets has always nauseated me. I looked away, under the pretext of providing cover for the team. I was a bit nervous and asked to execute the criminal once and for all. He was already turning into a monstrosity.

The guy was becoming a monster as he departed for a better world—in the case of outlaws, the path must be the other way around; he was departing for a worse world. At the moment of passage, a kind of metamorphosis happens to the dying—so you'll know I'm not an idiot, I should mention that it reminds me of a Kafka story by that name, about a guy named Gregor Samsa who turns into a cockroach. I'm not trying to show off, that'd be ridiculous. I'm saying it so you won't be misled by your own prejudices. In the metamorphosis in which a scumbag becomes a monster—as we say in the BOPE—the son of a bitch seems to regress, becoming a child and starting to cry for his mother. It's goddamn hard to take. Maybe that sounds funny. But there in the favela, in the theater of operations—your nostrils full of gunpowder, body parts scattered on the ground—it's not funny.

That's when I got a surprise. Not just me, our entire group. Captain Ângelo didn't authorize the execution. He raised his arm. It was the order not to shoot. He went up to the perp, kneeled beside him and asked, inches from his ear, "Do you accept Jesus?" He repeated it, raising his voice: "Do you accept Jesus?" The poor bastard said yes, he accepted. What else could he do? Even I would've done the same. Yeah, it's just what you're thinking: the captain was an evangelical Protestant and took his religion so seriously that when we'd go up into the favelas on our incursions, he could barely keep from shooting every time he saw the statue of a saint. He would see it, smash the porcelain image, and grumble, "Idolatry, blasphemy," and other imprecations, but we could never hear all that well.

"Captain, shit, Captain, doing that is gonna make the residents hate us even more," one of us got up the courage to say once when he was demolishing the saints.

"No problem. Better to be hated than to tolerate the

worship of graven images. They're the devil's work. They're the reason crime never stops growing."

Before I met Ângelo, I'd seen everything: firing at rats in the barracks, firing at dogs, firing at lowlifes, firing at boom boxes at funk dances, firing at the street lights—when we were equipped with night goggles—but firing at saints was something new.

The thing was that we wanted to execute the fucker and get the hell out of the favela. It was late and the bad guys might be regrouping for a counterattack. We weren't about to take a corpse downhill with us, much less a guy in his death throes but with still enough strength to shout something en route and make more trouble for us. The answer was to do what we usually did: execute and get our asses out of there. We reasoned with the captain, but he was adamant: "We're not going to kill the young man. He accepted Jesus. He's going to recover."

We called the civil police helicopter. This was a rare procedure, extremely rare. We only called for the helicopter when we were surrounded, in especially serious circumstances. Or when one of us was badly wounded and the location prevented any other kind of immediate safe removal. Even rarer was using airborne to remove the body of some outlaw. It had to be in extreme situations. For example, if the hill had been important to the drug lords' hierarchy and the body, if handed over to the residents, would serve as the excuse for protests.

The chopper arrived. It couldn't land. There wasn't enough room. The trees were in the way and the terrain was irregular. The crew members lowered the litter. They thought the guy was dead. When they found out he was alive, they refused to hoist him up. I understood. Deep down, I agreed with them. Take him away, why? Send a chopper there, for what? All of it to save the life of a criminal and take him away and send him off to the penitentiary for a short course to perfect his criminality, for a graduate degree in resentment and hatred? All of it so he would one day be back on the streets to murder and steal?

After a lot of back-and-forth on the radio between Ângelo and the helicopter crew, and after a few threats—the captain seemed suddenly possessed by a legalistic spirit—they took the outlaw away. The next night, the hospital was invaded and he was carried off by his accomplices. He was no longer useful, so he probably didn't last long. I don't know if his soul was saved, but his body didn't have much of a chance.

Justice Delivered

Cássio was a character. Captain Cássio. Anyone who didn't know him, seeing him ascend the favelas, leading BOPE teams, courageously grasping his rifle and risking himself for his comrades, would get the wrong impression of him. At first he seemed kind of arrogant, a would-be intellectual, looking down his nose at everybody, with a manner like David Niven, that old-time actor with the thin mustache, the one Nelson Xavier or André Vali would mimic quite well if they put on a tux and spoke with an English accent. Cássio had a certain air of what my grandfather would have called a scoundrel and my father would call a vulgarian. He was closer to Jece Valadão* than to Charles Bronson, but he loved a happy ending—an ending that for the accused was predictable and always unhappy. Just like in the Bronson *Death Wish* films, in which

---

*Jece Valadão (1930–2006), was a Brazilian actor noted for his roles as an unsympathetic, macho user of women.—Ed.

the 427 outlaws who raped and killed his daughter are eliminated one by one by the lone avenger, the vigilante for threat-
ened families. Let me explain why I said the "accused."

Cássio wanted to be a lawyer. Nothing wrong with that.
Many good people who work for the police dream of a better future. Who doesn't want more prestige, power, and
money? Nothing unusual in that. It's natural. If the guy has
a solid base, is intelligent, studious, can count on support at
home and doesn't lose sight of his objective, it can work out.
Don't a lot of good people from the police take the exams for
the Department of Justice? So why not the bar or even a
judgeship? The dream was legit—but Cássio himself was out
of order.

The captain would climb up the favelas carrying a folding
chair, the kind movie directors use. He would get to the place
he planned to occupy, and while waiting for the rest of the
team to do a sweep of the area, he would order the soldiers
who stayed with him to tap into a power line and hang a
lightbulb right above the chair. He would sit there, take a law
book out of his backpack, open the damn book, and start to
study—taking notes and everything, in total calm. He could
spend hours like that.

I took part in one of the night raids led by Cássio. I was
responsible for finding the weapons and drugs and arresting
the traffickers. We didn't accomplish much. After almost two
hours, we'd rounded up only one lowlife to take to the captain, who was reading, seated erect in his director's chair under the jury-rigged light and, of course, duly protected. The
outlaw had a rifle, a pistol, and about a kilo of cocaine. The

guy had been adopted by the local drug trade after he had to flee his own favela, which had been taken over by a rival faction. He wasn't from there. That made our job easier. Nobody would cry over him or mourn him with candles, raising a stink; there would be no sobbing sister, no aunt tearing out her hair, no fainting mother.

When I took the case to the captain, he applied the formula to the letter: "Let's try the accused." He handed out roles: I was to be the prosecutor; the accused would act in his own defense. Cássio determined that we'd form a 360, a complete circle of protection, to avoid attacks and prevent surprises. I related the incident as if I were in front of a judge. I imitated a prosecutor and asked for a conviction. Rehearsing the highfalutin language and choreography of the courtroom, the captain, as judge, gave the floor to the accused. The guy didn't understand a thing. He said he wasn't a trafficker, that he had the guns and drugs because the local drug gang, seeing the police approaching, wanted to burn him, precisely because he'd always refused to go along. Cássio wasn't at all happy with the lowlife's gall. He felt the guy was insulting the judiciary and playing the BOPE for fools. After a short time, he said he was ready to pronounce the verdict—those very words, pronounce the verdict. And he pronounced. The criminal was sentenced to capital punishment, to be carried out immediately.

The outlaw looked baffled, not knowing if this mise-en-scène was for real. Now the captain rolled up the sleeves of his imaginary robe, because it was time to play the part of executioner. The lowlife trembled and begged for mercy, but that kind of behavior always displeased Cássio: the sentence had already been given and brooked no appeal. The captain ordered Private Lobo to take the trafficker's own gun, then he solemnly repeated the sentence, authorized the poor devil to say any last words, and ordered him silenced with a bullet in the forehead. "Let's go," he ordered. Court was adjourned.

Domestic Justice

C amargo was one of our best commanders. He was firm and fair, and he didn't allow the BOPE to be used for the administration's propaganda machine, which was accustomed to delegating to the media decisions about our priorities. Thanks to people like him, our battalion resisted corruption for many, many years. Although in general the police were becoming discredited, we remained an island of excellence and credibility. That's not just cheap demagoguery. It's the unvarnished truth. If it hadn't been for that credibility, none of the rest of that life, or this story would make sense. An outside observer doesn't have the slightest idea of what goes on inside the barracks, on the operations, and above all, in the heads and hearts of the police.

Sometimes it's painful to confront the plague of corruption, especially when you have to cut into your own flesh to stop the disease from infecting your entire body. It's like amputating an arm or a leg to save your life. The difference is that in the BOPE, after the mutilation, the body regenerates itself: another arm grows, a leg is reborn. People go back to being what they were before. Within limits, of course, because the scar is there, the memory remains.

One scar we don't forget is Lisboa. Before entering the BOPE, he was a civil policeman, and he never left behind certain friends from the old days. They were friendships that led to no good. Besides which, he was going through some serious financial problems. His family had some kind of major issue. No one knew what it was, but he would often complain about life—which, in fact, wasn't uncommon, considering the salaries we received. In his case, things seemed more complicated than normal. Until, at the end of an operation I commanded, Lisboa came up to me, head down, speaking in a low voice: "You know what it is, Captain"—I was already a captain by then—"I've been wondering if it'd be possible to let me have one of the rifles we captured. You know that's not my way, but after all, it's not going to be needed, and it would help me get my life back together. A weapon like that's worth a lot of dough, and my situation—" I ordered him arrested on the spot, opened the procedure to expel him from the BOPE, and reported the case to Colonel Camargo.

Two months after the incident, back on the job but assigned to bureaucratic duties while awaiting internal disposition of his case, Lisboa got himself into another mess. Camargo was advised by P2 that Lisboa, with the help of his old comrades at the precinct, had put together a network for trafficking of weapons. The evidence left no room for doubt.

Colonel Camargo called the officers together, and we had

to make the painful decision. The next morning, as he came off duty, Lisboa was killed, at the door to his house, by two men on a motorcycle.

The sole witness to the vigilante action told the press: "Lisboa seemed to know the two men on the bike, because he stopped, calmly, when they called his name. He went up to them like they were friends. Dawn was breaking and the street was deserted. I didn't give it any thought and went on my usual way, in the opposite direction. Suddenly I heard a shot and the roar of the motorcycle. I turned around and ran toward Lisboa, but he was already dead. The shot came from a professional, right between the eyes."

It wasn't a matter of justice, strictly speaking, but of cutting off institutional gangrene and sending a message to Lisboa's comrades. In fact, Lisboa's indisputable guilt wasn't our greatest concern. If it were, perhaps it would've been enough to apply the punishment stipulated in the penal code and in the regulations of the corps. But the unwritten law is more important when it's a question of honor and the objective is reaffirming the integrity of a collective history. Anyone who thinks the real world consists of visible powers, written laws, and money is mistaken. What's most important isn't spoken, isn't written, and isn't recorded.

The family was helped and shielded from the truth. The funeral offered the full honors befitting the memory of an honorable soldier fallen in the line of duty. We made every effort to see that the sons of our comrade inherited that inspiring legacy.

The Other Side of Revenge

Sergeant Juarez was on his way back to the transport vehicle in the Boa Esperança favela on Governor's Island when a sniper from the drug traffic blew his head open from behind with a long-distance shot. The emotion of his team infected the whole BOPE, where he was one of the best-loved veterans.

We officers could barely keep the soldiers' reaction in check. To tell the truth, we were as upset as they were. It wasn't just hate or indignation; it was fury. We, too, thought that the retaliation had to be immediate and radical. Every one of us had been wounded by that cowardly and humiliating shot. The battalion's honor was at stake, in addition to the memory of our comrade. It was time to put into practice what we'd learned in the training for special operations: "Maximum violence, death, and upheaval, in the far rear guard of the enemy." We were trained to turn into wild dogs. Fine then, the moment for ferocity had arrived.

We formed a contingent of officers to speak to the commander on behalf of the whole group, after the burial. We
wanted revenge. Colonel Camargo said yes, of course, to react was necessary and legitimate; he shared our feeling. But
he thought that caution was called for, because operations of
that type had provoked devastating consequences in the past,
involving the deaths of innocent people and political crises of
international proportions, with disastrous effects on the image of the police. He preferred a more "rational" solution—
that was the word he used, it's not me talking. He repeated
the old saying: "Revenge is a dish best served cold." And he
continued more or less this way: "We're not going back to the
Boa Esperança favela today. We're going to plan a beautiful
operation, one that develops over time, to wipe out the entire group, one by one, but with surgical precision. We're war-
riors, not butchers."

We argued, but it did no good. We left the commander's
office unresigned. We sat down in the officers' quarters.
There were nine or ten of us. We had to come up with a way
out. How could we face the soldiers and tell them nothing
would be done? That we had to stick our tails between our
legs and that it was the sensible thing to do, that it was "rational"? We summoned Juarez's team and some other available men. We'd take care of this our own way.

One of us had a friend in the army weaponry depot. We got
hold of twenty rifles, ammunition, grenades, and night-vision
gear. We agreed to meet at midnight at the public school near
the favela. We were in plain clothes, in unmarked cars. I had
to threaten the watchman so he'd open the gate. We picked a

classroom. Gomes unfolded the map, pointed to the traffick-ers' usual location. He knew the place well. We discussed our plan of action. There were twenty-four of us. We selected Gomes to lead the op and handed out the other assignments. We would hit the favela in three groups, occupying the main arteries. A fourth group would ascend the neighboring hillside and take the upper part of Boa Esperança. They would force the lowlifes downward until they fell into an armed encir-clement in the lower part of the favela. We put on our hoods and prayed for the soul of our dead comrade.

The strategy and the tactics worked to perfection. No one escaped, with the exception of Juarez's killer, who had already fled the community, precisely because he feared reprisals. No one challenges the BOPE with impunity. The Skull has a name to uphold. Eight criminals were executed in the name of justice.

We descended the favela in peace, returned the weapons, and were never called before Internal Affairs to deal with the matter. For all practical purposes, no operation ever took place. No BOPE weapon, even if subjected to forensic exam-ination, would indicate our participation. Our faces hadn't been seen. The night watchmen wouldn't dare testify against us. Even so, the lowlifes had no doubt who we were. They al-ways know very well when they're facing the Skull. We jot-ted down in our notebooks the name of the guy that got away. The traffickers had given him up. We'd find him sooner or later, wherever he was.

In late afternoon the next day, Colonel Camargo called the four officers closest to Juarez for a conversation in his office.

We went in and complied with all the formalities that the situation demanded: we saluted and stood at attention in front
of the desk of the commander, who barely noted our presence, rapidly lifting his eyes, and raising and lowering his
head almost imperceptibly. On the desk in front of him were
scribbled papers, next to military medals and family photo-
graphs. We looked like a firing squad, except that there, at
that moment, we were the ones condemned. However much
we criticized and distanced ourselves from the formalities that
hierarchy imposed, however much privately we were the first
to ridicule the lay religion that is the military police with all
its rituals, the fact is that, in the face of authority, everything
changes: Who wouldn't shudder? You might think that the
cause of my shaking wasn't military hierarchy but the guilt I
felt from what had happened the previous night. You'd be
wrong. There wasn't the least bit of guilt. Didn't the memory
of Juarez merit that response? Wasn't the honor of the corps
worth something? Guilt is what I'd have felt if I'd been a coward. That's the truth.

"I feel bad about what happened. I believe it was my fault,"
said the colonel in a faint voice, in a tone that wasn't his, an
unusual pitch.

I couldn't have agreed more. The one to blame was the
colonel.

"I feel really bad," he repeated, getting up from his chair.
He went to the bookcases against the wall opposite the door
and stood there with his back to us. He took out a book,
opened it, turned his head toward us and ordered us to

stand at ease. He leafed through the book and turned his head again.

"You may be seated. Sit down." He pointed to the sofa on one wall, and to the chairs in front of the desk. "I'm not feeling well and"—walking toward us—"I want to talk to each of you, man to man. This isn't the colonel speaking, much less your commanding officer, it's a Christian, a servant of God. Do you believe in God?"

We four policemen, called by the colonel for that strange visit to his office, sank into the sofa and the chairs. The prolonged, unsettling silence smothered the room. I had the sensation that we had plunged through the bottom of the ocean, toward the center of the earth. None of us dared reply. I confess that I began to be more frightened than if I were being really chewed out, reprimanded for the kind of screwup that's completely beyond repair. It was justifiable to avenge a comrade executed in cold blood by bloodthirsty criminals. Wasn't it? Maybe it wasn't legitimate, but it was justifiable.

"You," he said, addressing me. "Do you believe? Do you have faith?"

I almost answered "Thank you." I know that doesn't make sense, but so what? Nothing was making sense. I stuttered and stammered, "Uh-huh."

"Uh-huh, what? What's uh-huh? What're you trying to say? Do you believe or don't you?"

I said, "Yes, sir, of course. Why?"

"Because what I'm about to tell you isn't of this world. It can't be understood using the logic of this world."

Rattled, confused, dumbfounded, I nearly said, "Uh-huh, of course, thank you very much, yes, sir."

"Why are you looking at me like that?" the colonel challenged me. It seemed that he was reading my mind. The more tangled up I got, the more his radar followed my trail toward the center of the earth.

"I, I do know, sir."

"Know what, Captain?" he probed again.

"Not everything in this world has its reasons . . . This world, I mean, isn't entirely rational."

"Do you believe in spirits?"

"Yes, sir."

"I repeat: Captain, do you believe in spirits?"

"I believe in spirits, yes, I do, sir."

"Very good. Any doubts? Does anyone here in this room have any doubts about spirits?"

Silence.

"Are there any atheists here?"

"No, sir," I replied. I think my desire was just to break the silence. I have a certain difficulty dealing with silence in the face of authority—it gives me the feeling that a grenade is about to explode at any moment inside my head. When he would scold me, my father used to interpret my silence as indifference and disrespect. The result was that my silence was usually followed by a smack in the head. A grenade inside my head.

"I'm not asking you, Captain. You already answered. I want to know what your comrades think."

Luckily, Captain Irley kept the ball rolling. "There're no

atheists here, Colonel. Everybody here has faith in God and believes in spirits. We're not saints, Colonel, but I can guarantee you that no one here's an atheist."

The other two, Paulinho and Miro, nodded in agreement. They were sitting side by side on the sofa, sweating buckets, with signs on their foreheads that said We Fucked Up. If the colonel had persisted just a little more, if he had applied just a bit more pressure, I'd be willing to bet they'd have broken down and confessed to original sin. It didn't even seem like they'd been trained in the BOPE and passed the Charlie-Charlie test—the CC, for "concentration camp," test, about which more later. I riveted my frowning gaze on the pair, hoping their eyes would meet mine, to send them the message that the least to be expected from two grown men was manliness. If they hadn't turned yellow on the hill, why would they give themselves up to the commander? Equally important to avenging Juarez was respect for the pact of loyalty among partners. I felt like shaking the two sons of bitches and yelling: "Goddammit! Shit!" I looked at Irley, searching for support, as if to say: you can't trust anybody.

"All of you believe. That's good. That makes it easier," Camargo said. He came around the desk with his hands behind his back, his eyes on the floor. He seemed to be thinking as he spoke. Speaking to gain time, while he calculated.

"Very well," he continued, sitting down in his chair behind the desk and staring at us, one by one. "I believe in spirits and speak to you as a servant. I'm carrying out a mission. A mission that demands great energy and, above all, humility."

He lowered his gaze, rummaged through the disordered

papers, rested both hands on the top of the desk, closed his eyes, then opened them and went on. "For many years I've been doing religious work, away from here. I don't bring my private life to the barracks. I don't mix my career in the military police with my personal things, much less with spiritual experiences. I'm a medium. Camargo is a medium. I work at the Light of the World Center. I go there with my family. The one invoking the spirits, doing the psychography, incorporating the entities, isn't the colonel, isn't the commander of the BOPE. The one doing the psychography is Camargo, you understand?"

"Yes, sir," I rushed to get him back to his narrative in order to avoid another interrogation. I felt relieved. He was the one doing the confessing.

"So then, you'll understand that now it's Camargo who needs to ask you something. It's not the colonel, it's the man, the servant of God, the guy who carries on his shoulders the cross of a mission."

He took a breath, paused, looked at the top of the desk, shuffled or organized the papers, then stared at us again and continued. "Last night I couldn't sleep. I didn't close my eyes. I tossed and turned in bed. My wife found it strange, because I usually sleep like a log. I've never had insomnia. I'm not the type to have insomnia, you understand? I went to the living room and turned on the lamp. I wasn't feeling well. At first I thought it was my heart, but I didn't want to worry my wife—she wakes up early, earlier than me, to take care of our grandson. I began to realize it wasn't anything physical. I got a glass of water, drank it, and felt that what was wrong with me was fucking anguish. So much so that the water washed away the discomfort. When I realized that water was the so-lution, I deduced that the problem wasn't of this world. It was spiritual, do you understand? Is anyone here a Kardecian?"*

Before I could fill the void with something foolish, Irley said that his godfather was an assiduous reader of Chico Xavier, but the colonel didn't hear him. I don't *think* he heard him, because he went on talking.

"Kardecism is a science. A Christian science, you under-stand? Of course it has religious aspects, but it's still a science. It has nothing to do with that craziness of macumba.† Spiritism is very demanding. You have to prepare, study—it's not for ignoramuses."

"My godfather used to say that too"—Irley was insisting on the story of his godfather, but the colonel wasn't the tee-niest bit interested in the scientific culture of my colleague's family. He quickly trampled on Irley's comment.

"I drank a second glass of water and let the channel open. I sat down at the table with pencil and paper, shut my eyes, put my right hand over my eyes—I'm left-handed, you know—and began to scribble, writing, writing. When you receive—"

"My godfather read me *Our Home*, by the spirit André Luiz, which Chico Xavier transcribed," Irley interrupted again, more and more an intimate of the colonel.

---

*The Frenchman Hippolyte Léon Denizard Rivail (1804–1869), writing as Allan Kardec, was the founder of Spiritism. Laying claim to being a science more than a religion, its beliefs include reincarnation and communication with the dead.—Ed.

†An animistic religion brought to Brazil by African slaves. The term is often con-sidered pejorative.—Ed.

"Right, *Our Home* was the first great work . . . You don't know what you're writing, you don't see the message the spirit transmits. It's the spirit who writes using human hands. That's why the one writing is called the medium."

"The means"—it was Irley again, punctuating the commander.

"The means, exactly. When I regained consciousness, know what I found? Know what I read? Do you have any idea who the message was from?" Camargo didn't wait for Irley's answer. "From Juarez."

I confess that, at that moment, I felt a cold sensation run down my spine and couldn't think of anything to say to break the chill. Irley also gave up. So it was up to Camargo himself to end the silence.

"From Juarez, yes, gentlemen, from Juarez."

After looking at each of us, the commander read the message. I admit I've never felt good about these things. I felt gravity pulling the room down. I had to grip the arm of the chair and clench my teeth to control a strong urge to disappear. In the message, Juarez, in words very much his own, his typical way of talking, asked his comrades not to avenge his death, saying that one misfortune was enough by itself, that it wasn't what he wanted, and for us, please, to sleep on it, let our heads cool, pray for him, and take care of his wife and children. And not add more corpses to his story.

"I insisted on reading it to you because, deep down," the colonel continued, "the message is directed to you, officers he admired, to whom he was always loyal and in whom he always had confidence. I felt it my obligation to act as a bridge between him, wherever he is, and each of you. Let's pray for the soul of our brother, Juarez."

Colonel Camargo stood up. Irley, Paulinho, Miro, and I leaped up, awaking from a kind of daze. The commander said a few words. We closed our eyes and lowered our heads. At the end, we repeated "Amen" aloud. He asked us to reflect on that message a thousand times before taking any rash action. And he added: the best homage to the memory of Juarez would be to respect his wishes.

"I'm going to visit his widow later today, but I'm not going to say anything to her about this message. It's best for this to remain among us. I trust you. You may go."

Camargo insisted on shaking our hands, as if feeling the need to seal a pact between us.

Silently, we left the office. In the hall, we walked with our heads down. No one could say anything. We've never spoken of the matter since. I've never talked about it with anyone. It was as if I had to bury the memory of the meeting, the psychography, the message, the colonel's office, perhaps because it all had the effect of resurrecting Juarez, whose words have never ceased to frighten me.

Two Floors

Corporal Nestor and Private Amparo were descending the Conceição favela, in Rio's West Zone. The rest of the team had already left the hillside, taking with them a sizable cache of weapons seized in the operation that night. After a powerful incursion by the BOPE, without prisoners or deaths, the community was enjoying a postcard serenity. Everyone knew the outlaws would stay away for some time. Day was breaking and the workers were leaving their shacks and heading for the streets, eager to get started on the tasks of the day. With a feeling of mission accomplished, Nestor and Amparo were thinking about coffee with milk, bread and butter, and the sleep of the just. At their backs was the hubbub of lunch pails, children, bags, and dust.

Because a policeman is tuned in twenty-four hours a day, on duty or off—I think that even when we sleep we're on the alert—our comrades noticed something odd in the appearance of two youths. So as not to waste the trip, they searched the guys. They were brothers. One of them was carrying a pistol and swore he wasn't a trafficker.

"I'm not part of the movement, no, sir. I'm just a holdup man. I don't have no other weapon, I don't."

He swore he didn't know anything about the traffickers' weapons. Amparo put the squeeze on him. "You either turn over the weapons or you end up in a ditch."

The guy was scared: on the one hand, he knew very well that you don't screw around with the BOPE; on the other, by giving up the weapons he might get off, but he'd never escape his accomplices, whether in prison or in the favela. He'd be treated like a CI—a "Criminal Informant." The truth is that he resisted, denied, swore he was nothing but a shit-heel robber, that he didn't have anything, his only gun was the one he was carrying. His brother was trembling and swore he wasn't involved in what the other one did or didn't do, that he was a working man—the usual bullshit.

Nestor decided to take them home. "Let's see if you hand over the pieces or not. Where do you two live? Let's go there."

They went up a winding alleyway and entered a small two-story house next to a dead end. A living room and kitchen, cramped and dark, separated by a greasy navy blue curtain. The refrigerator was in the living room, next to the television. A torn sofa and a chair, on a carpet with Venetian motifs: gondolas, bridges, canals. A wooden staircase off to the side, steep. One of the brothers kept saying that their mother was sick, a stroke had left her a paraplegic. She spent her days at home and it would kill her if she found out her sons had a problem with the police. Nestor, who was paternal and understanding, played counterpoint to Amparo. "If you hand over the weapons, nothing'll happen to you or to your mother."

The door squeaked.

"Who's there?"

A woman's voice came from upstairs. The story about a sick mother was probably true.

"It's us, Ma. Nothing to worry about. The police just came to see if anything's wrong here," said the guy with the pistol, who was taller and a bit older.

"Stay up there, ma'am. We don't need anything from you," said Nestor.

"Now cut the shit and give us the rifles. Where are they?" said Amparo, the bad cop. "Come on, goddammit. We don't have all fucking morning." And he smacked the shorter one in the face.

"Shit, man, don't belt me. I'm telling you I don't know nothing about no weapons. The only weapon's that pistol. I'm telling the truth."

"Don't fuck with us." Amparo struck him with his gun butt and gave him a kick in the knee.

The youth bent over and started to cry. "I don't know about any fucking weapons. I don't have a piece."

The woman upstairs shouted again. "The boys are workers. We're an honest family. There aren't any guns in this house. Leave them alone."

"Keep outta this, goddammit," Amparo answered, and then he raised his voice: "Shut up, you whore. If you don't shut that filthy mouth of yours, I'm gonna beat the shit out of these sons of bitches."

"It's better that you stay calm, ma'am; otherwise, things can get hairy," said Nestor, in the hieratic voice of a priest of public safety.

"What about you, you piece of shit?" said Amparo, bitch slapping the taller boy. Nelson Rodrigues* says a bitch slap doesn't hurt, but the sound is humiliating. I can't say whether it hurt or not. Given Amparo's strength, I just don't know.

Now Nestor piled on. "Give us the fucking weapons."

"Sheesh, I already told you I got nothing to do with that, I don't know nothing," said the shorter, more fragile one. He went from crying to sobbing like a child, which drove Amparo nuts.

"Give it up, fucker, or I'll blow your head off right here and now."

"Don't shoot, for the love of God. My sons, for the love of God. They're my boys. Our Lord Jesus Christ." The woman was hysterical. It didn't help matters. Her prayers didn't help. Or her appeals. Just the opposite; the shouts of the pious woman, echoing like a church choir, made Amparo furious. He reacted in the same language, bellowing like the God of the Old Testament: "Shut your mouth, you bitch."

He pointed his rifle at the column to which the stairs were attached and fired to frighten the youths and their mother, and to restore order in the place. What happened, by one of those tricks of fate or bad luck, was that the bullet ricocheted and went into the back of the neck of the boy who was cry-

*Nelson Rodrigues (1912–1980), Brazil's most important playwright, was noted for his hard-boiled subject matter and rather cavalier treatment of his female characters.—Ed.

ing. The explosion pumped adrenaline into the players, accelerated time, destroyed Nestor and Amparo's balance, raised the volume of the woman's cries, and paralyzed the taller boy. Seeing the traces of his brother on the wall, he turned green, yellow, blue, and white.

"Sons, sons, who fired that shot? For the love of God, what happened?" Strident howls followed from the mother, who guessed the worst.

"I give up. The pieces are in the water tank," the survivor said, staring at Amparo.

"Too late now. Where's this leave us, huh?"

Amparo knew there was no way out. Therefore he had to go on shooting. Nestor knew it too and started firing. The boy ran through the kitchen and the living room like a drunken turkey on Christmas Eve. He begged, shrieked, climbed onto the sink, slid down the sofa, jumped over the refrigerator, pushed over the TV, and the noises mixed with the agitation of the woman on the second floor, who was following the spectacle by the sounds. It seemed unbelievable that so many shots would be necessary in such a small space. Imagine two or three uncontrollable horses, condemned to wage a life-or-death struggle inside a modest house: an archetypal confrontation among Greek gods, Cyclopes, and unicorns, moving heaven and earth, lightning bolts, fire, winds, and oceans. Genesis and the Apocalypse inside four walls: floor and ceiling spattered with blood, bones, shards of glass, blocks of plaster, pieces of wood and cloth, fragments of brick, images diffused in the clouds of dust, full of gunpowder and seared flesh.

The boy fell, grabbing the curtain, his eyes wide open and motionless.

When Nestor and Amparo closed the door, nothing but the mother's voice could be heard. One mistake breeds another. In this case, a stroke of bad luck demanded an unwanted action: it made no sense to allow a witness to live. The woman was saved because she saw nothing. Sometimes, it's us or them. We don't always do what's right or what we'd like to do. The results aren't always the best. Don't think that Nestor and Amparo were insensitive monsters. I'm sure they also suffered from the slaughter. That they had nightmares. They took tranquilizers to get to sleep. But eventually you get used to it.

Bloody Boots

I remember a soap opera, in the Mexican style, a really corny drama with a title to match: *Blood Wedding*. Oh, wait. No, it wasn't on television; it was a novel by Nelson Rodrigues, written under one of those incredible pen names he invented, like Suzana Flag. By now you must be thinking that I'm obsessed with Nelson Rodrigues. It's true. I really am. In this case, though, with a slight twist and some goodwill, the bloody wedding could very well be attributed to García Lorca. Good taste and bad taste separate and overlap, depending on your perspective. It's all very relative. You don't need a Ph.D. in ethics to know that. But that doesn't matter. What matters is telling the story, the strange story of Corporal Alves's boots. Or Private Alves, because at the time of the boots he hadn't been promoted yet.

We were at the courthouse, assisting in the transport of a dangerous prisoner to testify in a trial. We were talking outside the hearing room, because the corridor was practically empty and the situation was under control. Colleagues were with the prisoner, inside the room; others were stationed at the entrance to the building; there were also comrades at the strategic points—stairs, emergency exits, et cetera. A camera system, monitored by another colleague, completed the job of vigilance. Therefore, no problem in exchanging a few words. I say this so you won't think we were sloppy hacks chewing the fat on duty. Please don't confuse the BOPE with the cops you're used to seeing around.

At a certain moment, Alves whispered, "Did you see who just went by, Captain?"

I'd seen a young man being pushed in a wheelchair, in handcuffs, led by a military policeman.

"So?" I asked.

"You didn't recognize him?" insisted Alves. "I'm amazed. How did that son of a bitch survive? That's Naldinho, the guy from that thing with the boots."

"Naldinho? Are you sure? Incredible. He looks like another person."

"Of course, Captain. He must've lost over forty pounds and he's at least a year older."

"It's already been a year since that operation?"

"At least. Besides that, the ordeal must've aged him several years. I don't know how the guy survived."

"To tell you the truth, Alves, neither do I."

"Think he saw us?"

"No way. His head was down when he went by. He looked like he was under anesthesia."

"You think he's lost it?"

"Lost it, Alves? No. Naldinho was always kind of retarded. I've never seen a trafficker who was any kind of genius. Have you?"

"No, Captain. But I'm worried. You think maybe he saw us and pretended not to? That's all we need, for the son of a bitch to come back to life and fuck us."

"Stay cool, Alves. Just let it go. It's our word against his, and don't forget that the courts are always on our side. Did you ever see a resisting-arrest charge cause us any shit?"

Corporal Alves had to agree. To tell the truth, I was speaking firmly to try to convince myself. I wasn't all that sure that the son of a bitch hadn't seen and recognized us. Even though we were armored against that kind of shit.

Naldinho's case took place in the Murici favela, in Niterói. Alves was still a private, as I said earlier. He was the point man and I was in command. I don't remember whether I was still a lieutenant or already a captain. The fact is that the eight of us were invading to catch or eliminate the traffickers, who were making life hell with their night raids, in which they would descend the favela to set up false roadblocks in order to steal cars and belongings from drivers and passengers, especially any weapons they found. And anyone who was armed was killed immediately, whether or not he was a cop. If he was a cop, the level of cruelty was higher.

Our ascent had been well planned. We surrounded a nearby favela, Coréia, conspicuously, giving every indication that we would invade with maximum force. But our target was Murici. During the day, we had scheduled with the 22nd Battalion to do a sweep of the terrain. We didn't explain the reason behind it, but we asked them to kill every dog they came across on their way up. We made up some cock-and-bull story about a rabies epidemic in the favela, with the blessing of the secretary of health, and stressed the need to not share the information with the residents, to avoid panic. I don't know if they swallowed that crap, but they smoothed the way for us, guaranteeing silence for our nocturnal incursion. A long trek uphill, without a single bark. The hawks—young boys working for the traffickers who were responsible for keeping watch—were deactivated, because all our attention was supposedly focused on Coréia. The field couldn't have been more favorable. Even so, as always, we climbed taking every precaution: the point man advancing to the next strategic location, from which it was possible to visualize the next stage of the incursion, and so on. Alves would signal to the second in line and to me; I would select the most appropriate action at each moment, trying to follow as much as possible what we had planned.

In one of those strange and complicated situations—but that's, after all, what the point man is for—turning the corner at the end of an alleyway, and after stepping into an uncovered manhole invisible in the darkness, Alves was surprised by a trafficker who came down armed. Alerted by the noise, the lowlife fired at the shadow he could barely make out because he was at the other end of the wide courtyard.

The alley emptied into that courtyard, which was reasonably well lit and surrounded by two-story houses, the samba school rehearsal area, lampposts, electric wires with thousands of illegal taps, and a few isolated trees planted by the authorities. Sons of bitches. All of them, the traffickers on one side, the politicians on the other. I don't know if it's actually that way, with two sides. Sometimes it's the same side, the gang is one and the same. It's organized crime, the crime that penetrates public institutions, just like the doctor ordered. But let's put that aside, 'cause war's about to break out in front of the rehearsal area.

Alves wasn't hit, and he got the lowlife. We ran to back him up, looking for cover behind posts and trees. The traffickers opened fire, covering an outlaw assigned to rescue their wounded henchman. They threw a grenade. Private Rodrigues leaped close to the place where the grenade fell, instead of far away from it like an amateur would have done. He protected his head, near the ground, and survived. His agility saved him. He was hit by shrapnel, but nothing more serious. We stepped up the pressure and forced the enemy to retreat.

The first lowlife writhed, bleeding like a pig. We advanced and formed a 360. The lowlifes realized they were dealing with the BOPE and fled. The dying man was our booty. The shot had opened his belly and he had spit up his guts. I stuck the rifle barrel against the bastard's face, and he still had the strength to ask me not to mess him up. Outlaws are terrified of dying disfigured, because then there can't be an open-casket wake. Just as I was about to apply the coup de grâce between the eyes, at the angle that kills most quickly, a female resident opened her window and started giving me a hard time.

"Don't kill him, don't kill him! The police are gonna kill the boy! The police are gonna kill him! Murderer!"

If there's anything that pisses me off, it's that.

"Close the window, you cow, or you'll die too, you whore." I yelled and pointed the gun upward. The woman closed the window and turned out the light. I regret having to use vulgar expressions. It would make no sense to lie and pretend that, at the time, I was cool enough to say, "Madam, if it's not asking too much, could you be so kind as to close your window, because I have to execute this citizen and you're distracting me?"

The woman closed her window and turned out the light, sure, but who says she didn't go on watching and maybe even photographing or filming? There was no way now to complete the job. The thing to do was to descend with the bleeding pig. The lowlife would probably buy it before we reached the wagon. Our only concern was Rodrigues. He said he was all right, just injured in the hands and arms, but with explosions you never know. There are cases in which the person absorbs the impact and suffers an internal hemorrhage but doesn't realize it; he starts bleeding without knowing it. We pulled the pig down the hill, making no effort to spare the son of a bitch. Again, it's too bad, I know, but that's how it was. When we got to the bottom of the hill, as we waited for the ambulance, Alves couldn't control himself and stuck his foot into the red, white, and gray mass hanging from the lowlife's belly. And he added a curse: "There, now the son of a bitch won't get away. There's a shit-pot of dirt, crap, bacteria, and germs. Swallow that shit, you fucker."

This is really in poor taste, I know. Disgusting. It's what I call dirty work. But it sure as shit happened. Now you understand why Alves turned white as a sheet when Naldinho passed by us at the courthouse a year later. The guy survived. When it's not your time, it's not your time. There's nothing you or anyone can do about it.

Sniper

L ike all the best combat forces in the world, the BOPE
has its sniper, the guy who can trim a cat's whisker with
a shot a quarter mile away, even in the turmoil of a kidnapping. Our sniper was Duque, Sergeant Alceu Duque dos
Santos. Late one evening, he climbed up the Nazareth favela
with us, determined to try out his new Remington M24 7.62
NATO high-precision rifle with free-floating barrel and
Leupold scope. We reached the side plateau of the hill, from
which we had a wide view of the movement in the favela.
The incursion was preventive. We'd gotten word that the
lowlifes running the local drug trade were planning a raid and
wreaking havoc in the area. With the BOPE breathing down
their necks, the creeps wouldn't be crazy enough to play with
fire. We took night visors and got ready to spend the night.

While we were settling in, occupying the strategic points
and planning a cleansing action to rid us once and for all of
the lowlifes in that community, Duque was amusing himself

with his powerful 7.62, polished, elegant, swinging back and forth on the bipod supporting it. He looked like a happy kid pissing at the stars on a summer night, after his first screw with the hottest girl in town. There he was, turning that incredible Leupold scope in every direction, striking a pose as a hero of the nation.

"Duque," I said, "I think you've been watching too many war movies lately. Are you trying to play cops and robbers? All that's missing is a sound track with the whine of bullets cutting through the sky. What do you keep looking at? The favela is quiet, there's nobody out there. The bad guys already know we're here. You can relax."

"I know, Captain, I know. It's just that from here, using the scope, I can also see the Bugre favela perfectly."

Fine. I had other things to worry about. I called Torres and Vargas to work out some details of the plan of action and forgot about our sniper.

It wasn't long—maybe half an hour, forty minutes—before Duque called me, clutching his weapon, his right eye glued to the telescopic sight.

"Captain, Captain. I think I've got an outlaw in the crosshairs."

"But you're looking outside the favela."

"Right, Captain. I think I've identified a lowlife there in Bugre."

"In Bugre, man. But you can tell he's an outlaw? How do you know?"

"I can tell, Captain. Take a look with your binoculars. The guy's got a rifle. I mean, it sure looks like a rifle."

"It sure looks like a rifle?"

"More or less."

"What do you mean more or less? It's more or less a rifle?"

"It's a rifle. A rifle. You can plainly see the long barrel. It's a rifle for sure. Just take a look, Captain. Check it out."

I aimed my binoculars, got down to the level of the rifle, chose the most appropriate position, glued my eyes to the lenses, but I didn't see shit. Not a rifle, not a person, all I could see was a milky mist, a slow-moving haze in a cloud of sand.

"I can't see a fucking thing, Duque."

"You will, Captain. Adjust them just right. Take a look at that rock. You see that big sharp-edged rock up there? Now come down in a straight line, past the houses, the bicycle, keep going down the hill, the green area, and that spit of land . . . There. Do you see it?"

He reached over toward me, lifted the binoculars to his eyes, fiddled with the focusing rings, and exclaimed, "There. Now look at him. Take a look."

I looked, concentrating my vision for all I was worth. I saw a vaguely rectangular form that seemed to move, but I wasn't certain if it was a person, or if it was actually moving, much less if it was carrying a weapon.

"You're nuts, Duque. You're seeing things."

"No, I'm not, Captain. It's a guy all right, and he's armed."

"Let the guy be, forget it."

"Sheesh, Captain, he's smack in the crosshairs. Let me squeeze one off. Just one."

"Listen to yourself, Duque. Forget it, this is silly."

"But, Captain, the guy moves like an outlaw, I know those types. He's a lowlife, yessir."

"Shit, I said forget it."

"Jeez, Captain, he's standing there real still, quiet as can be, like a little bird just asking to be shot at. Just one. Let me send him just one little love note."

"Duque, have you given any thought to the shit that would come down if you're mistaken? If it's not a rifle at all? If it's a cane? Or a piece of wood? Or anything else, goddammit? Besides which, at this distance you think you're going to hit your little bird? For God's sake, flip the record. Relax. Drop that shit. Go stretch your legs. Get a drink of water. Come help us finish the plan."

"Jeez, Captain. It'd just be one tiny shot. This weapon's the eighth wonder of the world. You can't miss. Look at the son of a bitch over there, right there, calm, not moving. Captain, he's asking for it."

"Let it go, goddammit. Stop pestering me, Duque."

Pow. It was a single report.

Duque had been overcome by a compulsion. He looked like someone on drugs. "I got the son of a bitch, Captain. I got him. He's on the ground. The guy's on the ground."

"Mother*fucker*, Duque. Who gave you the order, for shitsake? Didn't you hear what I said?"

"Jeez, Captain, he was asking for—"

"Get the fuck over there. I'll go with you."

I ordered several soldiers to accompany us.

"Let's see what you've gotten us into."

We descended Nazareth in a dead run. We crossed a few

streets and arrived at the base of the Bugre favela. It appeared peaceful, either because we were nearby or because we had carried out, days before, an operation of the black-box antibiotic type: broad spectrum. We'd left no stone unturned, so to speak. Although, if Duque was right, perhaps some microbe or other had resisted and was already starting to grow again. It was always that way. We went up cautiously, professionally, but at high speed. I had already sweated an amount equal to the entire month's rainfall. We finally arrived at the area where Duque had supposedly hit his target. A bunch of people were standing around a guy lying on the ground. Everybody ran as soon as they saw us. The guy was alive, crying and clutching his pelvic region. A few yards away, his balls were floating in a pool of blood, strewn and shattered. Beside the poor devil was the rifle that only Duque had seen. Seen or imagined, beats me. The moral of the story seems to be this: for a sniper, intuition is more important than aim. I thought that Duque was going to brag and give me a hard time—among us, camaraderie went much deeper than rank. But he wasn't happy.

"Fuck, Captain. Shit. I'm still not used to that weapon. What a mess. What a dirty trick I pulled on the guy. What a fuckup. This isn't what I wanted. If I'm on target, the guy wouldn't have felt a thing."

Skull

When I see some authority from Public Safety on television handing out bullshit, I'll admit it pisses me off. In general they're politicians, a bunch that usually beat their chests and bellow out totally hypocritical, moralistic speeches. When the problem is criminals, the line is always the same: "We're going to investigate and bring them to justice, whomever it hurts." When we, the police, are the target, the shilly-shallying goes more or less like this: "We shall immediately remove from his position anyone who dishonors the uniform he wears. The integrity and history of the institution must be preserved." The worst part is that our superiors in the police often act like politicians themselves. And even become politicians, at the end of their careers. That's fine, I've got nothing special against politicians. They're like the police, either honest or dishonest. It's case by case. You can't generalize. But I'll admit it makes me sick when I see certain demagogic farces and manipulations. What revolts me more than anything is hypocrisy. It can be fatal.

One day I was shooting the breeze with a friend, Franco, and the subject came up. We recalled a revealing case. The conversation began with Franco telling me this: "Shit, man, it's gonna be the coolest thing. I'm gonna do it here, in the arm, near the shoulder."

"What's it going to be? A mermaid? A heart with an arrow through it? The name Duília?"

"No way, bro. Don't fuck around. It's gonna be a man thing."

"An anchor . . ."

"No goddamn anchor, man. Don't give me a hard time. It's gonna be a skull. Naturally."

"That business of tattoos doesn't make sense to me. Why are you doing it?"

"Lots of guys in the BOPE are getting a skull tattoo. I've had phone calls from colleagues who did it and they're proud of it. It's important, man. It's our pride, our honor. It's forever. Just like being a member of the BOPE. It's something that stays with you forever. It's like it was a medal. It's our flag. Time passes, we get older, leave the BOPE, leave the police, but the history isn't wiped out. The pride remains. And when we bump into each other, one of these days, when we're already retired, we'll remember proudly. It's our fucking symbol. Our religion."

"And what if you suddenly discover that a handful of sons of bitches have been manipulating your pride? Are you going to wash off the skull to keep from looking like a fool?"

Franco looked at me with an expression half pissed, half quizzical. I explained. "Have you seen today's paper?"

"And?"

"Have you seen it or not?"

"I've seen it."

"What did you think?"

"About what?"

"The shot, for God's sake. The tragedy—I don't know what to call it. Over in Vigário Geral. Didn't you see that boy shot by Captain Plácido's team, by our brave BOPE comrades?"

"The singer? I know, I've met him. Everybody in the community there admires him. He's a super example for everyone. And he's a damn good singer."

"So then, what do you think?"

"I think it's sad. Horrible. It must've been an accident, fate."

"Fate, my ass. I spoke to Plácido this morning."

"Was it on purpose?"

"Of course not. He's devastated. But it might as well've been. Deep down, you could say yes, it was intentional."

"I don't get it."

"You know that the people in the Department of Public Safety are dying to catch Matias Matagal. Society wants blood vengeance. The governor is demanding the bastard's imprisonment at any cost. He demands it every day, all the time. The secretary says he's going crazy; he can't stand the pressure any longer. You can just imagine the heat the commander-general of the military police and the head of the civil police are taking."

"I can imagine."

"At times like that, you forget everything: technique, the law, work methods, everything. You want results. Results at any cost."

"Well, depends on the results, for chrissake. Blowing off the leg of a guy who's got nothing the fuck to do with anything, and who's an idol in the community—that's a shitty result."

"That's the point. You hit the nail on the head. What happened in Vigário was literally a shot in the foot."

The previous evening, 9 P.M., office of the BOPE commander

The red telephone interrupted Colonel Rubilar's meeting with four officers and his second-in-command. Together, they had just watched the tape of the newscast and had discussed alternative plans for an especially delicate emergency operation. Half of the newscast had been taken up by the funeral of the Rio businessman, who'd been kidnapped and murdered while in captivity after being brutally tortured. Agitation gripped the city, the state, and the country. Rio had become the capital of violence. There was even a solemn reading of an editorial demanding an end to impunity.

"Rubilar, what happened?" said the voice on the phone. "I've been informed that the BOPE still hasn't arrived at Vigário. The governor is calling me constantly. He's beside himself. He's also been told by the civil police that Matias is in Vigário. The commander-general promised that the BOPE was on its way."

"Mr. Secretary, unfortunately we can't undertake an incursion into the favela at this time. Today is Friday. It would be irresponsible. Technically, the conditions aren't right. There's a funk dance tonight. A large number of people are moving around the community. Under those conditions an invasion can only lead to disaster."

"The disaster would be to wash our hands of it, Colonel. What's the BOPE for?"

"Mr. Secretary, with all due respect, the BOPE exists to solve problems, not to create new ones. We are responsible for competently seeing to the public's safety. The last thing the BOPE wants is to cause you headaches. You and the governor already have enough problems. Society won't take any more, and it's clear that we have to act. The BOPE doesn't refrain from intervening, nor does it shy away from risking the lives of our men. We've been trained to carry out the most difficult missions. But I cannot, we cannot, be accomplices in an irresponsible action. I would be a poor counselor if I were to tell you that the operation is viable. It is not, Mr. Secretary. Unfortunately, it is not. And what I'm stating is based on a strictly technical examination of the situation. I'm telling you what I already told the commander-general of the military police. If you think it relevant, I can repeat it to the governor himself. I can explain everything, in technical terms."

"Technical, Rubilar, technical? What are you talking about? What planet are you on? Don't you understand the seriousness of the situation? Rubilar, the governor is cornered. The people are desperate. The federal government is considering intervening. Intervening, Rubilar. You know what that means?"

"I do know, Mr. Secretary. I understand your anguish—"

"Then how can you sit there and come up with technical arguments? Is desperation technical? Is federal intervention technical? Was the murder technical? I don't want to hear about technical. The only thing technical I care about is the result. I want that scum Matias Matagal; I want that monster, dead or alive. That's what the governor has decided. It's what the people want, Rubilar. I order the immediate deployment of the BOPE to Vigário Geral."

"Mr. Secretary, please try to understand my situation. It's not a matter of disputing your authority or that of the governor, or of the commander-general. What I can't do is give an order that will lead to disaster. The Special Operations Battalion is different, sir, not only because of its firepower but also because of its training. What distinguishes us is not only force but technique, because force, when it's efficient, is an outgrowth of technique. Therefore, in combat the BOPE wounds fewer and kills fewer, is wounded less and killed less. I'm aware that you know all this, but I'm taking the liberty of sharing this reflection because my resistance to deploying the men under my command in this situation is a manifestation of responsibility."

"It's a manifestation of insubordination, is what it is. Let's put our cards on the table, Rubilar. By all rights, I shouldn't even be talking to you. Observing rank, I would only speak to your superior, the commander-general of the military police. I called you out of deference to the BOPE. You don't seem to have understood my gesture and don't seem to realize what's at stake. That being the case, I have to be blunt: it's either me or you. Matias is in Vigário and it's necessary to hunt him down. If not you, the BOPE will do it under another commander. You have thirty minutes to invade Vigário."

The secretary hung up. Rubilar placed the phone on the hook and grunted something inaudible. The officers and the second-in-command continued to watch the news in silence, waiting for words that didn't come. The colonel yanked the receiver off the hook and dialed the number of the military police general command.

"Commander, it's me, Rubilar. He called. I just got through speaking with him. That's why I'm calling you. He wants the BOPE in Vigário, now. I told him what I'd said to you, but there was no way around it. Commander, please, this is very serious. Do you want a catastrophe on your record? I don't. My officers agree with me. Any serious professional, Commander, knows it makes no sense to execute an operation improvised at the drop of a hat, from one minute to the next, in the middle of a community dance, with hundreds of people milling about. That's not what we teach our recruits. The BOPE can't be the instrument of an irresponsible adventure, Commander. Please, talk to the secretary. Talk to him again. Tell him it's a technical question. Why don't you try to get in touch with the governor?"

Rubilar listened in silence. He muttered one last "Yes, sir" and hung up. He turned to his subordinates, almost holding his breath, and said, "Politics. The commander-general said he can't do anything. The decision is political, not technical. Fuck the community. Fuck the BOPE. Pol-i-tics."

Saturday, 11 A.M., hospital corridor

Family members of the singer mingled with journalists waiting for news from the surgery center. Voices raised in conster-
nation and revolt merged. One account was heard.

"He was in the car when the BOPE armored vehicle came
into the favela. He said that when he saw that searchlight from
the armored truck focusing on his car, he told his girlfriend
not to move, and he slowly opened the door, shouting that he
was coming out, peacefully. Lots of people came past, running
everywhere. When he put his foot on the ground and began
getting out of the car, that's when the burst of gunfire came.
He didn't feel anything but the violent blow and the damp
warmth of blood spreading under his pants. He told his girlfriend he'd been hit, but she didn't believe it. She refused to
believe it. He fainted before he began feeling pain. It was hell.
God willing, he'll recover movement and walk again. But the
other two boys didn't even make it to the hospital. They
died next to the wire fence, near the Peace House."

The most popular radio news program in the city informed
listeners that the BOPE commander had just been relieved of
his duties by the secretary of public safety. According to the
secretary's spokesman, favela residents were also citizens and
the community of Vigário Geral deserved the same treatment
that the police employed with the population of Leblon. In
a telephone interview, the secretary stated, "The BOPE police lacked technique."

Politics

olonel Leme was a born politician. More than that, he was a diplomat. His colleagues joked that he acted as his own minister of foreign relations, twenty-four hours a day. He was polite, affable, prudent, and above all, wise in the strategy of rising in his chosen career. He had learned how to say whatever his listener wanted to hear. Which isn't easy. It requires mental agility and the ability to anticipate the other person's expectations. Of course, sometimes in trying to bring harmony to the irreconcilable, Leme would end up displeasing everybody.

When he was commanding a battalion in the state capital, Leme was called to a trailer that the military police had set up at the entrance to Maracanã Stadium. It was a bright Sunday on which to wage a battle of flags: a classic Rio football game. The crowd that jammed the stadium didn't always bring with them just their team's T-shirt and their readiness to cheer. The skinny guy detained in the trailer was proof of that. Under his shirt he had a Taurus 9mm pistol, illegal for civilian use.

The corporal and the sergeant who arrested him handed him over to Major Roger with the satisfaction of someone who finds a needle in a haystack. The man was named César Castro or Carvalho, something like that, the name of a major operator, a big fish. He might not have been a lowlife with a rap sheet or some famous outlaw, but neither was he a minnow. The cops showed themselves—and their superiors—that their work was important, serious, honorable, and competent. That's what's known as pride. And it's priceless.

César, the skinny guy, was arguing with the major: he needed to call a friend who'd resolve the problem. He used his own cell phone. He spoke at length to someone. He seemed to be in more trouble with his listener than with the police. Some forty minutes later, the trailer received an illustrious visitor: a member of the Chamber of Deputies arrived. Simpatico, shaking hands like a celebrity, good-looking and self-assured. He was in a hurry. He couldn't miss the game. His votes came from football, that factory of passions and interests that ignites the nerves of the tens of thousands of fans who crowd into the bleachers and the grandstand of the noble old Maracanã. He demanded to see Colonel Leme. He needed to talk to the colonel immediately. A deputy doesn't negotiate with majors.

Leme entered the trailer, panting. "Deputy, what an honor to receive your visit. A pleasure to see you again."

The topic was the skinny guy. "Why arrest an upright individual?" asked the deputy, as if he were delivering a speech.

Yes, he guaranteed that, despite the absolutely illegal and in-
explicable weapon, this man was a law-abiding citizen.

"But, Deputy, please understand, the crime is stipulated in
the penal code. It's very serious. This isn't just any gun. How
can I let the man go? How can I not take him to the precinct
and book him? There has to be an investigation."

The deputy's tone rose a notch. He argued. He repeated
himself, reiterating each point of his contention that this was
a man of integrity. He knew the guy's background, his relatives, his life. He put his word on the line in his testimony.
What was at stake, in the end, was his word, his credibility.
Could the colonel be doubting the statement of an authority, one who was in addition a fraternal friend of the military
police, an intimate of the commander-general and even,
dare he say, a friend and admirer of Leme himself?

The colonel started to think it over, hesitating, stammer-
ing. Even so, he still tried to resist. "Deputy, having your esteem is a privilege both for the corps and for me personally.
I would never doubt your testimony. Nevertheless, you must
understand, the fact being so serious makes this a delicate
case. You understand that it's not just the two of us in the face
of that fact. My subordinates did their duty and detained your
friend. You can imagine what they'd think of me and of the
very institution they serve . . . I know you know what I'm
talking about and understand my situation. No one more
than I would like to accommodate you, but in my position,
you understand . . ."

The deputy didn't back off. Just the opposite. He demon-
strated that he was uncomfortable and somewhat irritated.

He used the adjective *inflexible,* resorted to the expression *ill will* and even conceded that the situation merited the extreme qualifier *ungrateful,* given how much he'd done for the military police in the state legislature.

The colonel excused himself for a moment and called Roger. "Major, we have before us a peculiar case that requires tact. We have to think, above all, of the institution. It's more important than one or another arrest. This search isn't going to lead to anything. I would be irresponsible if I allowed it to create an embarrassing situation for the corps in the legislature. Furthermore, the deputy gave his word. He guaranteed that the guy's not an outlaw. So, Major, the best thing is for you to tell the sergeant and the corporal to let the man go."

Politely, Roger asked the colonel to give the order directly. He disagreed with the procedure and couldn't accept losing face with his subordinates. Naturally, he didn't answer the colonel in those words. But he subtly got the message across. So much so that Leme found himself obliged to speak to the sergeant and the corporal directly. He swallowed his embarrassment, squared his shoulders, and hid his shame behind the mask of authority. His subordinates got a hands-on lesson in politics.

After the storm, the calm. Leme felt more relaxed when he returned to give the deputy the good news. It was time to gather the fruit. He had won the deputy's goodwill once and for all. One never knows what the future holds. It's always good to be prepared. Who knows whether he might someday be nominated for commander-general or even state secretary? Political support would be indispensable.

"Deputy, in recognition of our friendship, your personal integrity, and your well-known contributions to the military police of the state of Rio de Janeiro, I've found a solution to the situation: the young man is free. I've already ordered the record expunged. Officially, the episode never happened. The gun will be placed on the list of apprehended items, and that's it. You can go and enjoy your Sunday."

The colonel's triumphant smile collapsed, felled by the deputy's reaction: Leme hadn't understood a thing. The deputy needed to take the gun with him. The gun was as important as the skinny guy. The representative of the people raised his voice. He called Leme's solution true lack of consideration, gall. When the deputy discovered that nothing more could be done, because the weapon had already been sent off to the pertinent sector, he left brusquely. The skinny guy followed him and looked back, before slamming the trailer door. The colonel had suffered his greatest setback in years. A setback too big to fit into the stadium. How could he face Roger, the sergeant, and the corporal? How could he avoid the story spreading through the corps? What could he do to prevent the deputy's counterattack? He felt more vulnerable, there in his bunker, than the one hundred thousand fans he was there to protect.

Fate in the Middle of the Street

The military police didn't always mean the BOPE to me, though I never had any doubts about my calling and had always dreamed of the day I would pass the test and receive my small skull badge. For several years I served as a military policeman in different battalions in Rio de Janeiro. One of the most important moments in my life occurred at the time I was billeted in the 23rd Battalion, responsible for the area extending from Jardim Botânico to Gávea, passing through Lagoa, Ipanema, and Leblon, not to mention Rocinha, Vidigal, and neighboring areas. My D-Day took place when the commander of the 23rd ordered me urgently to Rua Marquês de São Vicente: "There's a demonstration by PUC students blocking traffic and causing a humongous jam."

The troop I was responsible for wasn't all that clean, which bothered me in this situation, mostly because on the other side were the flowers of the Rio bourgeoisie—those wonderful middle-class girls from PUC, the Catholic university*—and the daddy's boys who snorted coke on Saturday and marched for peace on Sunday.

The commander warned me, "Just remember what you're getting me into, Lieutenant. Go slow. If you bust heads of any of the heirs of the city's elite, I'm going to be the one paying the price. At PUC there's nothing but priests and important surnames. Keep your men under control. Get the street opened and don't cause any confusion."

"Yes, sir" was what it occurred to me to say, while I was thinking about the shit that is our country—pardon the unpatriotic heresy. In fact, if my father were alive, I wouldn't have the courage to write that, just like that, with such candor. But what can I do? Is the country shit or isn't it? If the toothless poor blacks come down from the hillsides and close off the avenue, the order is to go all out, beat the shit out of them, and if things get rough, shoot first and ask questions later. But if they're the spoiled children of the South Zone, blond and bearing surnames found on street signs, the treatment has to be five-star, VIP policing, because if things get rough with them, the tightrope breaks on our side. . . . In this case, on my side.

You can imagine my mood as I got out of the wagon and ordered my troop to disarm and keep their distance. I was by myself, heading toward the leaders of the demonstration. My goal was to order that band of faggots and hysterical girls off the street. Shit, those sons of bitches have homes of their own,

---

*PUC is the abbreviation of the Pontifícia Universidade Católica (Pontifical Catholic University) located in Rio's Gávea district.—Ed.

their laundry done, a guaranteed future, a first-class private university, and they still want to jerk the chain of people who need to work, by blocking traffic, shouting themselves hoarse to parrot the most ridiculous slogans. At least if they had been subversives at the time of the dictatorship, if they had risked their lives, or even sacrificed their comfort, had taken up arms . . . It's true that I'd still go on hating all of them. . . . Thinking about those things made me remember that these were the same cowards who ended my father's life and, by proxy, destroyed my mother's life. But this wasn't a good time to think about that. There's a time and a place for everything. At that moment, the less I thought about such things the better. I had to maintain calm and quell the disturbance, without firing a shot. It wasn't going to be easy. If one of my men raised his hand, it was certain that some photographer would climb the nearest tree, and the picture of the po-lice vi-o-lence would be on the front pages the next day—and I was the one who'd get fucked. Me, then the commander of the battalion, then the commander-general of the military police, in that order. Starting at the bottom, of course—which is to say, with me. Therefore it was best to keep a cool head.

I approached with a firm step, exorcising the ghosts that plagued me. I tried to focus on my mission. The mission. Looking around and walking firmly, starting to analyze the situation and evaluate the tactical alternatives available. As I approached the front line of the demonstration, my attention was drawn to a figure who in passing seemed familiar. He separated himself from the rest and disappeared, swallowed up by the crowd with flags and banners. I focused my gaze and identified him among the faces, banners, placards, shouts, and air horns, a definitely recognizable figure. *Hold on there, isn't that Nelinho? Shit yes, it is Nelinho. Of course it is,* I thought. It was. Nelinho in the flesh, with that shit-eating grin of a good-for-nothing, a gap between his teeth, straight hair—incidentally, his great trump card with schoolgirls. *Shit, it is Nelinho.* He was the leader of this piece of crap. Maybe he could give me a hand and help me resolve this mess.

Of course it had to be him, I should have suspected it. He loved screwing around. He was crazy about confusion. I'll bet he got involved in that demonstration shit just so he could screw some belle. But how could I approach a good friend, an old buddy, in the midst of the enemy army, when the friend was nothing less than their general, the head honcho? If I called the students' leader Nelinho, I would be discredited among my guys. If I called him Nélio, worse still. He'd feel insulted. He'd be pissed, and with good reason. He'd conclude that I was stuck up and didn't acknowledge my friends anymore, that I'd changed, become the authority figure, that kind of thing. And if I said Mr. Nélio Braga, that's where I'd feel really ridiculous. Imagine, calling Nelinho Mr. Nélio Braga. Who ever heard of such a thing?

Suddenly, he saw me and started running in my direction. We were some fifty yards apart. The march was moving forward slowly, swaying to the sound of the youths' favorite anthems, toward Santos Dumont Square in the Jóquei neighborhood. I was coming from the opposite direction. The initial stretch of Marquês de São Vicente, where the multitude was heading, was empty because traffic had been diverted farther back, in Jardim Botânico. Cars following the same route as the march had no choice but to go along with them, at a snail's pace. So Nelinho encountered no obstacles and was able to run to embrace me in the deserted space. The closest witnesses were crammed into bars, stores, and the windows of buildings. My squad had stayed two hundred yards back, more or less at the intersection of the street and the square.

"Man, man, son of a bitch, I don't believe it!" he shouted, coming toward me jubilantly. "Motherfucker, it's you. Awesome! Gimme a hug."

"It wouldn't be good, Nelinho. Not now. It won't go down well for me or for you. Later we'll have a cold one together and talk about old times."

"Shit man, it's great to see you. How've you been? You disappeared, you don't send word, you don't go to the beach anymore, you don't go to football, you disappeared from the parties, don't answer messages. Fuck, I've missed you. How's Dona Luiza? And Carlão?"

"Everything's fine. I have been kinda out of sight. Heavy workload, you know? But you look like you're doing great. Surrounded by beautiful women, for a change, in this parade of golden girls."

"Sheesh, what's that, man? This is serious business. The cause is just. In fact, you ought to take off that uniform and join us. Just kidding . . . Corporal Anselmo did that, and look what happened . . ."

"Who?"

"Never mind."

"Nelinho, you could very well give me a hand. Since you're in charge of things, you could help me free up one lane of traffic. Everything would be resolved without any problem. I would carry out my mission the way it should be, and you would show you're a good negotiator, seeing to it that the demonstration goes on and all the rest."

"Lemme talk to the guys. I don't think there'll be any problem. But see to it that you don't vanish again. Promise you'll call me. I'm still at the same place, living with Mommy and Daddy, as you used to say . . ."

As we talked, the march was coming toward us. When we reached our agreement, we were very close to the front line of the demonstration. So much so that Nelinho, who dashed back to the front of the march, had to pull three or four by the arm to the side of the street, move faster than the mass of people, and form a huddle. It was the only way of creating a kind of shell for the emergency deliberation.

When there were only a few yards left before the crowd enveloped me, I turned my back to the front of the line and returned quickly to the end of the street where my squad was. Nelinho had left me standing by myself in the middle of the road, and for some moments my question became a strictly symbolic one: if I walked alongside the leadership, I would give the impression of helping the demonstration; if I remained immobile, I would be engulfed by the mass of people and disappear, running the risk of receiving a, shall we say, less than hospitable reception in the belly of the mob; and if I walked backward, facing the front line, I'd be playing a pathetic, not to say acrobatic role—with the added risk of tripping and presenting the photographers with their shot of the day: the hilarious fall of Public Safety at the feet of disorderly students.

Nelinho concluded the negotiations and came running back. "Lieutenant, Lieutenant."

I stopped and turned around. The march continued on its way. My friend held out his hand, feigning formality and acting out for the cameras what could be interpreted as the celebration of an accord. He winked and freed up one of the lanes. For all practical purposes, I was the one freeing it. I got the credit because, after all, I was the authority and it was my arrival on the scene that changed the situation, to the benefit of public safety, as one reporter put it, according to the account my mother gave me of what she'd heard on the radio. I preferred not to relate the story of Nelinho, so as not to discredit Dona Luiza's son.

When traffic began to flow along the left side of the lane, an older man came up to me with the air of a big brother. "Lieutenant, allow me to introduce myself. I'm Father Raul de Matos, vice-president of PUC. Congratulations on your masterly handling of the conflict. You acted with great skill and sensitivity."

I swear he said masterly. I'm not exaggerating.

He continued. "I noticed that you dialogued with the leaders of the student movement, listened to the young men and women, pondered, argued, negotiated a solution, and produced an efficient outcome. In all truth, Lieutenant, you provided a class in crisis management, a lesson on the just and efficacious comportment of the police in a democracy. You, Lieutenant, are the embodiment of the police of the future, the police on the side of the citizenry, guaranteeing rights and liberties. What a difference, Lieutenant, what a difference from the behavior that we habitually witness every day in Rio de Janeiro. Here not repression by the state but protection of the citizenry. Congratulations, Lieutenant."

As he was talking, I smiled, a bit embarrassed, because it's always good to hear praise. But don't think I gave up my critical spirit; I didn't. I know very well where priests' harangues lead. In any case, I was surprised by what he said after all the soft soap.

"Lieutenant. Are you studying?"

"I'd like to, Father, but you know how it is . . ."

"Would you like to attend the university?"

"My dream is to study law, Father."

"Then it's agreed. Come look for me. Here, take my card. Don't fail to look me up. PUC insists on offering you a full scholarship to study law."

I thanked him, put the card in my pocket, and went on taking care of traffic and public order on Rua Marquês de São Vicente as if nothing had happened. But my head was far away. I confess I felt like crying, shouting, hugging my comrades. Did I already mention this? I don't think so. Studying law was my dream. Always was. What I'd told the priest was no exaggeration. It was a dream that had been postponed for lack of dough, and problems at home. I thought about my father and imagined him hearing the news.

I ran my uniform sleeve across my face. Lots of smoke, the smell of gasoline. Pollution irritates the eyes. And makes you emotional as hell.

A Good Student

There are wars not only on the outside, that objective place where things occupy space and follow the laws of nature, independent of our will. There are also the conflicts that are fought inside us, dividing our will in half. Whether the field of battle is our soul, or our mind, it's all the same. It's all the same, so to speak, because what characterizes this intimate game is precisely the balance of words, with their liquefied, spongy, vaporous, fluid meanings: their imprecision and their snares.

This is the way I experienced my entrance to PUC; it was a field battle. The battleground was me. On one side was my desire to realize my dream of college, of studying law; on the other, my desire to *postpone* college and the study of law. Maybe you understand what I'm saying, if you put yourself in my place. Day-to-day police routine is tough. A frantic rush. Physical exercises, deployments, roll calls, sirens, pressure, risk, stress, confrontation, getting chewed out by superiors, doing the chewing out on subordinates, always pretending that you're in control of everything. Combine this daily life of a Brazilian Indiana Jones with the routine of a student—the mental landscape of the readings, the slow rhythm of classes, the winding curve of digressions, the haziness of concepts—it's not easy.

Therefore, pressed by police duties and the small tasks of each week, I kept postponing, procrastinating, putting off the long-awaited—and dreaded—moment of enrolling. For no discernible reason, a year went by between my meeting with Father Matos on Marquês de São Vicente and the practical steps that would finally transform that invitation into my formal enrollment.

What actually happened was this: I knew it would be hell doing my job at night in a favela, walking the tightrope between life and death, and then spending the morning at PUC, listening to people badmouth the police. I knew that I wouldn't fit in, even though my desires would be similar to those of my future colleagues. Even calling them colleagues sounds bad, sounds wrong. Deep down, by even thinking about PUC I felt I was betraying my comrades in the corps.

I know there's nothing wrong in wanting to study—just the opposite; I know that studying is the most natural thing in the world, and that my intellectual development and cultural improvement and all that crap could even be useful in the police force, et cetera, et cetera. There was nothing wrong, there was nothing bad about it, but something wasn't clicking, didn't sit right, didn't compute. I didn't know exactly what it was. But let's put that aside for now, since I'm beating around the bush and it's making me dizzy. Maybe you're starting to think that in the next chapter I go into psychoanalysis. Shit, think whatever you want about me, okay?

Almeida's Wife

Deceive me, Copacabana, I like it. It's hard to resist the charms of the area and its clandestine enchantments. The conventional cops who get established in the 19th Battalion sooner or later wallow in the excess of women, stars, gossip, shows, booze, strippers, and foreign languages, fueled by white or black, according to the tastes of the customer and the willingness of runners, squeegee men, bouncers, and cross-dressers. Blow and grass, cocaine and marijuana, white and black; the neighborhood hallucinates at night. The girls who work in the nightclubs and massage parlors usually maintain an ambiguous relationship with the police. They like cops, especially the younger ones, because they feel attracted and protected, but they fear blackmail. They feel they're under the constant risk of being forced to have sex with a policeman for free. How could they demand payment from such special customers?

Some conventional cops—I must admit that some Skulls

are like this too—have a weak spirit and flesh weaker still, or are romantics and fall in love with prostitutes. That's what happened to Sergeant Almeida. Fat, short, very ugly, middle-aged, he seduced one hell of a woman. "Almeida's wife . . ." "Ah! Almeida's wife." That was the talk in the mess hall, on the shift, the rounds, the patrols. "What a wife Almeida has!" "Have you seen Almeida's wife?" Almeida's wife opened up territories, conquered new lands, colonized frontiers, and supremely occupied the collective fantasy of the troop.

Almeida left nothing for her to desire, this colossus he had on a leash. Every cent he earned went directly to the woman's expenses. He spoiled the woman rotten, like a pet goddess. It was all about her, always her, her above everything, her in first place. He bought a decent car. Modest but decent. She couldn't go around in the dilapidated Dodge that was all the sergeant had left after the division of property from his first marriage. He gave her an apartment in her name, a good apartment, simple but comfortable, in Flamengo. Almeida preferred to keep her away from Copacabana as much as possible, at least during the day, even though his conjugal arrangement guaranteed respect for the professional life of his beloved. Late at night, after seeing to the desire of her last client, she would telephone Almeida, who insisted on picking her up wherever she was. He took pleasure in doing so, found great satisfaction, said he felt useful as a provider and husband by taking his wife home after work. He would leave early. She would sleep until two in the afternoon.

One day, Almeida was summoned urgently. He was supervising the workshop of his battalion, the 19th, when he received the call. His wife was on the line and wanted to speak with him. It was 10 a.m. Strange, very strange. He came to the phone, pale—it was in the days when human problems accompanied the rhythm of wired phones. Nothing serious, thank God. She just needed the car, because she had an appointment at the beauty parlor and wanted to do some shopping at the mall.

"Right away, sweetheart. It won't be more than twenty or thirty minutes. Kisses, my love."

He left in a hurry, thinking about Azevedo, his steadfast comrade in joy and sorrow, in sickness and in health, as they liked to say. Could Corporal Azevedo leave the warehouse for forty minutes, an hour? He couldn't. Azevedo was loaded down with work, and his helper had left to take his pregnant wife for an examination. Bad luck. Almeida was also jammed up. His commander had given him a task that couldn't be postponed. The solution was to call Guedes, recently arrived to the battalion, who was still getting acclimated to the workshop, doing a bit of everything to learn the ropes.

"C'mere, son. Do me a little favor and I'll take over some of your work, okay? Get my car, that red Siena over there, and take it to my place. Give the key to Dona Samantha, in 702. You can park in the garage. Make it fast, 'cause she's in a hurry. Here's the address. You can't go wrong. Do you know your way around Flamengo?"

Eleven o'clock, noon, and no sign of Guedes's return. Almeida went looking for Azevedo for the two of them to have lunch:

"These young people are fuckers," said Almeida. "You ask

them for a favor and they take advantage. That kid leaves me by myself, in the middle of the workday, knowing how much I still have to do today. He's probably somewhere walking along the beach."

"Are you sure he got the route right? Have you called Samantha?"

"Yeah. Nobody's home. That's a sign the car already got to her. If not, she'd either have called or would be home, waiting."

"Right."

Two, three o'clock. Nothing. Almeida began to worry.

That night, at home, before dinner, Almeida looked out into the street from his living room window. Samantha pouted to her husband before leaving for work and demanded air-conditioning. It was a personal characteristic of hers. "Everybody has their own way," Almeida told us later. "She likes the air. She can't stand heat. We're very different. But love is in those little things, isn't it? We have to learn to live with differences. I can stand the cold, I can stand it perfectly. I've adapted."

Almeida was in anguish, staring outside. He couldn't get Guedes out of his head. He detested mistrusting his wife, but his head was going to blow up if he didn't say something. He decided to speak.

"Sweetheart, that young man I sent to bring you the car, did he treat you well? Did he respect you? I admit I got worried, because he was supposed to return to the battalion, but he didn't, and I got to thinking . . ."

Samantha didn't like to be controlled. She detested it. If there was one thing she couldn't stand, it was suspicion. She hated control, jealousy, that sort of thing. She wouldn't allow it. And furthermore, she was a professional and Almeida himself had promised, had sworn, never to meddle in her work. Besides which, the young man was clean, polite, and willing to pay in advance.

Almeida hid his uneasiness. After all, Samantha was right. He turned his head to the side, as he habitually did in certain situations, and thought, *If it's that way, professional, that's fine.* To each his own profession. He kissed Samantha on the forehead. He didn't want her going to Copacabana with anger in her heart.

Brizola

"Kill Brizola?"
        "That's right."
"Are you crazy?"
"Not me. Us. It was a group decision."
"You're all crazy."
"Crazy but not cowards."
"Are you calling me a coward?"
"Is it crazy to want to comply with the law? To fight crime and madness? If it is, then yeah, we're crazy."
"You *are* crazy. Since when is killing the governor complying with the law?"
"If the governor violates the law, if he impedes the carrying out of the law, blocks the fight against crime, doesn't let the police act, ties our hands—"
"And since when has Brizola tied our hands?"
"He's imposed complicity on us, forced us into passivity. What kind of cop am I? What kind are you?"

"What are you trying to say, man?"

"We're forbidden to climb the hills, invade favelas, catch traffickers . . . Am I right? Hasn't he tied our hands?"

"Of course not. You're talking nonsense."

"No? Isn't it true?"

"It's not like that, man. Not at all. You just don't understand anything."

"No?"

"No, of course not. This must be something you got from those reactionary uncles of yours who miss the military dictatorship and hate Brizola."

"Okay. So tell me something: Can we or can't we, huh? Is or isn't the BOPE authorized to go into the favelas and collar the bad guys?"

"What the government doesn't want, and we shouldn't want, is for us to go into the favelas all the time, causing a bloodbath, killing and getting killed over nothing."

"'Over nothing'? Whaddya mean 'over nothing'? Fighting crime is nothing? Defending the law and society is nothing?"

"You still don't get it, do you, man?"

"Get what? You're the one who's spaced out. I always thought you leaned to the left. Any day now you're going to join an NGO and start talking about human rights."

"Shit, man, how dumb can you get?"

"Have you bought your little thong for the summer? And a simple white T-shirt for the peace march?"

"Right-wing extremist."

"Ah! So now you show your true colors."

"What true colors?"

"Don't you see what you just said? You think I didn't hear?"

"What did I say, for shitsake?"

" 'Right-wing extremist.' You called me right-wing. Say it like a man. Or maybe you've been taking a few tokes, smoking a few joints? Son of a bitch. That's all we needed. You of all people, a serious guy, becoming a junkie?"

"That's a load of shit. There's no talking to you."

"But I'm not here to talk with you. To tell the truth, all this blah-blah-blah is a waste of time, it's idiotic. I'm here to carry out a mission."

"So, spit it out."

"We're going to kill Brizola."

"There you go again with that insanity."

"That what?"

"That insanity, madness, craziness."

"Okay, change the fucking record. You keep coming back to the same place. It's not crazy. We've already gathered the basic facts."

"Even if it wasn't insane but was just and necessary, don't you realize it's not easy to kill the governor of a state and get away with it?"

"Like I said, we've already done the preliminary groundwork. And I'll repeat it one more time so you can get it through your head: it's not me, it's us. It's the BOPE, I mean, the cream of the BOPE. It's us. Including you."

"Oh, that's just great, that's all I needed. You guys are off your rocker and want to drag me down with you. Very funny."

"It's no joke. It's serious. I'm talking seriously. We're talking seriously. And you're involved, whether you like it or not. Because, my friend, given it's a maximum-security mission, anybody who hesitates is fucked. We're not going back or allowing defections. Any defection will be treated as high treason. And you know very well what that means."

"You guys have gone mad . . . Or else, maybe not. Maybe some political group has gotten to you. Is that what it is? Are they the same ones who wanted to blow up the gas reservoir? Those 'sincere but radical' types? The ones who killed that sergeant at the entrance to the Riocentro? What's the next step? Blowing up a newsstand?"

"We have a map of his daily movements. We've found out he has relatives in Santa Teresa. He goes there once or twice a week. As you see, nothing is impossible. If it's well thought out and well executed, the plan is perfectly workable."

"Son of a bitch. What've I gotten mixed up in?"

The group couldn't meet just anywhere. Caution was necessary. If there was a leak in something like this, we'd all be fucked. Including me. At the time, I was just a supporting actor. That's why I was merely a witness to that exchange. Before I realized it, I was already up to my neck in the conspiracy. I wasn't very clear about Mauro's and Olavo's arguments. My head was spinning. I had the impression they were right. I agreed with what they were saying, and my neurons were turning to jelly. All that was left was for me to act. I was responsible for finding a room to serve as headquarters. We forbade phone conversations or mentioning the plan outside our clandestine HQ. The rules were inflexible: we were not to arrive together, or in uniform, or take our cars, and were never to take the same route twice to arrive at the meeting place. The group would be kept to the minimum number, to reduce the risks of being ratted out or discovered by counterintelligence. The members of the group were policemen of the most absolute reliability. The coldest one was Diego. The most cerebral was Sabino. The most experienced, Walter. So, drawing up the initial plan fell to Sabino. Diego would handle the execution, and Walter would supervise the overall project. I took care of the heavy lifting.

Whenever we thought of Sabino, we thought about his mother at the same time. She was always with us, in spirit. It's very common to share intimate thoughts in the trenches. Sometimes you have the feeling that every word you say will be testimony to posterity, and the most inane babble sparkles like some kind of mystical flash. Okay, maybe I'm exaggerating a little. But what I mean is that we talked about ourselves more than we probably should have, about our girlfriends, wives, and families. Sabino's most unforgettable character was his mother. Dona Rosália was brought up so often, in so many different situations, that she had come to be part of our conversations even in Sabino's absence. We appropriated Dona Rosália into our own lives, to the point where we knew what Sabino's saintly mother would say in each new situation, even in contexts that had nothing to do with either of them. Sabino attributed part of his skill to his mother. The equilibrium and serenity that gave him a more mature aspect came from his mother. He didn't say this; we deduced it. Dona Rosália's wisdom filtered into her son by osmosis, through DNA, or by day-to-day teaching. By extension, to some degree we all became her long-distance apprentices. We had never met her, but we'd probably be able to identify her a mile away. How many times had she saved us? Through the prudence of her son, she got us out of some real jams.

Saturday afternoon, there we were, the Brancaleone army, hunched over the map of Santa Teresa. A blazing sun shone on the boiling coastline. Nobody would have been interested in our bunch of discreet crazies, family men in Bermudas obviously off to do weekend shopping. In any case, we couldn't be seen through the closed curtains. To breathe, we had the ceiling fan and cold water. Sabino arrived late. Sabino was never late.

"I bring bad news," he said.

It's funny to call silence palpable, but that's what it was— and so intense was the unmoving activity of that silence, that it seemed to drive us out of our heads. I immediately thought the worst: our meeting place had been blown through some error of mine.

Sabino clicked his tongue. He did that when he was nervous. "It won't work. We have to abort."

"What do you mean? Why?" I don't remember who said what or in what order, but we all jumped on Sabino: What do you mean, abort?

"Just that, abort the operation. My mother thinks it's very dangerous. She thinks it's madness."

Silence again. Diego was the first to speak. "You told your mother?"

Sabino nodded, gazing at the floor and raising his lower lip until it covered his upper lip—another of his habits.

"In that case, we'll have to kill your mother too," Diego reasoned, with the practicality that was his hallmark.

The room exploded in a tumult of voices and arms, with everyone on his feet.

Brizola died in 2004, of natural causes, without ever knowing that at the beginning of the '90s, Dona Rosália saved his life.

Sex Is Sex

I want to say this: sex, to me, means one man and one woman. There are guys who like screwing several women at the same time. There must be women who prefer the opposite: several men at the same time. Fine. That's her problem and theirs. I'm no nun. I know about everything. I know that homosexuality is part of human nature. Not of mine, but I don't condemn anyone for their sexual preference. It's an intimate thing. Within four walls, anything is permitted as long as it's consensual. I'm not going to go into some moralist speech about it. Because from what I've seen, the heralds of morality and tradition are the worst.

I'm saying all this for a very simple reason: when Lieutenant Santiago cornholed a lowlife in Andaraí with a broomstick to get him to confess where the weapons were, he wasn't promoting a sex scene, like many good people from the police were saying. It wasn't sex. Beats me just what it was, but sex it wasn't. By the way, the guy ended up turning over the

guns. In any case, I think Santiago had a certain gift as director of porn films, a sort of perverse thing: before cornholing
the leader, he surrounded the drug site and arrested everyone:
the fireworks signalers, the lookouts, junkies . . . everyone.
Then he ordered the men to lower their pants and told the
girls to blow them all. He staged a veritable choreography of
debauchery.

The guys were lined up shoulder to shoulder, their pants
down. The girls were positioned in front of them in a paral-
lel line. Three or four yards separated the sexes. Eyes locked
on eyes. Everything very severe, methodical, symmetrical, and
disciplined. They had to lower the straps of their dresses or
push up their shirts to show their breasts. Some were chosen
for the thankless task. If you thought that those chosen, by
some incredible coincidence, were the girls from the favela,
you're right. The white middle-class girls were spared. They
just had to watch. I'll leave it to you to decide whether this
was racism or pragmatism. Or both. You don't mess around
with daughters of the middle class and get away with it. And
there's something else. Santiago warned them all: the boys
who couldn't get it up would take a beating and on top of
that, be charged.

I don't know if he was trying to be original, by punishing
the group with the maximum moral penalty, which is humiliation, and playing with variations on the word *mouth*. The
fact is that it all turned to shit. He was accused by his own
colleagues, the officers were furious, the rank-and-file cops
were indignant. Not because of the guy he cornholed. That
seemed like part of the police operation. Unorthodox, but po-

lice work, because the aim wasn't pleasure. The objective was practical and suffering was a method. But playing dirty, with humiliation and forced sex, was too much. I'm not the one saying that. As I said before, I don't judge, evaluate, denounce, or criticize, neither myself nor others. My mission is to relate what happened. It's a kind of midwife work. Except that in this case what's born is truth. I'm bringing it into the world, and each person can deal with it as he likes.

The atmosphere was one of general revulsion with Santiago. Even though no formal action was taken against him, there was tension in the air, a climate of embarrassment. Nothing else. At least until the next chapter, which began with the visit of three community leaders to the battalion. They wanted to formalize a complaint to Internal Affairs. As always happens, the news spread through the corridors at high speed. Santiago found out about it right away. To make sure that's what was happening, he removed his name from his uniform and went to the Internal Affairs waiting room. He went in casually and asked the three if they were there to make a complaint. They said they were. Santiago looked at them one by one and replied with professional coolness, as if he were the host, asking them to wait a while longer. The officer in charge would see them in a few minutes.

He left the battalion and stationed himself at the first corner, in a recess of the lot at the end of the long wall surrounding the old police complex. An hour later, the three men from Andaraí came near the corner. One of them was taller and walked more slowly, a little behind the others. Santiago put a bullet in his head. He warned the survivors that next time they wouldn't be spared, then walked back to the battalion. The climate, which was already not good, soured, and the commander decided to punish Santiago, make an example of him, as the authorities like to declare when they're at a loss about what to say or do.

Santiago was called to the colonel's office.

The relationship between the two of them had never been the best. It was a long story that had begun a year earlier when Santiago arrived at the battalion, transferred from the interior to the state capital because of a dispute with the mayor of the interior town and other municipal authorities. I knew him because he'd tried to get into the BOPE three times and was always volunteering for operations that involved some kind of cooperation between the conventional police and the Skulls. He failed three times because of heights. Later I'll tell that story.

In the interior of the state, in a small town, as a brand-new, virgin lieutenant, full of love to give, proud of the uniform he wore and the power he embodied, the center of female attentions, still with great illusions about the police and its sacrosanct combat against crime, he had the misfortune to bump into a bookie who was jotting down bets, leaning conspicuously over the trunk of a police car.

Santiago knew that it was a delicate matter anywhere in the state, especially in the smaller towns, but he saw no way out. It was all or nothing. He couldn't allow the shameful arrogance of the gorilla bending over the police car in broad daylight, lest he lose his authority.

"What're you doing? Show me that notebook. And your documents. I want to see your documents."

The guy didn't move. He raised his eyes from the paper, examined the young lieutenant from head to toe, and continued writing his notes.

"Do I need to take other measures? Didn't I make myself clear? Get away from there this second and hand me the documents."

"I work for Eliseu. I'm Eliseu's man. If you're new in town, you'd better get informed right now so you don't do something foolish."

"I don't care who you work for. Haven't you noticed that you're talking to a police officer?"

"Fuck off, boy. My boss gives orders to your boss. If it's dough you're after, you're making a mistake. The system here's different. You don't get anything. Eliseu doesn't like working with retail. Everything's set up with your boss. You make your deal with him. And don't hassle me, unless you want to wake up with ants in your mouth."

He turned his back and went on with his notes.

Santiago kicked the small table and chair that were on the sidewalk and hit the guy in the knees with his billy. The guy crumbled before he could resist. Santiago placed his gun against the bookie's head and made it clear who gave the orders in that shithole.

"You're under arrest, you son of a bitch. Disrespect for authority."

He handcuffed the guy, shoved him into the wagon, and took him to the precinct.

The next day, he ordered a roundup of all the bookies in the area for which he was responsible.

As he expected, the commander of the local battalion called him in for a chat. "Understand something, Santiago. Things are different in the interior."

"From what I've been seeing, Colonel, they don't seem all that different."

"But they are, Lieutenant. It's just that you haven't gotten acclimated yet, you still don't know the rules of the place. You'll understand soon. Those small-time lawbreakers don't do the city any harm. In the local culture they're respected, they contribute, they're orderly. In a way, indirectly, they pay your salary. For you to have an idea, unlike what happens in the capital and the larger cities, they don't want anything to do with slot machines, drugs, or the prostitution of minors. The bookies, many of them are ex-convicts, are out there doing their job honestly, trying to get by. What are we supposed to do, force them back into crime? Close doors? Who would benefit from that?"

"When you say that in a way they pay my salary, do you mean the way I'm thinking?"

"Lieutenant, I can't know what you're thinking, I can only say that your attitude isn't contributing to public order."

"Colonel, if you care to know, I didn't intend to arrest the guy. I don't want problems, and I'm not looking for trouble. But you don't know what the scene was like. The guy was sprawled all over the car, in front of God and everybody, in the middle of the street in broad daylight. It was him or me."

"Very well, Lieutenant. But don't let it happen again. You'll have no reason for regret. Our salaries are unworthy of the importance of our societal function. Therefore, there's nothing more just than for us to raise the worth of our profession—without sacrificing public order, of course. You'll come to see that life in the interior has its advantages."

Santiago wasn't prepared for that conversation. He was a policeman with a calling. You know, the guy who takes his training seriously and goes out into the field firing on all cylinders? So much so that his dream was the BOPE. He had a full head of steam and all those beginner's convictions. The talk with the commander was a bucket of cold water in his face.

He decided to pretend he misunderstood and went back to arresting bookies. The colonel called him in again. This time he greeted him, as was predictable, with a darker expression.

"Listen here, Lieutenant. Here's the way it is. If not the nice way, then the bad way. The mayor called me. I got a reaming out because of you. I occupy this position only because of the political arrangement between the government and city hall. If you must know, I'm not the one getting paid off, it's the mayor, the government, the secretary, the commander-general. My cut is tiny. Partly because I'm not greedy. I divide up my slice. Since you've chosen to remain outside, you'll pay a price for it. If you want to be more Catholic than the pope, live with it. It's your problem. Except that I can't allow the problem to go on being just yours. If you don't know how things work in the police, it's time you learned. If you don't like it, get out while the getting's good. Your transfer comes through in forty-eight hours. I'm giving you leave so you'll have time to get your personal affairs in order. You're going to the capital. If I were you, I'd start getting ready for the

move. One of these days, in the future, we'll talk again. You
may go."

Santiago told me he had a lump in his throat. A mixture
of anguish, depression, and revolt. On the one hand, he had
been prepared for that outcome. He had imagined a result
more or less like that. On the other hand, he had nursed a certain hope that the commander would propose an accord that
would save him and respect his legalistic leanings. Deep
down, he had still harbored the expectation that the commander would retreat to a more moderate posture, at worst
dividing up the city and authorizing him to maintain a
bookie-free zone in the area under his responsibility. It would
have been a reasonable compromise—he thought so. At least
to keep up appearances.

Just try understanding the mysteries of the human soul. I
have no such aspiration. I therefore don't let myself be impressed by Santiago's rapid metamorphosis. He arrived in the
capital, back in our jungle, because of his resistance to the
prostitution of the police. That's not me saying it; he's the one
who used the expression. And that's precisely where the irony
comes in. After six months of getting established in the capital and two years before transferring to the battalion at whose
corner he killed the guy from Andaraí, Santiago was no longer
the same person. Copacabana had melted away his puritanical rigor. The beach, the hookers, the tourists, the opportu-
nities. Who knows what else. In the 19th Battalion, Santiago
changed into the character that we in the BOPE call the typical conventional. Except worse than that, much worse, as

you'll see shortly. A kind of conversion in reverse. He gave himself over to worshiping the pagan god, or over to pantheism, to hedonism. Beats me how to define it. Better to put it plainly: he opted for depravity, immorality, libertinism. He came to represent the worst of the conventional police. Everything that my comrades and I in the BOPE hated most. And the result was that every Friday, there was Santiago, overseeing the pickup of the take from illegal gambling and the "special posts."

The special posts varied according to the characteristics of the neighborhood. The saunas, nightclubs, and massage parlors are the most common examples, especially those that prefer not to be bothered with police raids to check on the age of the party girls or the boys who service johns. It's common knowledge that after the second raid, customers who have a name to protect disappear for good and the business goes down the drain. Abortion clinics and the unlicensed auto repair shops that invade the sidewalks and block the streets are also good sources. Irregular parking lots and fixed locations for street vendors, brokered by impresarios in the field, generate a lot of dough. The police live off what's illegal. The more disorder there is, the greater the take for the conventionals.

You might think that's funny, but we in the BOPE didn't see any humor in it. We were disgusted by all of it. While we were risking our lives in the nighttime war, the most shameless, most mediocre corruption machine turned and turned, fattening the dirty cops, their paunches more and more rotund, their spirits softened by bribery, their souls literally sold to those devils.

In a short time, in addition to this retail-level corruption, Santiago discovered the most promising veins in this field of business: taxi vans, illegal private security, wiretaps, video-poker machines and slots, the old but always profitable "animal game" illegal lottery—to which he had been introduced, traumatically, in the interior—and the "grease," meaning deals with traffickers. In one sense, I could say without exaggeration that he progressed from retail to wholesale in dirty dealing. He became an expert, a pro, a master in the art of extortion, blackmail, deception, and manipulation. He also learned how to pull the strings inside the corps to get transfers to the most coveted battalions, at the most convenient moments. This ability took him from the 19th to the 23rd Battalion. He went wild in the South Zone. Next, he withdrew strategically to the area of Andaraí, where he got himself into that imbroglio with the blow jobs. Since he was nobody's fool, each of Santiago's transfers corresponded to a movement of the chessmen in the game he was playing with I-don't-know-who. With the gods, his fantasies, his delusions of power, the traffickers, the politicians, the colonels, the owners of the police?

Some days after murdering the guy who had denounced him, Santiago was called in to the commander's office. He stayed locked inside for more than an hour. He left in silence.

The official version verified the first hypothesis that the command's spokesman had given the media: the traffickers were to blame; Santiago was innocent. In other words, the official communiqué stated that the victim had been caught in an ambush by the Andaraí traffickers, who were getting revenge for having been denounced. The murderer and his accomplices would be arrested momentarily. The subject was never mentioned again.

Discourse on Method

Illegal private security, the big business of precinct chiefs and colonels; clandestine vans and buses; bingo; wiretaps, both legal and illegal; the slot machines that lay the golden eggs and multiply like rabbits; the venerable "animal game" lottery, worn and antiquated but still going; and the thousand and one transactions with traffickers, in all their exuberant variety, from the so-called grease in the favelas—the payoffs either daily or with each police shift—to the most ambitious and riskiest deals, or shall we say the most strategic. Sometimes those webs get tangled and link up with politics, which makes everything juicier—and more explosive. I didn't make up the story I'm about to tell. I heard it directly from some of the main players. It's like that in the police—everything is known, nothing is hidden. At least not for long. It's hard and gratifying work that fills you with pride and shame, floods you with massive doses of adrenaline and takes you to the heavens on a kind of psychedelic trip, frightens you to death and saves you—at the very least it saves you from Sunday afternoons in an armchair in front of the TV, that shallow grave dug on the installment plan.

It's true; policemen, especially the BOPE, are cadavers on lay away. But who isn't? It's best to take off the masks, retire the rhetoric and the good feelings. In the trenches of our daily holy war, squeamishness quickly gets swept aside. You're impregnated with the acid smell of your colleague's urine. Everything circulates: saliva, come, blood, shit, pus, and stories. On risky operations, the best and worst emotions spew out like vomit. Time becomes a rubber band that contracts and expands. Words gush out, they happen. Afterward, you wipe your mouth on your arm and dry the dripping saliva. So it's no big deal that everything is known, everything acknowledged. And it all lies entombed in the dark cavern of mutual forgetting. For better or worse, that's the way things are in the police.

Santiago boasted of having staged, involuntarily, a spectacle worthy of World War II, Korea, or Vietnam. It was one of the more sordid stories.

He was already a seasoned cop, as we say. That is, mature, experienced, some years on the job. The opposite of the "moderns," those who came into the corps later. Like a good veteran, he would offer advice. That's what he did, or thought he did, with a major who was transferred to the conventional battalion to which Santiago was assigned. The major was in fact younger than him. Rank sometimes does that. Santiago was a captain; the other man was his superior, a major, but Santiago was older. This can happen in various ways.

For example, the major probably entered the academy young and got promoted quickly—promotions aren't automatic. There's a lot of politics involved in the process, as well as other *petites choses*. The major, whose name was Coelho, had come from the interior, too. And he landed in the capital with his beak wide open, famished, dying to set himself up as fast as possible. Santiago changed or was changed by the capital and by the police; not Coelho. Judging by what's known of his background, Coelho had been born that way. He immediately realized that Santiago was the Man. One Saturday, when Coelho was substituting for the colonel commanding the unit, he summoned Santiago.

"Come in, Captain. Have a seat. Care for a cigarette? At ease. If you want to smoke, I don't mind."

"No, thank you. I don't smoke."

"Would you like something to drink?"

"No, not now."

"You know, I'm a very human type of guy, Captain. A common man. Of course, I respect rank, but you know how it is. Everything in its time and place. Also, I'm not one to think that, I don't know, because I'm a major and you're a captain . . . It's not like that. Life isn't like that. It has its twists and turns. I'm not a guy, I mean I don't consider myself a guy, who's all that experienced, but I've learned a few things. Are you following me, Captain?"

"Naturally."

"Well then. That's what I meant. I've learned a few things. That today we're up, tomorrow we're down. That it doesn't do any good to bang your head against a brick wall. That a barking dog never bites. Does it? Isn't that right? You may speak frankly."

"That's right."

"So. That's why I say: better to look after ourselves and not go around playing the gadfly to humanity, wanting everything to be perfect, pointing out the sins of others, trying to save the planet. Is that right or not? You may speak. Say something. Be frank."

"Exactly."

"So. That's why I say: everyone knows himself for who he is. I'm not going to pretend I'm something I'm not. Is that right or not? Eh? You may speak, Captain."

"Right."

"So. I think we understand each other wonderfully, Captain. Don't you think so? Eh?"

"Absolutely."

"I think so too. Absolutely. It's better to work like that, isn't it? Better that way, understanding one another, sharing things, cooperating, than hounding, causing confusion, pressuring, raising problems, humiliating people. Is it or isn't it, eh?"

"It is."

"So. It was because I was thinking along these lines that I called you in for a frank conversation, man to man. Know why I called you in for a conversation man to man? Eh, Captain? Do you know? You may speak."

"No, Major."

"I called you in for a frank chat, man to man, because I wish that had happened to me when I was a captain, and because that's what I'd like to have happen today, understand? I'd like for the colonel to call me in for such a conversation. I thought you'd like to talk with me that way. Was I right? Eh? Speak, Captain, no need to be inhibited. Was I right or not?"

"Absolutely."

"So. That's what I deduced. That's why I say to you, Captain—are you sure you don't want to smoke? Do you mind if I smoke? . . . One day at a time. What good does it do to arrest those poor devils that we arrest, eh? Can you tell me? They're a bunch of poor devils. If we add up everything they steal, it doesn't come to a thousandth of what the big guys swipe, quietly, or even with pomp and circumstance. Those son-of-a-bitch politicians, eh? Does it or doesn't it, Captain?"

"It doesn't."

"That's why I say: we have to look out for ourselves. What good does it do for us to kill, do our homework, everything correctly, pack the jail with people, pack the prisons, kill traffickers the way you would mosquitoes, fill up the cemeteries—what good does it do? Tell me, Captain. For what? Those kids who sell drugs barefoot are skinny, poverty-ridden poor devils who don't have a pot to piss in. They can't even grow a beard. They're nobodies, small fry. What for? Tell me, Captain, you may speak. What for? Eh?"

"Right."

"Isn't it true? Is it or isn't it? They're up there on their hills, selling drugs to the scum in the street. But we don't beat up on the upper-crust kids, do we? Eh, Captain? Do we? No, of course not. We're not stupid. Society shoves those small fry from the favelas into a mass grave, and we're the executioners, we're the gravediggers, Captain. Am I wrong, Captain? You may speak. They're pure, those sons of bitches from the elite and the politicians. They're the ones who snort, smoke, live large, and we kill and get killed to keep the streets clean. It's shitty, Captain. Really shitty. The police do all the dirty work, Captain. Isn't that true? Or am I lying, by some chance? You may speak."

"True."

"So, Captain, that's why I say: a bird in the hand is worth two in the bush. What do you say? Do we or don't we have to stay in control and look out for what's ours? Eh? You can speak, be frank. I'm being frank. It's like I'm saying, Captain, a bird in the hand. Far be it from me to judge others. People take care of themselves. Do they or don't they? If everybody took care of himself, wouldn't everything be better? Eh? Sincerely, I think it would. So you can rest easy, Captain. You can rely on me. You have a friend here. I don't want to come here and impose my will, making decisions. I'm military but I'm also democratic, understand? I believe the first thing an officer must do when he arrives at a new unit, with the responsibility of command, the first thing is to listen to his subordinates, his comrades, listen with an open mind, understand? What do you think? Do you believe I'm right or not? You may be frank."

"You're right."

"Then we're beginning to understand each other, aren't we? Are we or aren't we, Captain?"

"Right."

"Excellent. In this case, I feel I owe you all a demonstration of my democratic spirit. Don't you think it'd be a good idea, eh? Eh, Captain? I feel I owe the troop some proof: a demonstration of how I desire perfect integration with the men under my command. The same positive relationship that I plan to establish with my superior in rank, Colonel Penido, I want to construct with my subordinates. The troop has to understand that. Do you agree?"

"Absolutely."

"Done. So, we've arrived at a consensus. We're going to do things that way. You go on doing as you have been the things you consider necessary. I have no intention of interfering, right? You got it? I'm not going to interfere. Just the opposite. I'm not here to get in the way or to impose anything. I'm a tolerant person. I don't like to create problems, understand? I don't want to create problems for anyone, right?"

"Right."

"Excellent then. Everything is agreed. We're on the same page. I don't want to receive anything that isn't fair. Look into what you all used to pass along to my predecessor, and I'll adapt. I'll adapt. I may discuss a detail here or there, but nothing that will create difficulties to our entering into an accord, right? How much do you all make here per month? Is it by the month or by the week? I would guess the bulk comes from the traffic, because this zone has lots of favelas. That's good, isn't it? But there must be lots of vans too, the animal game, bingo, slots, massage parlors . . . Are there many nightclubs around here?"

"Major, things here don't work that way. You've just arrived from the interior, where everything is more direct, simpler, more organized: the mayor appoints the battalion commander, the colonel takes his team, the head of the animal-game lottery introduces himself, he helps finance the mayor's victorious campaign—because he helps all the candidates precisely to avoid taking chances—in general the people who control the slot machines are the same, and when the drug traffic organizes it has to get the okay from the established powers and negotiate its place. Everything fits. By reaching an agreement with some, everything falls in place. Not here. It's much more complicated. For openers, the traffic here doesn't pay out to everybody. The commander, for example, doesn't like taking from the traffic. He just takes from lawbreakers. He accepts a little payola—lately the vans have been bringing in a lot—but he doesn't like negotiating with the drug traffic. He's a hard nut, you know? He converted not so long ago. He's in the puritanical phase, you know?"

"Yes. I understand."

"So, the best thing for you to do is to introduce yourself. Because there's no doubt that in this area of the battalion the greatest potential is in the traffic. But you have to introduce yourself."

"You mean, I go there, call on the bums, get them all together . . . Won't that look bad?"

"No, it's not that. You have to show how much you're worth. I mean, you have to justify the price they're going to pay. They're going to pay according to the risk you represent, both to their lives and to their business. To be more direct, if you'll allow me: if they don't judge you to be dangerous, they're not going to hand over the dough. The people of the movement in this region are hard as nails. For example, Corporal Mazinho and Sergeant Mosca have a field day and rake in a pile of money. The people know that when they're on duty, if there's no grease, heads will roll, up there and down below, where the drugs are sold and on the street. Now, Sergeant Neves, Pereba, Ruizinho, that team doesn't cut it. They like to shoot the breeze with the favela girls, have a cold one in the bars, and eat barbecued cat. That team comes away with small change and that's it. That's why I'm telling you, the thing here is highly individualized. Each one has to show his worth and sell his merchandise. It's not enough to just show up and present the bill. With all due respect, Major, that's not how it works."

The major fell silent. He frowned, appeared to be sulking. He dismissed Santiago without the previous exchange of pleasantries. So much so that Santiago began to wonder if he had laid it on too thick. But what was done was done. He didn't want to give the impression that he couldn't reach an agreement with the major, but when all was said and done, from his point of view, that of a professional in the matter, cooperation didn't mean carrying the other guy on his back.

Sunday night, Santiago was hastily summoned. Colonel Penido, commander of the battalion, had been informed by P2 that Major Coelho was upsetting the applecart in the largest favela on Governor's Island. He wanted Santiago there, immediately. The order came in the strident and hysterical tone Penido normally used when his neck was on the line. All because word was that the press had already been informed and reporters were on their way to the island. Penido bellowed into the telephone the hypothetical Monday morning headlines. Santiago suggested that the editions had already gone to press at that hour.

"On Tuesday then, Santiago, imagine the headlines on Tuesday. And what if *Fantástico**decides to scoop the competition with a live TV broadcast?"

"*Fantástico* doesn't do live coverage, Colonel. Rest easy. I'll get there before the press."

A pro when it came to money, slapping people around, the media, the corps' internal politics, military psychology, Santiago considered himself the greatest. A professional.

He did get there before the media. And that was the salvation. Salvation for Penido, for Coelho, and even for Santiago himself, because any drastic change in the pieces on the battalion chessboard would disrupt all his plans.

The population of the favela was gathered on a long, wide plateau that formed a vast courtyard, almost an Indian village, with shacks in a near-circle, elliptical in design. There were hundreds of dwellings in the narrow streets that rose and descended, but that was the central space, where all the neighboring paths converged.

The doors and windows, all of them, were wide open, and the lights inside were on. The families, in pajamas and underwear, had been expelled from their houses. Men, women, old people and children, were facing the front walls of their houses, their hands in the air. Policemen were rummaging through drawers, closets, packages, mattresses, stoves, and refrigerators,

---

*A popular Sunday evening television program.—Ed.

waving flashlights, shooting into the air, kicking and smashing rifle butts into objects. Clothes were thrown onto the ground and stomped on. Books, photos, and magazines were tossed into a black bag before being burned. Kitchen appliances were being destroyed, and the adolescents, all of them, were being driven by billy blows to the squad cars. Coelho was commanding the spectacle through a megaphone, declaring himself the new person responsible for law and order in that pigsty. He ordered his men to punish the residents' protests with blows to the back and legs.

When he finally managed to work his way to Coelho, Santiago gave him the message, almost between clenched teeth: "The commander sent me to tell you that you went astray. You've overdone it. This operation is too much like the actions the Nazis took against the Jews. It can turn into real shit, Major. It's more efficient to go one at a time, house by house. More discreetly. Without so much hullabaloo. It doesn't draw headlines, there's no risk, and the return is immediate."

Fiscal Policy

"What an absurdity."

Ornelas observed as the boss, Silas, grasped the cell phone in his right hand as if he was about to strangle it, and ran his left hand through his thick hair.

"What an absurdity."

The boss paced from end to end of the small room that served as headquarters for the Mangueira drug traffic, from which could be seen Maracanã Stadium and the outline of the mountains, in Rio's North Zone.

"You gotta be shitting me."

Ornelas shook his head in concern and looked at Nivaldo. It wasn't anything good. When Silas talked like that, it wasn't anything good.

"What an absurdity."

Nivaldo couldn't stand it any longer: "Shit, Silas. Spit it out, for chrissake. Talk like a man."

"Don't bust his balls, Nivaldo. Can't you see the guy's pissed?"

Ornelas was the right-hand man of the boss and felt he had the duty to protect him.

Nivaldo looked at Ornelas with an expression that said, "Fuck you, ass kisser." But it was only the expression. He preferred nonconfrontation. The atmosphere was too tense already. Better not to provoke anything.

Ever since he'd had a girlfriend from Rio Grande do Sul, Silas had been using *che*. There was nothing for it.

"But it's an absurdity, *che*. It's not done. It's playing dirty. Shit, it goes against everything we agreed on, everything."

Ornelas remained seated with his legs thrown over the back of another chair and his arms crossed. He stared at the boss, who made faces at him as he paced, listening to his interlocutor on the phone.

"Who's Silas talking to?" Nivaldo whispered to Ornelas.

"That son-of-a-bitch captain."

"The one who came up here to arrange the grease?"

"The other one, the stronger one. The one who thinks he's a tough guy."

Silas spoke again. "That's absurd, I can't accept it. How can I accept a deal like that? If I do, I'm discredited. And how can I trust the deal? You want war, we'll go to war. What don't play is you jerking me around. You came here yesterday, didn't you? Your partner called me, like we agreed, and I had the weapons deposit all set up for you. Did I or didn't I? Hold on, hold on. Tell me, did I or didn't I? Wasn't that what we agreed on? You guys came up here, made a big circus, hauled off twenty rifles, and put on that cool show for television down on the street. Did you or didn't you? I seen it all on RJ-TV. A huge success. Hold on there. Hold on. Listen. I seen you there shooting your mouth off, giving interviews and all that shit. Okay, what the hell. Everything's cool. Everybody does his part. Everything's good. Wait, man, wait. What's that got to do with me? That's your thing. I got nothing to do with it. It's your problem. No. No way. What was the agreement? What the fuck was the agreement? Shit, this way we're never gonna understand each other. This way's gonna end in shit. Listen to what the fuck I'm saying. Lower your voice. Lower your voice, goddammit."

"Shit, it tanked. You can start getting the troops ready," Ornelas whispered to Nivaldo, who couldn't resist and declared war in his own style.

"Give him hell, Silas. That's the way. Go all out. Fuck 'em. You gotta talk tough with them guys. Only thing them pigs understand is bullets."

"Shut the fuck up. Can't you see the boss is up against it?"

Silas continued. "No, no way. Listen, man. Admit it. Admit it. It's one big-ass double cross. It's unfair. Ain't there no rules anymore? Don't anybody respect nobody else these days? Does a guy's fucking word mean anything at all? Ain't there no goddamn justice anymore? Can't you trust anybody? What would you do in my place? I'm talking serious, goddammit. No, I *don't* have to understand. You're the one who don't fucking understand. Am I maybe speaking Greek? You call me up asking—just listen—asking us to collect twenty rifles, set up the deposit in the place we agreed on, and you'd come and get 'em, just like we'd agreed on. Right? So then. Didn't you guys show up here? Did you find everything we'd talked about? Wasn't it all done with complete honesty? Did we or didn't we do our part? Okay, that's what I'm saying, man. Exactly. So? Didn't you come and go in total calm? And didn't we shoot into the air, responding to your shots, everything cool, everything right, just like the doctor ordered? To us, grease means fucking grease. That's why we're established, with a name that's respected in the area. You yourself said on TV that the operation was a success. Well, was it or wasn't it? It got you on RJ-TV and headlines in today's papers, all nice and clean. So then . . . Now it's time you did your part. Like we agreed. Whaddya mean, you can't? Whaddya mean, there's problems? What's that to me? Did you ever think about what if you'd gone into the favela yesterday and I had set up an ambush for you? I *know* that it'd lead to shit. I know that. But what you're telling me is shit too, for chrissake."

Ornelas whispered to Nivaldo, "The son of a bitch don't want to give 'em back."

Nivaldo nodded, sitting on the edge of his chair, and lit a joint. "Want a hit?" he asked Ornelas, who got up from the chair, took the joint, and went to the bed. He took a toke, while Silas paced in circles and stuck his left hand into the pocket of his Bermudas. It was a habitual gesture when he needed to concentrate on difficult decisions.

Nivaldo turned toward Silas. "The son of a bitch don't want to give 'em back?"

Silas covered the mouthpiece of the phone and answered, "He wants to charge."

"Charge?" Nivaldo raised his voice and the verb *charge*, repeated, echoed through the shack.

Ornelas commented in a soft voice, "I don't believe it, man. I just can't believe it, man. You can't trust nobody. You can't believe in nothing anymore."

Silas went on circling, until he stopped and supported his right foot on the chair in which Ornelas had been sitting before joining Nivaldo to smoke the joint. It was his turn to talk. He wanted to put an end to the matter and reestablish his authority.

"Look here, Santiago. We're gonna talk man to man. I got no way out. I'm gonna have to buy the guns back from you. I got no way out. I know you knew I'd end up accepting, 'cause you know that I know if you don't sell 'em back to us you'd sell 'em to the Third Command.* And you know that I can get by without them twenty rifles, but I can't make it easy for them other guys. If the guns stayed with you, I wouldn't give a shit. I wouldn't buy back a fucking thing. I'd leave 'em there just for the pleasure of not negotiating with you. I'd write 'em off as lost weapons. Fine. They'd end up in the Arms & Explosives Division, that gun cemetery you guys got there in the police. But I know it ain't gonna be that way. And I know that you know I know it ain't gonna be that way. That's how come you had the balls to make me that kind of offer. Okay then, Santiago. It's a deal. I'll pay. I'm buying them. Yeah, all twenty. All twenty rifles. That's right, I'll go

---

*The Third Command is one of the three criminal organizations operating in Rio de Janeiro.—Ed.

along with the price. Yeah, in dollars, of course. Right, I understand the arithmetic, yeah. But don't play me for a fool, for shitsake. Don't give me that crap about a friendly price. You can order them sent. Right. Yeah, I understand. Okay. I'll tell the guys here. I'm gonna tell 'em it's not a buyback; it's just a tax for returning them. Leave it to me, I'll tell 'em. Now, in exchange, you can tell your people that 'fiscal policy' can go fuck itself."

Silas hung up the phone, kicked the chair, grabbed the joint from Nivaldo's hand, took a drag, and stood looking at the sun setting behind Maracanã Stadium.

Betrayal

It was a special request from Colonel Hugo Flores to the BOPE. The commander had ordered me to visit the colonel, inform myself about the demand, plan the requested action, and distribute the assignments in case carrying them out ran past my duty time. It was a long trip from downtown to the West Zone, especially in the Rio heat. Actually, as a friend of mine says, Rio has only two seasons: summer and inferno. We were at the height of inferno—something no Dante could find fault with. You must already be imagining making that trip in January, crossing the arid suburbs. Fine and good, except that our wagon doesn't have air-conditioning. That must be why it's called a personnel vehicle. Remember that, in addition to comfort, your automobile with AC kicks off an instantaneous upgrade in status: you gain the right to be an individual, and maybe even a citizen, rather than being called an element. All this only applies, of course, if you're white.

I'm not going to be a hypocrite and pretend I live in a racial paradise. And I'm not just saying that because I'm black and the victim of prejudice. Millions of times I catch myself discriminating too. When ordering people off the bus, you think I choose the middle-class blond kid with blue eyes, all dressed up for his English class, or the black kid in Bermudas and sandals? And don't try to make me feel guilty. I adopt the same criteria that govern the fear of the middle class. The police selection follows precisely the pattern of fear instilled by the ruling ideology and spread by the media. No, that's not Marxist jargon. Later I'll tell you why I can assure you I have nothing to do with Marxism, communism, those things. Later. Each story in its own time.

We left off where I had to get to the West Zone, because Colonel Flores was waiting to assign me the special mission. It was morning, early, but planning an operation isn't easy. You have to dig up the pertinent information, work with maps, topography, and all of that takes time.

On second thought, I'm going to hold off a little on getting to the West Zone, so I can give you a more realistic picture of this question. Let's leave Colonel Flores waiting a bit longer and accompany a patrol that some of my colleagues were on in Tijuca.

They were returning from a raid on a drug site in the Galinha favela, descending in their wagon down a deserted incline, their headlights off. A car was heading up. It was suspicious. People in favelas don't own imported cars. They turned the wagon with a sudden movement, got out with guns in their hands, and aimed their flashlights inside the car. Two flight attendants and two crew members from a well-known airline, still in uniform; they were doubtless arriving from one trip and apparently looking to take off on a different kind of trip. Flustered and nervous, the women quickly confessed: yes, they were there to buy drugs, but they weren't traffickers. Users prefer the label of addicts, because it has the advantage of making the crime into a sickness and the perpetrator into a victim. Fine, it was obvious they weren't traffickers. But even so, Lieutenant Diogo didn't relent. He was furious with that hypocritical middle-class complicity with criminals. Potheads finance the outlaws and then march against violence.

He ordered everybody out of the car. He realized, with his experienced police antennae, that the women were married, but not the men. Deduction: they weren't couples. That was all he needed to know. The appropriate procedure was self-evident. He chose the better-looking of the women.

"Listen here, you little whore. So you came here to smoke, snort, and screw the boys. Your faggot of a husband is going to enjoy knowing that your flight is just starting. Where's your cellular? There, call the cuckold, I want to speak to him."

The woman was crying as if she were being beaten.

"You too," he addressed the other woman. "Dial the number. Let's do a conference call with the cuckolds. Call your husband, you whore."

The guys tried to intervene with that "let's be reasonable" crap. This infuriated Diogo. At that moment, any word could be the last straw. The problem was that instead of coming from the men, the last straw came from the more gutsy of the two women, who decided to pick up the gauntlet, saying the lieutenant was staging the scene in order to up the price of their freedom. She caught a slap that whirled her around on her axis before felling her to the ground. Dizzy, she was lifted up by the men, while the weaker woman dissolved into sobs. The team realized what was happening; in a way, it was as if the lieutenant had struck his own group. They found the slap indecorous, unnecessary, and cowardly.

"Shit, Lieutenant, hitting a woman?" Sergeant Ávila voiced the general feeling. "A woman?" He made this compassionate comment after the flight attendants had left, released by Diogo, who also felt he'd overplayed his hand, so to speak, and had relented on the educational phone calls to the cuckolded husbands.

The moral of the story: You don't hit a woman even with a flower?

No. It was Diogo himself who clarified. "You keep looking at me with that expression and muttering, but I'd like to see if it was some badly dressed, kinky-haired black woman. I doubt you'd come to me with such scruples. Anybody who can swear he wouldn't have had his fun with the poor bitch, and wouldn't make a point of adding a kick to the thumping for good measure, let him throw the first stone at me."

As you can see, skin color is our compass. And in this we're merely modest and faithful followers of Brazilian culture. I've never forgotten this little story, because of its didactic nature. In any case, enough of general considerations. I can no longer put off the arrival to Colonel Hugo Flores's battalion. Let's see . . .

I got out of the wagon at the battalion courtyard and was

received by the commander's adjutant, who took me to Flores, on the second floor. I've always found the spatial organization of the military police incredible. It seems more like a government office building with purely bureaucratic functions. The general staff is a long way from the office of the commander, which isn't connected to the operational sectors, which in turn receive calls like a hospital, as if knowledge of criminal dynamics and their prevention were none of their business. Equally impressive is the number of police involved in absurd tasks. For example, checking the phone calls made from the battalion to the outside. Not to mention the personnel that repair the squad cars, the teams that take care of the kitchen, the cleaning people.

There are hyperactive commanders who run you ragged. But there are also the ones who call in female police officers to give them manicures and pedicures and who spend their time setting up their own businesses—in general, these are private security agencies under the names of their wives or relatives. It's even funny: on Monday, the higher-ranking officer gives a dressing-down to his subordinate, applying the medieval disciplinary norms, unyielding when it comes to hair length, lenient when it comes to robbery, extortion, murder, et cetera. On Tuesday, the two can be found at the security agency, as owner and employee, in other words, as accomplices in an illicit action—because, as you know, policemen in Brazil aren't allowed to moonlight in private security. On Wednesday, back at the barracks, the soldier has lost respect for his superior and looks on the whole farce of military order with irony and repugnance. And downhill we slide.

When I first began to understand all that, I dived headfirst into the entrance test for the BOPE. I'm not a thief, and I have no calling as a civil servant. In fact, I'm more disgusted by dirty cops than by outright crooks. But I let it go. I figured I'd write about it one day—after they kicked me out of the corps.

I went into Colonel Flores's office, saluted, and was told to sit down.

"Captain, we haven't been able to get into the Cavalo favela. The traffickers have been very skillful at blockading it. They are many and they're heavily armed. We have good informers there, and we know the location of the weapons and who the leaders of the movement are. But until we manage to break the circle they've mounted in the lower part of the hillside, nothing can be done. Attacking from the top would require a special force, because the terrain is steep and may be equally well protected. I've never had so much difficulty with a police incursion. The commander-general's order is for us to occupy the favela. But it's impossible under present conditions. That's why we need you."

Flores was direct, polite, thorough, and professional. I was close to rethinking my image of him. The colonel, shall we say, did not enjoy a good reputation. Lots of rumors were circulating. It was said that he was linked to a notorious trafficker who headed one of the criminal factions in Rio de Janeiro. You can imagine what that means, but if you can't, I'll give you a hint: he was splitting the profit from the traffic, in exchange for certain guidance about the police incursions, in accordance with that criminal faction's interests. That type of alliance isn't uncommon: the police are used by one faction against another. One well-known tactic is to provoke a phony crisis in a favela run by a given faction in order to justify operations that weaken it or even expel it from the territory, making room for new business while retaining the old patterns. The benefitting faction seizes the moment to invade the favela, take it over, appropriate the drug site and the corresponding slice of the drug trade. And thus goes mankind. If you feel revolted, imagine what I and my honest colleagues felt when we discovered we were being used and that our lives weren't worth shit. Unfortunately, not all our comrades understand the process clearly. Sometimes they blame the politicians, not understanding that, more than the politicians' maneuvers, our comrades and our superiors, many of them, some of them—whatever—are the main ones responsible. And the media applauds the cops, playing the role of idiots and deceiving the suckers who pay the taxes that go toward our own paltry salaries. But don't jump to any simplistic conclusions: "Poor guys, they sell out because of low salaries." Bullshit. No fucking way. If that were the case, the federal police would be immune to those little problems. And they're not, as you must know. And the majority of the Brazilian population is poor but isn't corrupt.

As I was saying, Flores's first intervention almost swept away the image I had of him. I said almost. I'll admit I was expecting to meet a character out of a comic book, a petty small-time dictator, some operetta-type puppet. But at first sight he didn't seem like the caricatures—I'd never met with Flores in person. He wasn't as short as I'd imagined. Less paunchy than I'd supposed. Less coarse than they said.

Unfortunately, the imposture soon melted away.

"Major," he told an auxiliary, "show the captain what we know and give him that map. And put our hero to the test to see if he's a real man." He gave a laugh straight out of an animated cartoon and left, slamming the door. I pretended it had nothing to do with me and went over to study the map and the data put together by P2.

An hour and a half later, more or less, the commander returned. He waited until I finished presenting the first outline of the plan and then said, "Listen here, Captain. We're going to take advantage of the sweep we're doing tonight in the Cavalo favela to settle overdue accounts with a traitor, okay? So see to it you keep things under control, understand?" Turning to the major, he said, "Amarildo, set everything up just right, because it's time we wasted Múcio."

"Sergeant Múcio?" the officer asked.

"Shit yes. Don't act like a fool."

I was startled, but I chose not to believe what only *a posteriori* took on the trappings of reality. In that setting and in the midst of that dialogue, it seemed to me that Flores was trying to befuddle me just for the childish pleasure of screwing with my head. A small macho jest, maybe? The police force is a perpetual locker room. Either you adopt the language, verbal and body, or you're a fag. It's like school, with the aggravating factor of guns and official power.

I reviewed the plan with the major, left him the instructions for Flores's team, went back over the basics of the movements the BOPE would make, and left. On the way, I would stop by the firm of a friend to once again borrow eight night visors. Either you bust your hump or nothing gets done—and the risks increase. You think the state provides the necessary technical equipment? Forget it. I thought about calling the operation Trojan Horse, but it struck me as too obvious. The idea, in summary, was this: Eight men from the BOPE would invade the favela from above, silently, with the visors, surprising the traffickers from behind—they'd never been approached from the rear because they were protected by a high rock. We were good at rappelling and with the visors we could attack the traffickers' HQ. We would sweep the area for the ascent of Colonel Flores's group. At worst, the outlaws would flee to the lower part of the favela. If that happened, they'd make their way down disorganized and be overwhelmed by the regular military police troop, which would be already geared for battle. It could hardly go wrong.

In late afternoon I delivered the visors and the plan to Captain Técio, who would be taking my place that night. He would command the BOPE team, which was in charge of the Cavalo operation. I passed along all the details to him and left exhausted, dying to enjoy a romantic Friday night with my wife. All work and no play, you know.

Funny, though, something didn't seem right. I had the feeling that something was missing. I reviewed in my mind every step of the plan. It all seemed to fit together perfectly. Even so, I felt like I had a hole in my stomach, anguish, a voice communicating some unintelligible message. I couldn't rest or relax. In bed, however exhausted I was physically, sleep wouldn't come. I paced about the house ceaselessly. My wife couldn't get to sleep either, worried about me, sensing my anxiety. That's not a rare phenomenon. When I was taking part in the planning of an operation but wasn't part of the team, it was hard to disconnect. For reasons both good and bad, it's horrible to imagine defeat and it's awful not to be part of a victory. I turned on the radio, phoned, and finally managed to speak to Técio.

"It was shit, man. It was pure shit. I don't understand anything," he said.

"What happened? Didn't the operation go right? Were any of our men wounded? Did somebody die, Técio?"

"No, man, the operations couldn't have gone better. That wasn't the problem. A sergeant died. It was very strange. Goddamn, what a nightmare. He died in my wagon. A sergeant from Flores's battalion."

"Fuck. A sergeant? What was his name?"

"I don't remember."

"Where are you? I'm on my way to meet you. I need to clear something up."

I didn't remember the name that Flores had mentioned earlier either. I didn't remember because I hadn't taken seriously the threat he'd made. All my anguish may have been the disturbing presence of that threat, which echoed in my head like some kind of curse. The same way you feel ill when you eat spoiled food, you suffer when you don't really digest a piece of information, a word. It's a type of spiritual indigestion. The stomach and the mind get all churned up. I blamed myself for not having told Técio the story about the sergeant so he could be on the alert. Total shit. And I couldn't remember the guy's name. Maybe if I heard the name of the dead man I could tell if it was the same name I'd heard in Flores's office.

It was the same. Múcio. I had no doubt about it. The dead sergeant was named Múcio. Técio told me what happened that long night in the Cavalo favela.

"We went in up top, according to plan. We rappelled down, using our night visors. It was easier than we'd thought. We went down to the first attack level, then on to the second stage. Everything okay. No surprises. We descended to the attack platform. Everything was like it was supposed to be. The lowlifes were right there, around the house where the weapons cache was. We blocked the alley they'd have to retreat through and closed off the two points of attack in a pincer maneuver, exactly as planned. They barely had time to blink. We eliminated all or almost all of them. There were nine. We apprehended a good number of guns and several kilos of cocaine and marijuana. The other outlaws disappeared. They must've sought refuge in the houses and wouldn't be coming out anytime soon. Just the other way around; I believe that under the circumstances, they won't be able to reorganize the gang. The tendency is for them to abandon the favela."

"All that, beginning at midnight."

"Exactly."

"What about Flores?"

"Right, we advised Flores's people by radio that we'd make our way down calmly but on the alert for ambush. I told them to wait for us at the spot you marked on the map to regroup."

"Was there any problem on the way down?"

"None. Quiet as a cemetery. Just the dogs, but the noise

of them barking was good, it alerted people not to be stupid and come out of their houses. So we were wired, you know how it is . . ."

"And then, down below, you handed things over to Flores."

"Right. Everything was calm. The favela was like a desert. Everybody inside their houses. Total silence. Nobody would dare do anything rash. In any case, I pointed out to Flores's guy the safest way up. I explained I'd left the bodies up there. They might have problems with the families. Those things. There *was* one detail that seemed suspicious."

"What?"

"Flores's group was bringing two guys in handcuffs and hoods. He told me they were informers and it was necessary to pretend they were being taken prisoner and mistreated, to avoid future problems with the boys."

"I understand."

"I thought it was kinda funny, but okay."

"What about the guns you apprehended? Did they stay up there with the bodies?"

"You crazy? Not the guns. We took all of them with us."

"Ah! Good."

"What are you thinking? I'm no greenhorn. God only knows who Flores's cops are . . ."

"*I* know."

"I know you know, but what you don't know, and I didn't suspect, was that some twenty minutes after my team left, the radio announced an emergency in Cavalo. Fuck, an emergency in Cavalo."

"Fucking hell!"

"Exactly. We were relaxing . . . we were allowing ourselves to feel the effects of tension, fatigue . . . Hey, you know very well how that is."

"You went back."

"That very second. I think we got there in ten minutes, because the wagons broke every speed limit imaginable."

"And?"

"Take it easy. We stopped a short way outside the entrance to the favela. We advanced on foot to the start of the main street that goes up into the hillside. Flores was sitting on the sidewalk with a major. Calm as could be. They didn't have that tense look you get in confrontations. They seemed composed. There on the sidewalk, like they were about to play cards."

"You remember the name of the major?"

"No. It doesn't matter. They got up and pointed out the fallen cop to me."

"Where?"

"Just a little ahead, right at the start of the street that goes up into the favela, beside a wagon."

"It was the sergeant."

"Listen. They pointed to their colleague and said in the most resigned and natural tone that he'd been killed in the firefight."

"What firefight?"

"That's what I asked. They said as soon as we left, the traffickers started shooting. Flores's troop answered with heavy fire and the outlaws retreated. While Flores's group was advancing, forcing the bastards upward or dispersing them, the policeman was hit. He was killed."

"But—"

"Wait. Except he wasn't dead. I was so pissed at Flores's apathy, not even taking away his comrade's body, dumped there like some animal, that I ordered my men to cover me with heavy fire and crawled toward the guy. He was alive, man. Bleeding badly, but with a pulse. I shouted, called Dutra, and we dragged the guy. Let me tell you something. Something really strange. You know, when I shouted that the guy was alive, looking sideways at Flores and the major, I got the impression that the two were scared. They weren't happy or emotional; they were scared. They looked like a couple of half-wits, confused, unable to act. Shit, man, what fuckers. Their comrade there, bleeding to death, and they don't even check to see if he's dead or not. Fuck. Never saw anything like it."

"Was the MP ambulance already there?"

"No, and there wasn't time to wait for the ambulance. That asshole Flores probably took his time to call it. We had to put the man in our wagon and drive like crazy. We were desperate, man. It was horrible. Our colleague died in front of us, in our arms, vomiting blood. It was already too late. There wasn't time. Bad shit, understand?"

"I understand perfectly. And it all makes sense. Everything fits."

"What do you mean, you understand? What fits? Actually, it doesn't fit. Follow my thinking: we went away after sweeping the terrain. When we left the favela, there wasn't the slightest trace of the traffickers' ability to respond. The lowlifes who were left had dispersed, probably without weapons and with no idea of what had happened and would happen. Besides that, they'd lost a large number of henchmen—according to our calculation, we executed the most experienced, the leaders, the organizers. How could the fuckers go from being decimated one minute to taking the initiative the next, just like that?"

"I know how."

"Shit, man, it's impossible. There wouldn't be enough time. There wouldn't be conditions."

"I know, what I'm saying is that I know how it would've been possible."

"Don't fuck around, Captain. Besides which, there's this—and for me it was the weirdest sign of all: the key wasn't on the sergeant who died. When I saw that no fire was coming toward me, I felt calmer and went to check the wagon beside the sergeant. The keys weren't in the ignition and there was no sign of bullet marks. Flores told me the sergeant had just gotten out of the wagon when he was hit. But how could there have been a firefight if the wagon was undamaged? And the keys, why weren't they on the sergeant or in the ignition? Where'd they go? And why? Shit, man, nothing makes sense."

"Everything makes sense. I'm telling you. Everything fits. I didn't tell you, but I heard Colonel Flores comment to a major that they would use the operation to get rid of a sergeant."

"You're shitting me."

"It's true."

"Fuck, Captain, how could you not tell me something like that?"

"I don't know. I guess I didn't take it seriously, I don't know.

I should've told you. Of course. You can be sure I'll never for-give myself for it."

"But why?"

"I'm telling you I don't know. I didn't think it was for real."

"No, I'm asking why they wanted to eliminate the sergeant."

"They said he was a traitor, bought by the traffic."

"Can that be true? The story I heard is quite different."

"About Flores?"

"Yeah. What I know is that he has some very odd con-nections."

"So I've heard."

"I don't know, man. I don't know anything anymore."

The day dawned with the sky dark, an awful hot haze. My head felt like it would explode. I made a point of going to the sergeant's funeral that afternoon. I noticed that Flores and the major were uncomfortable. Colonel Ademar didn't leave the side of the open coffin. It was obvious that he was deeply moved. He was one of those old-school officers, respected throughout the corps. At the first opportunity, I went over and said I needed to talk to him, in private.

"Some other time, Captain. Come see me another day. To-day I'm in no condition to talk. I've lost a friend. Múcio served with me until a few months ago. He was one of the most hon-est, loyal, and competent police officers I've ever known."

I confess I was speechless and felt my legs shake. My vision blur. My view of the world shake.

The next day, Flores asked for help again. He needed us to retrieve some bodies that had been left on a high plateau, on a spit of rock. He advised that it was hard to get up there and, for his people, impossible to make it down with the bodies. He explained that they had killed some remaining traffickers in the Cavalo favela. The police went to the upper part of the favela, on the outside, but didn't come down because they weren't trained to rappel. They shot from above, because the outlaws must have been on top of the rock, down below. And the bodies stayed there.

It really wasn't easy to get to the site. Much more difficult was bringing down the bodies. But even that wasn't our biggest problem. Worst of all was the smell, the vultures, and the sight. I'd never seen anything like it, and I think I never will again. The story must have been a bit different from the version recounted by Colonel Flores. There were two bodies mutilated in such a way that I could find only one explanation: the two hooded men seen by Técio weren't informers; they had been taken to Cavalo to be executed. Except that the cops lost the handcuff keys and, so as not to leave any clues, cut off the men's hands.

Days later, Colonel Ademar received me. He listened to my story in silence. The blow was violent. He couldn't completely hide his emotion, which seemed to be a mixture of hatred, outrage, shame, and defeat. But he remained silent. When I asked him what I should do, he took a breath, thought for a moment, and said, "Captain, you have two options: denounce this incident to Internal Affairs and be hounded out of the corps; or resign and write a book."

We said good-bye. I left his office. I greeted the colleagues who assisted the colonel. As I was approaching the stairs, he opened his door and finished his advice.

"Captain, if you do write the book, don't forget to keep your passport up-to-date."

We both laughed and waved good-bye. The colleagues didn't understand the words, the smile, or the gestures. I myself would need time to understand a little better and in a more encompassing way Sergeant Múcio's sacrifice. The colors of life were getting murkier as I absorbed the episode. The more subtle tones began to become confused. Little by little, the borders were being erased by a succession of the most extravagant insanities. Reality was becoming more serious, more absurd, and less verisimilar. To the point where, a few years later, truthful testimony would no longer be distinguishable from delirium.

Two Years Later:
The City Kisses
the Canvas

The Players

Santiago had gotten into a few scrapes. Make that lots of scrapes, and good ones. He exceeded the average quota of trouble and underhanded tricks. He loved to brag about his deeds, arrogantly. My grandfather used to call it a case of loose lips. Santiago loved to boast. Whoever talks a lot says what he should and what he shouldn't. One day, fate settles the score. Especially because one account gets piled onto other accounts, from other sources, whether from the police or the criminals—another bottomless well of stories, in which you know everything and forget everything, for the sake of your own survival. The stories are swept into the trash. The problem comes when the rubbish accumulates and something stops up the drain. Sooner or later, some reporter plucks the rebel flower of truth pushing through the manure to raise its head—even in a swamp, there's the chance of a flower—and that's when the talker goes down.

Two years after the period in which the episodes related in

the war diary occurred, Santiago set the rattrap and wrapped sticks of dynamite around the pillars of the house. Here's your opportunity to see the major role of the BOPE from another perspective.

So you don't get lost in the dizzying story that's about to begin, a list of characters may be useful.

- ADEMAR CAMINHA VIANA TORRES—federal deputy for the state of Rio de Janeiro
- ALICE DE ANDRADE MELO—girlfriend of the BOPE policeman who narrates the war diary and the epilogue
- ALICE'S BOYFRIEND—a BOPE officer and a law student at PUC, the Catholic university. He is the narrator of the war diary and the epilogue.
- AMARILDO HORTA—state deputy linked to the governor
- AMÍLCAR—colonel in the military police of the state of Rio de Janeiro, codirector of the intelligence service of the Secretariat of Public Safety
- ANACLETO CHAVES DE MELO—warden of the Bangu-I maximum security prison
- ANCELMO GOIS—a columnist for Rio's leading newspaper
- ANDERSON—informer for the civil police, with ties to Amarildo Horta
- BABY—nickname of Carlos Augusto, Renata's friend
- BARROS, CHICO SANTOS, VILMAR, AND ZARA—BOPE policemen acting in Bangu-I maximum-security prison

- BRITO—partner of the illegal lottery banker Saramago
- CARLOS MEIRELES—former intelligence service agent; retired army officer
- CEZINHA—boss of the drug trade in the Alemão complex
- DINO—boss of the drug trade in the Rocinha favela
- DIVALDO SININHO—main adviser to Anacleto Chaves de Melo
- DORIS—Renata's neighbor
- ELPÍDIO—colonel of the military police of the state of Rio de Janeiro, head of the Military Office of the state government
- ÉRICO, ITAMAR, AND JÚLIO—friends of Baby
- FÉLIX COUTINHO—civil policeman
- FRAGA—commander-general of the military police of the state of Rio de Janeiro
- ÍNDIO—boss of the drug trade in the Mineira favela
- JAIMINHO ONÇA—nickname of Jaime Correia, Polinices's right-hand man
- JARBAS—super in the building where Renata lives
- JONAS—assistant to Índio, the boss of the drug trade in the Mineira favela
- JUVENAL—army recruit and former history student
- LEONARDO—Ecstasy dealer
- LINCOLN—civil police officer, assistant of Luizão França
- Lúcio Pé-de-Valsa Moraes—friend of Luizão França
- LUIZÃO FRANÇA—an official of the civil police of the state of Rio de Janeiro

- MARIA DO CARMO—corporal in the military police of the state of Rio de Janeiro, acting as secretary in Guanabara Palace, site of the state government of Rio de Janeiro
- MARQUINHO—diminutive of Marcos Paiva de Souza Carneiro, chief of staff of the Secretariat of Public Safety
- MAURO PEDREIRA—senior precinct chief of the anti-kidnapping division of the civil police of the state of Rio de Janeiro
- MICHELE—Moisés's wife
- MIRANDA—military police officer; Santiago's right hand
- MOISÉS—leader of the Red Command
- MURICI—assistant to Noca, the boss of the drug trade in the Maré complex
- NEREU—boss of the drug trade in the Coréia favela
- NOCA—boss of the drug trade in the Maré complex
- NUNO CEDRO—important businessman and friend of the governor, whose campaigns he bankrolls
- OTACÍLIO MALTA—civil police officer, principal assistant of Luizão França
- PEDRINHO—son of Santiago and Renata
- POLINICES VIEIRA DA SILVA—superintendent of the federal highway police in Rio de Janeiro
- RAMIREZ—BOPE officer; friend of the narrator
- RENATA FONTES—ex-wife of Santiago; mother of Pedrinho; social worker in the Bangu-I maximum-security penitentiary
- RINALDO—henchman who helps Dino flee

- RITA, RODRIGUINHO, AND MARCINHA—wife and children of Índio
- RIVALDO—boss of the drug trade in the Borel favela; former evangelical preacher
- RUSSO—trafficker and enemy of Dino
- SALES, SANDER, JUREMIR, CRICIÚMA, BERNARDINHO, and ADRIANO—civil police officers, assistants to Luizão França.
- SANTIAGO—captain in the military police of the state of Rio de Janeiro; ex-husband of Renata; father of Pedrinho
- SARAMAGO—banker of the illegal "animal game" lottery.
- SAUL NOODLES—reporter for TV Globo
- SILVINHO—a prisoner in the south wing of Bangu-I maximum-security penitentiary
- SUELY—day worker in the employ of Baby
- URUBU—assistant to Cezinha
- VAZ—officer in the civil police of the state of Rio de Janeiro and codirector of the intelligence service of the Secretariat of Public Safety
- VIKIE—assistant to Índio
- VITOR GRAÇA—head of the civil police

The secretary of public safety and the governor are indicated by their respective titles—therefore, nameless. COSR is the Coordination of Special Resources for the state of Rio de Janeiro, the unit that in practice functions as a kind of BOPE for the civil police.

A Petrobras gas station on Highway BR-101, interior of the state of Paraíba, July 11, 1:50 p.m.

Dino didn't know if his head was throbbing from the heat inside the car or from the pressure he was under, inside, outside, in his entire body, gnawing at his bones and chewing on his nerves. If he had ever read Nelson Rodrigues, if his tumultuous life had allowed him time to read, if the crummy school he attended had taught him to read anything worth the trouble, he would say: a sun strong enough to melt cathedrals.

That afternoon, the heat cracked the asphalt and raised a liquefied fog, a vapor in which things in the distance seemed to float. Dino couldn't travel at night. A matter of security. By day it was less risky. He felt great relief when he opened the door and stepped onto the stone floor of the gas station. Some shade at that moment, a glass of cold water, was all he wanted. He filled his lungs with the Paraíba air, air from his childhood, the oxygen of freedom. It was great to be far away and feel good again. Even so, he sensed a strange chill. He thought about his mother and the cloth pads she would plunge into cold water before putting them on his head when he was feverish. He thought about his mother, the fever and the ice, and realized his mouth was dry. He was thirsty. An electric current traversed his body and soul when he counted down the time left before he would arrive at his mother's home: three hours, only three hours, after three days of travel, this one with Rinaldo in that shitty car. After so many years. She didn't know he was coming, much less that he planned to stay.

He took a deep breath and recited the prayer that the mãe-de-santo* had recommended, back in Vitória da Conquista. Rinaldo left the attendant filling the tank and headed for the bathroom, behind the small bar, at the rear of the station. Dino noticed that there weren't any trucks and began to wonder what it would be like to become a truck driver at his stage of life. Maybe it'd be better than becoming a farmer, the occupation that killed his father at an early age. A very hard occupation, hard like the people of the Northeast, and their fate. His wasn't that different, when all was said and done. The life of the people of the Northeast was a war. Different from his, but only to a point. Dino went to look for cold water. If his stomach hadn't been so knotted from the agony of never arriving, he would even have gotten something to eat. He took a deep breath. It was good to be away, far away, and breathe without fear.

"Hey."

Dino was startled by the voice so close by.

"Hey, how are you?"

He hadn't noticed the presence of anyone. Where had this person come from?

"Don't you remember me?"

He scrutinized the guy, running his gaze from head to toe.

"I was the one who went to get the grease, several times, from your hands."

Even before hearing these words, Dino's professional eye

---

*Literally, mother-of-saint: a priestess of *candomblé* or *umbanda*, religions of African origin followed by many Brazilians, mostly in the lower socioeconomic strata.—Ed.

had identified a gun under the loose-fitting shorts of the guy with the soft voice.

"You don't remember? There in Rocinha. I'd go to pick up the dough from you. Vitor Graça is my boss."

Dino tried to think fast, act fast.

"Don't look back or you die right here. I'm going to disarm you slowly. You're in the sights of my partners. One move and you die."

Dino let himself be disarmed and went on trying to think of something, fast.

"Now get quietly into that brown car you see there in front of you. You'll find two men in the car. Another car with two more of my partners is going to follow us. Nothing is going to happen to you. You can relax. Dead, you're not worth anything. We want you alive. We'll take care of your driver. Just a scare so he'll keep his mouth shut for three days."

Dino looked into the guy's eyes.

"Mr. Vitor sends his regards. He'll be waiting for you in Rio. He wants to have a talk with you."

Dino remained frozen, pondering the meaning of those words. He didn't understand anything. Where had this guy come from? The gas station was deserted. Who was the traitor? In Rocinha, nobody knew anything. Even if they had tapped his cell phone, there was no way they could suspect anything. Besides that, he had taken care to swap out his cell several times and used prepaids, to avoid being tracked by the cell's signal.

"Start moving and don't look back."

Who had set up the snare? How had they sprung the trap?

How long had he been followed? Was there any way to escape? Was it really Vitor Graça's people? Maybe Russo escaped from prison to invade Rocinha and this bunch was part of his gang . . .

"I told you to get moving, goddammit."

BR-101, Kilometer 666, July 11, 3:25 p.m.

An hour and a half of travel. The brown car turned to the left, following the sign with the name of the city. The second car stayed with it like a shadow. Some two hundred yards later, it made a U-turn at the traffic circle and quickly passed a motel, a tire repair shop, an open savanna, and a group of kids in its cloud of dust. The driver knew the place. He accelerated toward the city and stopped in front of a bakery. It wasn't a bakery. It was a bus station. They got out, bought water, drank coffee. They offered water and coffee to Dino. The second car parked immediately behind. No one got out. The man who identified himself as a subordinate of Vitor Graça went to the car window and talked to a guy in dark glasses. His face wasn't visible, but his silhouette was: he was talking on his cellular.

The bus arrived, washed and blue, its paint shining. In the interior, buses don't do tourism: they take people places and make stops like a pilgrim at the shrines devoted to blessing and prayer. A vehicle for migration is what's necessary, and that's what it is. A world of people with bags and suitcases rose from the wooden benches on the sidewalk. Dino didn't know if the anguish was in the atmosphere that the travelers exuded or was merely his own. He drank water until it flooded his bones. He ran his hands over his mouth. His companions said nothing to him; they barely talked among themselves. All that was left was to guess what awaited him in Rio. The sign on the bus announced its destination: Rio de Janeiro. Sometimes closing your eyes and dying is preferable to the long wait. Wait for what? The future was bountiful, a prodigious future. He would have a future sufficient for stuffing himself on the trip back to Rio. And a long reality to digest, minute by minute, smelling of dust, urine, and vomit, watered with the crying of children and spilled milk. He thought about spilled milk and almost smiled. Better than blood. He picked up the newspaper left on the counter. It would be useful for fanning himself. He no longer had ideas, spirit, mind, gray matter. Only a skull, squeezed at the sides. His eyes throbbed and seemed to foam, fried like eggs in the sun. He almost smiled again. He climbed onto the bus with his escorts.

BR-101, July 11, 10:20 p.m.

Three of Vitor Graça's men had gotten on the bus with Dino in Paraíba. The journey would take forty-eight hours. The return to Rio would be faster than the outbound trip. The bus was economical and direct; there was no need to twist and turn to throw anyone off the scent. One guy sat beside him and two in the seats behind him. At the countless stops, everyone stood up to stretch his legs, get some food, have a sandwich, and perform all the rituals that characterize long journeys.

Little by little, heat and fatigue benumbed the bodies, and

the light of the backlands produced a kind of intoxication. Slowly, night swallowed up the broad plain, skewered by the headlights.

Dino plunged into the haziness of his memories, hunting for the face of the man who captured him at the gas station. He closed his eyes but left a crack through which he could see the profile of the man now sitting beside him, his watchdog. He narrowed his eyes and stared at him, from back at the station. He could still hear his mellifluous voice. Memories sprang up with smells and sounds. He put the machinery of his imagination in gear. "Yes, the son of a bitch was with me. He wasn't lying." When? Where? "Maybe, just maybe, it was him." He clenched his teeth. "Son of a bitch." He was thinking so hard he was afraid he might have said "son of a bitch" out loud, but he hadn't, or if he had, his hatred didn't awaken the dog sprawled beside him, growling in his sleep. Dino captured the image of the policeman in the darkness of an alley in Rocinha, returning to him the weapons he had taken the night before and receiving the prearranged grease.

Main bus station, Rio de Janeiro, July 13, 5:05 a.m.

Dino and the three men were the last to leave the bus. He expected to find the same hullabaloo as always: he would descend the two steps, be handcuffed in front of the TV cameras, and be thrown into the back of a police wagon with its warning light on; the wagon would then set out at top speed, followed by a cortege of reporters' cars, for the exhibition, live and in color, at the zoo of the Secretariat of Public

Safety. But there was nothing, nothing other than the customary movement, people getting on and off, pulling children by the hand, bags and suitcases. Dino stepped onto the platform, inhaled gasoline, swallowed his nausea, steadied his legs. No one, nothing. This didn't smell right. Prison was better than kidnapping. If nobody found out he was in the hands of the police, anything was possible. They could execute him and make his body disappear. Where was the record of his being captured in the interior of Paraíba? No one knew about it, no one saw. "If they wanted to kill me, they'd have already done it, right there. Why bring me back to Rio?" Experience fought with fear in the cloudy arena of his awareness.

"We're taking you to a hotel."

"Where, what hotel?"

"Right here, in the bus station. The boss is going to call you in a little while. Relax, take a bath. Have some coffee, and prepare yourself for a long day. You're going back to work. The soft life is over. Vacation's ended. The boss has to pay off his campaign debts, my friend. He needs you."

HOTEL AT THE BUS STATION, JULY 13, 7:30 A.M.

Dino, after a bath, some bitter coffee, and a half-cold ham-and-cheese sandwich, collapsed into bed. He reviewed in his imagination the chapters of his life: coming to Rio with his brother; adolescence in his uncle's house in Rocinha; his brother's ruinous cocaine addiction; the addiction driving his brother into debt and danger; Dino's horror of drugs and his disdain for his violent accomplices; the need to join the drug trade to pay his brother's debts; his rise in crime; his success and the enjoyment of power; the discovery that such a victory was a piece of shit; the desire to abandon everything and start over; the dream of getting away; the long planning for the flight; sneaking out of the favela in disguise; the journey to Vitória da Conquista; the visit to the mãe-de-santo; meeting with Rinaldo; the arrival in Paraíba; the emotion of crossing the border; the final stretch to his mother's home in Rinaldo's car; the encounter with the devil in that gas station; hell; the return to Rio; disaster, defeat, imminent death.

The ceiling fan made an annoying though regular noise, with a numbing effect. He tried without success to use the telephone. It was blocked. There was no window. Beyond the opening over the air vent was a dark interior space. It wouldn't be easy to escape. The men patrolling the door to the room would detect any unusual movement. He fell into a deep sleep. Darkness. Silence. Emptiness. Until he leaped out of bed, panting. He thought he heard sirens. The phone was ringing. It took him a few seconds to get his bearings. He answered the phone. Vitor Graça himself. It was really him, the head of the civil police. He recognized his voice and his way of speaking.

He wanted four hundred thousand reais by the end of the day and ten thousand a day, starting the following week. Dino would have to return to Rocinha and resume his role as boss of the drug trade. The goose that laid the golden eggs mustn't stop producing. The civil police needed that fertility, they depended on it. "I don't have four hundred thousand," Dino said. Use the hotel phone as much as you like, you'll find a way—was more or less what Vitor Graça told him. Dino didn't quite hear what was said. He was thinking about a way to pay the ransom and get out of there. Later he'd come up with a way to escape paying the ten thousand a day. Maybe by fleeing from Rio de Janeiro again. He imagined himself far away, and a wave of anguish suffocated him. Vitor seemed like a hydra, a leviathan with a thousand eyes. How could Dino start over, make time stop and get away? Would it be possible to start life again?

TWO MONTHS LATER, THE PANTRY AND KITCHEN OF SANTIAGO'S HOUSE IN ALTO DA TIJUCA, SEPTEMBER 15, 8:15 P.M.

The interphone rang. The security man at the gatehouse advised that the expected visitor had just arrived. Santiago placed silverware, glasses, and plates on the countertop by the sink. He went to the living room doorway and welcomed his guest warmly.

"Thank you for coming. I thought it best for us to talk where we'd be more comfortable."

"I prefer it also."

He offered a drink. The visitor thanked him but accepted only coffee. The host went to the kitchen to get the thermos bottle and cups, sugar, and cream. He served his guest and exchanged pleasantries, while testing for openings with his voice. Finally words and will converged on the same frequency. Santiago began to talk.

"You know that Vitor has always been a good friend to us."

"True."

"Right, he's been a loyal guy and it's very good for us to

have a person like him on our side. You know that. He's a class act. I sincerely think he'll go far."

"He's got what it takes."

"You took the words right out of my mouth. What it takes. He's resourceful and competent," Santiago added.

"He speaks well."

"He speaks very well. And if he *communicates* well, that's even more important, isn't it?"

"Without a doubt."

"He communicates very well. Nowadays, nobody can be head of the police without having a good appearance, photographing well, and being at ease on television."

"Without a doubt," agreed his visitor.

"Nowadays, without that, you don't get anywhere."

"Nowhere at all."

"And he has all that and class too."

"He has class, he definitely does," the visitor acknowledged.

"I'd say he could head any police force in Brazil, and then some: he can go very far."

"Yes, he can. Vitor can go far. He has everything you need. He's very capable, knows how to negotiate, gets along with everybody."

"There's nobody who doesn't like Vitor," Santiago added.

"Everybody likes him."

"And since he has everything it takes to go farther, why not give him a little push? If we want to lend him a hand, nobody's going to stop us."

"You think he can make secretary? Secretary of public safety?" asked the visitor.

"He can go farther. Look, Vitor can grow. He can grow a lot. He can go farther."

"You think so?"

"I'm sure of it. Look, it seems that he's been doing some research. His name scores well. Really well."

"He didn't get that many votes when he ran for state deputy."

"That was a fluke," Santiago explained. "He was very unfortunate. He had a lot of bad luck. The elections came at a bad time. There were lots of strong candidates with lots of money. You know that these days votes are money, election is dough."

"Yes, it is."

"He had very little money and he spent it badly." The host got to the point. "I wanted to talk to you, have a serious conversation, because I'm sure that Vitor has his act together and in the next election he'll go all out. If he gets elected, he'll decide who's secretary, he'll be in control of the civil police, he'll hand out the precinct captaincies, and we'll be able to work in peace. We know how to work, don't we? All we need is for them not to get in our way."

"That's true."

"He's a reliable partner. A partner in everything. He's a brother."

"What about the military police? What's the plan with the MP?" the visitor asked.

"That's the problem. Now you've put your finger on our problem. It's a tough nut to crack. More coffee?"

"No, thanks. The impression you get is that nobody gives

orders to the MP, nobody controls it. It's a small agreement here, another there, with us running behind and trying to patch things here and there and wherever."

"One tremendous retail operation."

"That's right, retail."

Santiago ventured, "So then, what we need is a global solution. Even if it costs a bit more, it'll pay for itself. This retail stuff is the kind of cheapness that ends up being expensive."

"Very expensive."

"I've given a lot of thought to the problem . . . You sure? No coffee, no tea? How about some Scotch? If you don't mind, I'm going to have some. I need to relax. These days haven't been easy. A real battle . . . But, as I was saying, I've given a lot of thought to this problem and I think—this is really fine Scotch, delightful; you don't know what you're missing—and I think I've found a solution. We're going to have to negotiate this with great care. The first step is to get rid of that commander-general, who doesn't play ball. We already have a candidate who's in tune with us. We'll promote a huge debate, with lots of media, which will entail some costs, something we'll also have to discuss. Vitor is going to invite police officials from outside the country, researchers, NGOs, universities, all those people. The motto will be: dialogue between the two police forces. We're going to hammer that theme hard. Our candidate for commander-general of the MP is going to rise precisely because he'll appear in the media as a defender of dialogue, a friend of the head of the civil police, a personal friend of Vitor's. Meanwhile, we'll attack the present commander-general. We'll plant items in the media, those things. We'll kill two birds with one stone: undermining Fraga and strengthening Vitor."

"What if Fraga goes along and turns into the champion of dialogue between the two forces?" asked the visitor.

"No problem. He wouldn't fall because of lack of dialogue, because of being against dialogue. That's bull. Demagoguery. It's just to give the government good cover. There's a trap set for him, a very nice one. A file, a beautiful file. It's almost ready."

"Very good."

"Professional, my friend. With us there are only pros."

"That's very good."

Santiago elaborated. "Yes. Our difficulty at the moment, in order to get everything under way, is to unblock Vitor's account."

"How so?"

"It's a figure of speech. Vitor has an excellent relationship with the movement in Rocinha. A movement, I might add, that's very successful. Competent. Efficient."

"Yeah, I know."

"The personnel's top quality. The traffic there doesn't use children, violence, or show off with gunfire. It's a mature thing, out to make money. They do their thing, don't cause any commotion, and make a lot of money. It's one hell of a machine."

"True."

Santiago got up, went to the pantry for ice, and from a distance pontificated. "But everything bad comes to an end, and nothing good lasts forever."

"Is Rocinha coming to an end?"

He returned to the living room. "A son-of-a-bitch lowlife, Russo, escaped from prison, some kind of deal with the penitentiary guards . . ."

"Those guys are murder."

"Murder. They're all penny ante. They'll sell out for chicken feed."

"They're something else . . ."

"The lowlife ran off and wants to take over Rocinha."

"Who for? Who's he working for?"

"That's not quite clear as yet. We're on his tail to find out."

"Didn't the boss there disappear, abandon everything?"

"He's back. Dino."

"He's back?"

Santiago dotted the i's. "Yeah, he's back. Vitor brought him back, to go on producing. Everything depends on Rocinha. Vitor's other businesses don't even cover expenses. He has his campaign debt, his debt to the deputies' slush fund, the government's slush fund, and he has to invest in expansion of the network. Everything you can imagine. It's a lot of responsibility. Rocinha is fundamental."

"Strategic."

"Exactly. Except that because of the confusion that lowlife Russo has stirred up, the secretary sent the BOPE there on a permanent basis. In other words, my friend, the BOPE is occupying Rocinha."

"I saw it in the press and heard about the story superficially, because it's not my area, you know . . . Shit, what a problem, eh?"

"A huge problem. Everything's closed down. You can't make deals with the BOPE. You know that. Frozen account, my friend. There's no way to negotiate with Dino. Dino himself is barely managing to keep the traffic going. He had to shut down the drug site temporarily. For now, he's working with just one runner. With the BOPE in Rocinha, business is way down."

"And?"

"And so I had to take action."

"To convince the secretary? But isn't he kind of a hard-ass?"

"Hard," Santiago conceded, "very hard, a real stumbling block. There's no way. Not by that route. The only thing to do is create a war in some other part of the city and draw the Skulls far away, a trick to force the BOPE to leave Rocinha and free up Dino's business."

"Create a war?"

"Yeah. To set one pit bull against another. Throw the Red Command up against the Third Command, in a theater of operations a long way from Rocinha."

"I like that, 'theater of operations.' But how?"

"By kidnapping the wife of the Red Command boss, for example. The issue, my friend, is that I have no means of doing that without your help. Without the help of all of you."

"Christ, you're playing hardball. You're asking a lot. This isn't a game. It's complicated."

Santiago laid his cards on the table. "Complicated and risky. But doable. With professionalism, it's doable. You're professionals, you control the federal highways, you have one fucking great communication system, and an enviable level of organization. You're loaded for bear. If you get into the deal, it's doable. I don't have the slightest doubt."

"I don't know. It's complicated. And I can't expose myself. You know that in my situation, because of the position I occupy, with the obligations I have . . . They're very serious obligations. Many people are depending on it. It's all a weighty setup, you know . . . The responsibility's very large. What were you thinking about the operation?"

"The woman has to disappear and turn up dead in a house belonging to the Third. All we have to do is invade a meeting of the personnel of Third Command, eliminate the guys, and leave the woman's body there. Before it hits the headlines the next day, the RC will already know about it. But we need to choose carefully. It won't do to wipe out the leadership of the Third, 'cause then there's no war. And only catching the small fry won't work either. It's a question of fine-tuning. We've got to get one or another big shit and push the guys into a confrontation somewhere far away from Rocinha."

"And have you arranged things with the enemy?"

"It can be done. It's complicated, but it can be done. What's at stake is very important. It's no accident that I asked you here to talk. This is heavy-duty, something for the first string. The starters. Vitor would be willing to split with you and your team the net from Rocinha during the summer. What we can't do is miss the timing. Summer's the big season for business."

Fifteen days later, Central Gallery of Bangu-I
maximum-security prison, September 30, 1:30 A.M.

The BOPE men in black pointed their hoses at the cells. The prisoners were still asleep, out cold with exhaustion. Captain Barros gave the command. The valves were opened. Jets of cold water gushed into the cells at maximum force, crashing into the bars and the steel corners, provoking a roar that muffled the shouts of the Red Command leaders. One minute was enough to soak body and soul. The prisoners would then have thirty minutes of repose while the policemen grabbed a quick lunch.

Editorial room of the highest-circulation—
and most prestigious—daily in the state of
Rio de Janeiro, September 30, 1:34 A.M.

The editor in chief spoke on the telephone to the secretary of communications of the state government.

"I'm not going to argue. I'm just saying that we can't hold off any longer. Tomorrow's edition has to be posted on the Internet, and I have to send the paper to the printers *now*. I can't wait any longer. You promised me confirmation of the scoop, and you know I can't run news like this without confirmation. I won't run it without confirmation. My job's at stake. Just imagine if I say that the mayor canceled classes in the public schools yesterday, unnecessarily, merely to spread panic and disseminate the impression that the traffickers have taken over the city. For purely political reasons. Have you thought what happens if I publish that H-bomb and it's not confirmed? You think I'm going to go along with you because you have pretty eyes or because you swear it's true? In the face of all the material, and there's tons of it, that we've gathered about the traffickers' actions, forcing the closing of stores in various parts of the city, why should I give preference to your interpretation? Of *course* it's an interpretation. And so far that's all it is. So far you haven't given me one piece of concrete, objective proof that it was a political maneuver by the mayor against the state governor. Who can guarantee it's not the other way around? How can I be sure it's not the state government that's trying to wash its hands and blame city hall? What do you mean there wasn't? Of course there was. It's been proved there was. Traffickers came down from the hillsides and ordered businesses closed. That's what happened. Either you give me some data to confirm what you're saying, or I'm putting the edition to bed. I can't wait anymore. If I don't send it to the printer immediately, there're going to be serious problems with distribution. You work in this field, you know about that."

Hospital receiving area, September 30, 1:45 A.M.

The first victims of the shock assault ordered by the state government arrived. Two men in their thirties. They were the veterans in the group. Cardiac arrest and other stoppages. Everything came to a halt except the organs of safety, the brave arms of the state in the maintenance of public order. Since it was no longer possible to ensure that businesses would open their doors and schools would resume their functions, better to concentrate on prevention, by drying up the source. That is, by wetting the source. Dousing the source until it lost its will to fight. The night before had been chaos. Deserted streets, businesses closed, traffic flowing, broad spaces empty and silent. The only voice heard, bellowing, was the media and the opposition: the city on the ropes, the city kissing the canvas; knockdown; throw in the towel; federal intervention, for the love of God. Some idea, "for the love of God"; a white flag or a cannon shot, fast; curtain down, fast.

Meeting room of the prison guards, September 30, 1:50 A.M.

Sixteen soldiers and officers of the BOPE were sitting in chairs around a table and on the floor. They drank sodas and glasses of milk. They talked about the VIP reception with which they had been greeted. Food on the late shift was a rarity. They hurriedly chewed the mortadella. There were ten minutes to go before the next bath. As Chico Santos listened, Vilmar commented to Zara, "If it was up to me, the bath would be something else. Definitive. This business of jets of water seems kinda strange. It doesn't seem like anything serious, it's not a manly thing."

"That's 'cause you're not on the receiving end of the hose."

"Yeah, but this hose business, I don't know."

"Quit bitching."

"Me, I'd rather take a slug in the forehead. A day and a

night getting pelted with cold water's enough to drive a guy crazy," said Chico Santos.

Barros ended the break. Time to go back to work.

Secretariat of Public Safety building, ninth floor, September 30, 2 A.M.

The movement remained intense. Advisers crossed waiting rooms. Secretaries walked down corridors carrying thermos bottles. Drivers nodded off while leafing through magazines in the reception area. Media advisers argued, crouched over monitors, navigating the Internet. The assistants closest to the heads of the two police forces said nothing to each other. No one dared enter the secretary's office. The red light was still on.

Office of the secretary, September 30, 2:05 A.M.

A coat and a tie hung on a clothes hanger behind the door of the private bathroom. The head of the civil police took the last swallow of his cold coffee. The commander of the military police furrowed his brow and read the small letters printed in the margins of the Bangu-I penitentiary blueprints, which covered three-quarters of the table. The three men who had the secretary's confidence talked softly among themselves, on the sofa. The red telephone rang with its unmistakable sound.

"Son of a bitch. You can't even take a piss in peace. Fucking hell. Marquinho, answer that for me. Tell the governor that the secretary is urinating. Ask if it's all right to urinate, whether urinating affects the executive's political image. Marquinho, I'm kidding, okay? Watch what you say."

Mineira favela, meeting room of the Residents Association, September 30, 2:10 A.M.

Índio tried again to make contact with Bangu-I. He swapped cell phones with Jonas, dialed again, and anxiously waited for an answer.

"No signal. Dead, dead."

"When I dial, it gives me 'outside the coverage area.' It don't even go to voice mail."

"Of course not, Jonas. Man, are you dumb. How can it go to 'voice mail,' for shitsake? Everything's blocked. The pigs have closed off the whole area around Bangu."

"So there ain't no way."

"Of course not, you dummy. Go round up the guys. Wake everybody up. Bring whoever's at the site."

"Should I call the lookouts too?"

"Of course not, asshole. What're you trying to do, fuck us? You trying to set up some kind of trap? Have you turned into some kind of snitch, you fucker? All the lookouts stay at their posts. More on the alert than ever. Spread the word that I'm calling a full alert."

"Can I call the people saying you're the one who's calling?"

"Of course, you slug. You know my name?"

"Índio."

"Well then, what the fuck is the problem? Índio is calling. Índio told me to call. Is that hard to say?"

"No."

"Then don't fuck around. Move, goddammit. *Run*."

Office of the secretary of public safety, September 30, 2:15 A.M.

The secretary looked out at the deserted Avenida Presidente Vargas through his office window, which reflected the movement inside the room. He cupped his hands in order to see Candelária Church at the end of the street. He thought about speaking of the massacre* but changed his mind. Images of the massacre filled his head. He again recalled Vigário Geral. When the memory of Carandiru† sprang up, his train of thought was interrupted by the ringing of the interphone. Marquinho rushed to answer it.

"Mr. Secretary, Colonel Amílcar and Director Vaz are here. They urgently need to talk to you. They've brought a special report from Intelligence."

"Send them in."

---

*On July 23, 1993, around midnight, a group of street kids was attacked by military police at the Candelária Church. Six youths and two adults died. Two policemen and a civilian were later convicted of the crime.—Ed.

†The former penitentiary where in 1992 a prisoners' rebellion was crushed by military police of the state of São Paulo; the police killed 111 unarmed inmates. The facility was demolished in 2002.—Ed.

Mineira favela, September 30, 2:18 A.M.

Índio rose to his feet. "Shut up, I'm going to speak. Is everybody here? Anybody missing?" He looked around, searching for Jonas. "Shit, Jonas? Where the fuck are you?"

Jonas slightly opened the door to the bathroom, in a recess behind the pillar in the room. "I'm listening. You can talk."

"Is anybody missing, goddammit?"

Jonas answered through the crack in the doorway. "No, everybody's here. The representatives of the brothers in prison and the most important friends of the community. Here you got only the bosses of the hill and reliable citizens. And our people here from Mineira, too, everybody's here. 'Cept the lookouts, so's not to make it easy for the Blue Command, in case they—"

"I know, man, I was the one who said it."

Jonas tried to fulfill his role as master of ceremonies, even from inside the bathroom. He raised his voice and shouted, enunciating clearly, "Okay, boys. Time to be quiet and listen to Índio. Índio, you have the floor."

He closed the door, and Índio took over.

"I called you because we've got a mission. We've lost contact with the brothers in Bangu. The operation was executed all day yesterday. We've shut down business in several areas and ordered the schools closed. Tomorrow's mission was going to depend on a phone call around midnight from Bangu. It didn't happen. The brothers are blocked. We're out of contact. In case of loss of contact, the order was to repeat tomorrow—I mean, today, 'cause it's past midnight—yesterday's action, and fire on some public building or the entrance to some hotel in the South Zone. For now, we're not going to wound anyone. The plan is to tell the press what's happening. The wives of the imprisoned brothers have to raise hell outside Bangu-I, in front of the TV cameras, with banners and all that shit. We gotta be prepared for the police deciding to make a show of invading some community. We've all gotta be in contact. Everybody is going to be on duty. Unity is our strength. If they take Mineira, Noca will organize resistance in Maré. If they invade Maré, Cezinha takes command in Alemão. If Cezinha goes down or if they take Alemão, leadership passes to Rivaldo, in Borel. If the cops show up in all the areas at the same time, Nereu will take over and give orders from Niterói, from the Coréia favela. Understood? Any questions?"

Warden's office, Bangu-I, September 30, 2:20 A.M.

A knock at the door. The warden, Anacleto Chaves de Melo, stayed in his armchair, watching TV, his legs resting on the small coffee table. He let out an unintelligible guttural sound. His main assistant, Divaldo Sininho, slowly opened the door, stuck his head into the opening, and informed the warden that the order had been carried out. He asked Anacleto if he wanted to speak to the prisoner right there. The guy was outside, in the waiting room.

"Take the bastard to the tomb. Open it, push his head inside so he can get a close-up feel of that womblike coziness. Then bring him here."

Wrapped in a towel, handcuffed, bluish, with purple lips, deep hollows under his unfocusing eyes, and sparse, unkempt hair, Moisés was led, stumbling, by three military policemen to a dark compartment at the rear of the storehouse, under a stairwell. The warden's assistant opened a small hatch in the wall, which looked like a garbage chute or a small interior window, two feet high by two and a half wide. He tugged on a silvery strap inside the wall; it was connected to a varnished platform of iron or tin. A kind of cot slid from the wall, emitting a strong sour smell that seemed like a mixture of urine, vomit, formaldehyde, and mold.

"Take a look at that, Moisés. You've heard of the tomb? A shallow grave to its friends. Look inside. Can you see anything? Stick your head in. Take a look."

One of the policemen turned on a flashlight and pointed it into the hole in the wall. Divaldo forced Moisés to bend down to look. He resisted the pressure on his neck and jerked his head back in an abrupt movement. Trying to straighten up, he lost his balance. He was pulled up by the men keeping watch on him.

"Let's go talk to Mr. Anacleto. He wants to talk to you."

They returned to the warden's office. They knocked on the door, heard a grunt. Divaldo repeated the previous scene, opening the door a crack and sticking his head in. He whispered something, withdrew and then ordered the policemen to go in with Moisés. Anacleto received them without getting up. He took his feet off the coffee table, turned off the TV, and began threatening Moisés.

"Your choice. Some get out of there alive, others don't.

They say the lucky ones die right away. I don't know. You can do the experiment and tell us later, if you survive and can still talk. Because the funny part is that guys who leave there alive seldom regain their speech. Oh, they talk, but they never again make sense. You know about that. If, a few hours from now, you all make the same row as yesterday, shutting down stores and other such funny business, you're going to rest in the drawer, the shallow grave, Moisés. Well, how about it?"

Moisés kept his head lowered. He didn't look at Anacleto.

"The rules of the drawer are as follows: One meal a day and one glass of water. The jailer pulls out the platform only some fifteen inches, enough to push in the plate and the glass of water. Remember that you'll be flat on your back, horizontal, like a dead person, all the time. He pushes the meal as far as your knee, so you can eat with your hands. You may be able to raise the glass to your lips, since you're thin. I recommend that you don't lose control. Anybody who becomes hysterical is fucked from the get-go. It does no good to cry. Whoever goes into the tomb only comes out after three days, just like Christ. The resurrection, remember? Nobody suffocates, because the drawer has holes in the bottom. No light comes in, but air does. The only ones who suffocate are those who become hysterical, or have bronchitis, asthma, those lung diseases. I hope that's not your case, because I want to be present when they bring you out alive, on the third day."

Moisés kept his head down.

"But you can avoid that needless suffering and save your life. It's up to you. If you decide to save yourself, you can use the phone here in the office to give the necessary orders. We'll hear what you say and monitor the conversation, of course. So, no tricks. Any attempt on your part to pull a fast one will only make your situation worse."

"I ain't got nothing to do with what's going on," Moisés stammered.

Divaldo interrupted. "Don't give us that, you bastard, we know very well that you're the man. No use denying."

Anacleto ended the meeting. Addressing Moisés, he said, "You don't have much time to think it over and decide." To Divaldo: "Keep him away from the others. Let him sleep a little. If he doesn't get some rest he won't be able to think. If he doesn't think, he won't be in any shape to consider things. Put Moisés to bed, Divaldo."

Office of the secretary, September 30, 2:25 A.M.

Amílcar and Vaz were sitting at the table on which they had opened a black briefcase and set up two small recorders hooked up to a laptop whose monitor was turned to face the end of the table where the secretary was seated. At the secretary's side were the chief of the civil police and the commander of the military police. Behind them huddled the few advisers who had remained in the room. The LCD screen showed a photo of a woman of about thirty years of age.

Amílcar was the first to speak. "Mr. Secretary, you'll enjoy seeing and hearing the bombshell we've brought you."

The secretary gestured with his hand, cutting short the introduction, and turned to his assistant in the room's semidarkness. "Marquinho, check if the light outside the door is on and tell them to hold all my calls. I'm not answering the phone, the interphone, nothing; I'm not seeing anyone, understand? I'll only take a call from the red phone or some urgent call from the BOPE command. You may continue, Amílcar."

The colonel spoke again. "The woman you're looking at on the screen is Renata. Advance to the next, Vaz."

Vaz touched a key on the laptop and the photo was replaced by another.

"Now you're seeing Michele. Renata and Michele: the plot of this drama, Mr. Secretary, revolves around these two characters."

While Amílcar spoke, different photos of the two women were projected in rapid sequence. He continued, "Renata is a social worker, thirty-two years old—"

The MP commander-general, Colonel Fraga, questioned his subordinate. "But that woman there, Renata, wasn't she that agitator from the prison guards union? When I saw the picture, I thought she was the one who threw fuel on the fire during the last revolt. Remember her, Amílcar?"

"It's her all right, Colonel. It's her. Except that she incited the guards because she thinks she's a political leader. Actually, she's no agent at all. She's a social worker. She must be a communist."

"It amounts to the same thing, Amílcar. Social worker and communist are one and the same," added Vitor Graça, the head of the civil police.

"Stop talking nonsense, Vitor. If you people go on interrupting Amílcar, how can the man tell me what he came to say?" the secretary said. "Shit, people, let the man finish. Go on, Amílcar, more objectively. Get to the point. Marquinho, get me a coffee. Hot. Say something, Amílcar, out with it."

"As I was saying, Mr. Secretary, Renata is a social worker, she's thirty-two, has a basset hound, a two-bedroom apartment in Flamengo—"

"Marvelous, Amílcar. That's just marvelous," injected the secretary. "The girl's dog is a basset. That's what I call first-class intelligence work. While the city is falling apart, the secretariat disintegrating, you sniff out the breed of the girl's dog. Wow, you can't beat our intelligence. Go on, Amílcar, go on, my comrade."

"Renata has a ten-year-old son and a very special ex-husband. And a small detail, Mr. Secretary: she works at Bangu-I."

"An interesting detail," said the secretary. "Now it's heating up. What's still cold is my coffee. Marquinho, for God's sake get your ass out of that chair, son. Do something worthwhile. See to it, damn it. I told you I want hot coffee. Doesn't anybody in this shitass secretariat know how to make coffee? Continue, Amílcar. Continue, it's getting hot."

"Right, yes, it's very interesting. Especially if you know who Renata's ex-husband is. Vaz brought his file. I'll leave the filet mignon to him."

"I thought the filet mignon was the other girl, who I wouldn't kick out of bed," said the secretary. "What's her name?"

"Michele. Yeah, quite a babe . . . But Michele is more dog-meat than filet mignon. She's twenty-seven, has a son and a daughter, and is married to Moisés, who's a prisoner at

Bangu-I. Moisés, of the Red Command. The interesting fact about Michele, Mr. Secretary, is that she was kidnapped."

"She *is* kidnapped," inserted Vaz, correcting his partner.

"That's right: she *is* kidnapped. Now you're going to understand what these women have to do with the chaos in the city. It's better for you to hear it for yourself. Shoot, Vaz."

"Mr. Secretary . . ." Vaz straightened up in his chair; he was hindered by the movements of the secretary, who helped himself to coffee, apparently ignoring the spectacle that the men from Intelligence were providing him. Vaz began again once he had the others' attention.

"This is the kind of work that fills you with pride. When we hear what people are saying about the police, when we read what's written in the press, it's painful, Mr. Secretary, it hurts, and our response has to be through our work, our competence, because—"

"Get on with it, Vaz; let's hear the wiretap."

"Of course, Mr. Secretary, that's what I was about to say. We're going to hear the tape. It's a phone call from Renata to a friend. She says—well, you'll see."

RENATA's voice, shaky, tearful, was heard: "I shouldn't be telling you this on the phone, but I'm so nervous. It's this: Could you do me a huge favor? A favor like you'd do for a sister?"

A MAN'S VOICE answered: "Renata, I'm getting nervous. You're making me more nervous than you. Say what it is you want, girl."

RENATA: "First promise me you'll do what I'm asking. Do you promise?"

MAN: "I promise. Sheesh, Natinha, have faith in me. Am I your best friend or not?"

RENATA: "Then promise you'll do exactly what I ask you to."

MAN: "God in heaven, I already promised."

RENATA: "I want you to go get Pedrinho at school, take him to your house, tell him that I was called away for work, on short notice, and that his granny can't stay with him tonight. He adores you, Baby. And the teachers at school know you. You've picked up Pedrinho before and have been to the school with me several times. There won't be any problem. Take good care of him tonight, don't leave him alone for a single moment. You promise, Baby?"

MAN: "Oh, Natinha, today? Does it have to be today? Why do you ask these things of me at the last minute? Today, this very evening, I have a date with Érico. This very night, kitten. After centuries. You know he's been running away from me for centuries. Oh, Natinha, not today. Ask for something else. Look, I'll pick up Pedrinho tomorrow and keep him till the weekend. How about that? You know I adore Pedrinho. How about it?"

RENATA: "You don't understand, Carlos Augusto."

MAN: "Eee! I see it's something serious. When you call me Carlos Augusto, the thing is really serious."

RENATA: "And it is, Baby. As serious as can be. I'm in deep shit."

MAN: "For a change, huh, sweetie?"

RENATA: "Deep shit."

MAN: "I'm guessing some hunk asked you out and you're ashamed to tell me 'cause then you'd have to admit you never told me about him. Fess up."

RENATA: "I'm speaking seriously. Why won't you take me seriously?"

MAN: "And since when isn't love serious? I think it's serious. I think it's the most serious thing in the world. Especially today, my dear, for me. I can't stay with Pedrinho. It's not just you, Natinha. I've got problems of my own, my honey men."

RENATA: "Pedro's father kidnapped Moisés's wife. That's all. You satisfied now?"

MAN: "Who's Moisés? God in heaven, who's Moisés?"

RENATA: "You're telling me you don't know who—"

MAN: "I don't. I don't have the faintest idea. Now, for a long time I've known and you've known what the father of your son is. Now that I mention it, I've never understood how you could marry that brute. I've heard all kinds of things about him, but kidnapping's something new. But what do you have to do with any of that?"

RENATA: "For heaven's sake, Baby. Sometimes it's like you're in another world."

MAN: "And I am. I don't get along with kidnappers."

RENATA: "I think you're not from this planet. From planet Earth. Planet Brazil. Planet Rio. Rio de Janeiro. Wake up, Baby. Wake up. Moisés is the leader of the RC. Do you know what the RC is or is that something else you don't know? Moisés is a prisoner where I work. We get along extremely well. We've established a very positive relationship. How can

I not tell him that? But if I do, what are Pedro's father and his gang going to do to me?"

MAN: "Lord in heaven, oh my goodness. How did you get yourself into a mess like this?"

RENATA: "I didn't get myself into it, Baby. Don't you understand?"

MAN: "But there's something I really don't understand: If you tell that Moisés guy, how would Pedro's father find out it was you who told? And there's something else I don't understand: How did you find out about the kidnapping?"

RENATA: "The two things are connected. That's the problem. I found out through Pedrinho. He spent the weekend with his father and overheard some weird conversations, things he couldn't make sense of, but I understood immediately—because you know that when Pedrinho comes home he tells me everything that happened at his father's house."

MAN: "Especially when his daddy and his daddy's buddies shoot into the air at the end of their barbecue, which is a very healthy manifestation of collective jubilation, isn't it, Natinha?"

RENATA: "I'm speaking seriously, Baby. Can't you take anything seriously?"

MAN: "And you don't find it serious that they fire into the air, in front of a child, after a barbecue, just to show off how macho they are and seduce the women there? I find it very serious."

RENATA: "So do I, Baby, but that's not what we're talking about. You don't seem to be able to focus in on things. Pay attention. Did you take your Ritalin today? Baby, pay attention. When Pedrinho tells me something, it mobilizes me—

and obviously this mobilized me like anything—though I tried to disguise it, I couldn't help but ask him a million questions. When he tells me something related to me, I suspect he tells his father later. I mean, Baby, he tells what he tells me and how I react to what he tells me. That's what children do. Baby, I'm going to have to hang up. Pick up Pedrinho. Take him to your place. Take care of him. Don't let him be alone. Forgive me, but this time there's no choice. Do it. I'm going to spend the night away from home. I don't know yet where I'll go. Until this business is resolved, I'm disappearing. Okay? Can I count on you?"

MAN: "What else can I do? What alternative do you leave me? What can I say?"

RENATA: "A kiss, Baby. You're wonderful. Don't let me down. Don't call me. I'm changing telephones. I'll call as soon as I can. A kiss. I'm going to have to hang up."

Mineira favela, meeting room of the Residents Association, September 30, 2:30 A.M.

Noca broke the silence that followed Índio's speech.

"I'm over here in my corner, listening. I came from Maré with Murici and the bros here. I been listening to Índio and chewing over what he said. When he got through talking, I heard lotsa people saying 'yeah,' 'yeah.' Fine, I'm with you in the thing, 'cept there's something here that ain't right. I don't like it. You're playing the general in this job, Índio, but this job don't have no general. If there is one, he ain't here, for God's sake. He's over in Bangu, paying for his sins. Maybe this job has a general, even more than one. Okay. But they ain't here. There ain't no boss here, Índio, you hear? You ain't the boss, I ain't the boss, or Cezinha or Rivaldo or Nereu. You understand, Índio? Our brothers in prison, some of them, if they was here, could make the rules. Moisés . . . If Moisés was here with us. But that wasn't God's will, so he ain't here. So then, no general and no boss. Understand? Let's start all over again. Say something, Murici."

"Índio, you didn't get through to our friends in Bangu 'cause you're trying to talk to the north wing, which is blocked. In the south wing, Silvinho is making contact as usual. I mean, not as usual 'cause it's raining there. But from time to time, he's getting through. And what he says is real different from Índio's ideas."

"Shit, I don't understand," Índio interrupted Murici. "You come here, Noca, with your people and all our friends from Rio, the Baixada, São Gonçalo, the interior of Niterói? You come here to question my authority in front of all our friends in the Command? What's your game, man? Wasn't the kidnapping of Michele enough? Are we gonna have more problems?"

Jonas picked up the cue. "Who's Silvinho to play the boss? What's Silvinho got in mind?"

"Don't fucking butt in," said Índio. "Shut your yap. Did I tell you to talk? Don't stir up any shit, goddammit."

Cezinha spoke up. "Shit, nobody here can have any doubts about Silvinho. What's this stuff? He's a partner and is connected to the process. If he talked to Murici and sent a message from inside, we gotta find out what the message is 'fore we decide what to do. Let's drop the rumors and the fag talk.

Nobody here's any better than anybody else. And we ain't here to decide who gives orders to who. We're here to follow orders from our friends in Bangu, who're there with Moisés. Tell us, Murici. What did Silvinho say?"

"He said we shouldn't do anything more. We done enough already. He said the clampdown in the penitentiary is real tight. Better to wait and see what develops. It's enough for now to send the women to demonstrate and complain to the press about mistreatment. Other than that, just to wait for new orders."

Noca took the floor again. "What's most important is this. Silvinho said nobody understood how come the police kidnapped Michele. It ain't dough. Why would the pigs do that just for some dough? They got their grease from the drug sites, their gun deals, they're all the time upping their cut, at most there's a free-for-all here and there, some shots here and there, but we end up coming to some kind of agreement. Money, they know there ain't no more we can come up with. And they know messing with Moisés's wife could only lead to trouble. They were just gonna cause a lot of commotion."

Rivaldo, who had been quiet the whole time, broke into Noca's reasoning with his inimitable manner of an evangelical preacher.

"Ah, there it is, my brothers. There's the heart of the matter. Jesus said: I am the way and the light, only through me can you come to the Father. That means this: only through Christ can one arrive at the truth. And Jesus Christ spoke to us and through us. The Holy Spirit enlightened Silvinho and blessed Noca. Through them, Jesus wafted onto us the vitalizing wind of truth. What is the truth, brothers? It's there, right before us. Thanks to God, thanks to Jesus and to the Holy Spirit, the truth has come to us, has made the long journey and after the arduous trek through the shadows of ignorance has arrived to us, here, this night. Praise God, my brothers. The crystal-clear truth is here: the pigs knew that messing with Michele would provoke immense confusion, great tumult, chaos. Is it not so? Didn't Noca say that? Yes, brothers. It is precisely that: the pigs wanted to take advantage of the confusion they have sown. They weren't after money. They were after confusion. Do you understand?"

Cezinha didn't understand. "So what, Rivaldo? What does it all mean? How come would the police wanna stir up confusion?"

Índio picked up the thread. "I understand what Rivaldo meant. I don't know if he's right, but I understood what he meant. The police want confusion. All that shit, for some reason, that's what they want. The pigs are the ones behind all this shit. Shit's in their interest."

"But what do they want with this?" said Cezinha. "What've they got to gain from shit in the city? Is it a political thing? Do they wanna bring down the government?"

"Or the secretary?" said Rivaldo.

"Or the chief of police?" said Noca.

"Or maybe they don't want to bring anybody down," said Índio. "Maybe the pigs have a plan to get somebody promoted. Or it could be some more complicated scheme that we got no way of discovering now."

Noca turned to Índio. "Ain't you the one with all the political contacts, Índio? Why don't you try and clear up this fucking mystery?"

"Exactly," said Rivaldo. "Where there's mystery, there is light and darkness. Let us pray. Let us pray for Michele, for Moisés, for our brothers in Bangu, for all our brothers, for our union. Then we'll go in peace. Tomorrow is going to be a difficult day. Let's rest and distance ourselves. Distancing isn't a retreat. It's a tactical maneuver that demonstrates prudence and wisdom. In the meantime, Índio will do his research."

"Tomorrow the meeting'll be there in Maré," said Noca.

"Day after tomorrow, in Alemão," said Cezinha.

"There ain't gonna be a fucking meeting day after tomorrow," said Índio angrily. "Don't you see how serious the thing is? It's do or die. All I know is that it ain't gonna last more than forty-eight hours. Everything's on hold till tomorrow night. Don't nobody make waves."

Office of the secretary, September 30, 2:45 A.M.

Vaz finisheed his account. "Michele has disappeared from the Providência favela, where she went with the two children to visit her mother. She left to see some female friends. She said she would return in late afternoon to pick up the kids. She didn't return. That was on Sunday, two days ago—I mean, three . . . It's already Wednesday."

"Did her mother report it? Were the police informed?" asked the MP commander-general.

"No, Colonel. You know how it is. The wife of the RC

leader disappears. It's a matter for the criminal general staff. Moisés's mother-in-law would never go to the police."

"Yes, I know. That's what I thought. That's why I find it odd that you have this information. Did you say Intelligence has been monitoring the incident since Sunday night going into Monday morning? It being such a serious matter, I find it strange how quickly the informants acted. In any case, congratulations."

"Congratulations my ass," said the secretary. "Congratulations, Colonel? Why congratulations? Beautiful job, Intelligence follows the case and lets that shit explode. What does it matter if they get the information faster, if we're only now getting access to it, after this goddamn mess already blew up? Was the kidnapping the work of the Third Command or that FOF, the Friends of Friends?"

"The Blue Command, Mr. Secretary," said Vaz

"What the hell is that? Have the bastards created another criminal organization?"

The head of the civil police savored the words. "Blue Command is the MP, Mr. Secretary."

"It's what the criminals call the MP," said Vaz

The secretary scowled: "And you in Intelligence, to show allegiance to your office, fidelity to your office, have started using underworld vocabulary?"

Commander Fraga nodded in agreement: "That doesn't help, Vaz. It isn't good."

"Sorry," said Vaz. "That wasn't my intention. I was just quoting what I heard from the criminals."

"Vaz didn't mean anything by it," said Amílcar. "He's loyal

to our military corps, from the heart. Sometimes I even forget he's a civilian. Really, he doesn't seem like one."

"Why, Colonel? I don't understand," said Vitor Graça. "You tried to fix things and only made them worse. Is there some problem with being a civil policeman?"

"Shit, enough of this foolishness," said the secretary. "Vaz, from now on, when you want to talk about the MP, say MP, understand? We've got enough on our hands with this vandalism that's taken over the city. I don't know how much longer I'm going to be occupying this chair. And that goes for you two as well"—he looked at Graça and Fraga—"if you keep up this squabbling we won't get anywhere. We'll fight one another and drown together, each one dragging the other under. Continue, Vaz. The woman was kidnapped by the Blue Command—"

"Yes, exactly, I mean, that's right, Mr. Secretary. Michele was kidnapped by the MP."

"You mean, by some military policeman, not by the military police as an institution—" said Fraga.

The secretary slammed his fist on the table. "Fuck it! Fraga, for shitsake. Fraga! You understood, didn't you? So don't fuck around. Go on, Vaz. And no more interruptions."

"Moisés's wife disappeared Sunday afternoon," Vaz continued, "and from all indications was kidnapped by military policemen."

"Excuse me, Mr. Secretary, but I'd like to ask Mr. Vaz a question," said Fraga.

The secretary remained silent, looking at the desk in front of him. He took a deep breath, then moved his right hand slightly, as if giving the floor to the MP commander-general in an ironic choreography.

"Mr. Vaz mentioned military police," said Fraga. "Where does that certainty come from? Couldn't civil police have been involved?"

The secretary glared at Fraga. "Again! How's is it possible?"

"Forgive me, Mr. Secretary, but it's an exclusively technical issue," said Fraga.

Vaz hesitated and looked at the secretary, who was silent. "We don't know yet, Colonel. As of now, we only know about the military policemen."

"The ex-husband of that girl who works at Bangu-I—" the secretary hesitated.

"Renata," said Amílcar.

"Is he with the police? The military police?"

"Exactly, Mr. Secretary. He's Captain Santiago," said Vaz.

BATHROOM OF SANTIAGO'S HOME, ALTO DA TIJUCA, SEPTEMBER 29, 7:18 P.M.

Santiago's shower was interrupted by the signal from his radio. He shut off the water, pulled a towel to his chest, reached out to answer the cell phone and listened. Then he began speaking in a slow, even tone. "Repeat the story calmly, Miranda. Don't be nervous. No point in getting nervous. Leave my house? Why? I have every type of security here. But why? What? Where'd you hear that? How'd you find out? Him who? Why? He told you himself? Okay. I understand, I understand. Now, stay calm, take a deep breath, take it easy.

No, no way. No fucking way. Have you gone crazy? Meet me in the fallout shelter. You do know, goddammit. Understand? An hour from now. Bring him along too. And make yourself scarce, Miranda. Make yourself scarce, got it?"

A FOUR-STORY BUILDING ON RUA DOIS DE DEZEMBRO, FLAMENGO NEIGHBORHOOD, SEPTEMBER 30, 2:50 A.M.

The interphone of apartment 202 rang incessantly. Finally, a woman's voice was heard in the small garden that separated the reception area from the sidewalk. "Who is it? Who is it?"

"Police. We need you to come down and open the door. It's nothing with you. Don't worry. We need to raid the apartment of a neighbor of yours who's a drug dealer. Don't you live in the front? You can take a look from your window. We need to check on a tip. We've got a search warrant."

"Is this some kind of joke? You wake up a lady with a family, at this hour of the night, to pull a prank? I never heard of such a thing."

"It's not a joke, ma'am."

"If it's not a joke, it's a robbery. You scared my son, you know that? Go away or I'm calling the police."

"We *are* the police, ma'am—hello, hello?"

After much pressing of the interphone button, they heard the same woman's voice again.

"I said stop, or I'll call the police."

"And I said, lady, that we're the police. We're here to check out a tip on drug dealing. You can look out your window. You'll see the wagon with its revolving light on. Tell me the number of the super's apartment, otherwise we'll have to break down the door."

"Drugs? In the building?"

"Yeah, drugs. Now what's the super's number?"

"It's 104. Mr. Jarbas. He's going to be furious. Don't tell him I gave you the number, okay?"

"No problem."

With the negotiations concluded, the matter fully explained, Mr. Jarbas descended the stairs grumbling and thinking that the savings he achieved by living in the condo maybe weren't worth it after all. As he climbed the stairs with the two policemen, he weighed the possibility of moving to a building with an elevator, contradicting his usual thinking on the question of price versus quality.

"Second floor," he announced as if it were necessary, thanking God that the trafficker didn't live on the fourth floor. He would have had to catch his breath before climbing the last two floors. "Second floor," he repeated, to eliminate any doubts. He preferred things to be clear, without ambiguities. That's why he detested delays and indiscipline. Jarbas took pride in the letter he'd written to *O Globo*, which the newspaper had finally published in 1988, about the ill effects that arise from the confusion between public and private. He had cited the example that had always seemed to him the most revealing: inconsiderate mothers who allow their children to play in the hallways. He knew the letter by heart, because he always read it aloud at family gatherings: "The mothers are worse than the children. Everything begins and ends with the family. The lack of discipline among the elders is the breeding ground of urban disorder. The stray bullet is the bastard child of the negligent mother."

"Mr. Jarbas, you have to stay here and go in with us. We need a witness. Where's apartment 203?"

"In the rear."

One of the policemen rang the doorbell of 202.

Jarbas couldn't contain himself. "Are you after Dona Renata, in 203?"

"I think that's her name all right," answered the policeman, checking the documents he was carrying. "Renata Fontes, apartment 203."

"I shouldn't say this. Especially to you and at a moment like this, but it breaks my heart to see these young women pay no attention to their family, not be able to maintain a decent family life, and wind up destroying themselves with drugs. That girl's a good person . . . at least she seems to be. It's a shame she doesn't have a husband, a balanced, normal life. She lives there alone with her son. These divorced women, you know. They entertain some friends who don't have much to recommend them. I'll bet it was her bad company. It breaks my heart but it doesn't surprise me. 'Everything begins and ends with the family. The lack of discipline among the elders is the breeding ground of urban disorder. The stray bullet is the bastard child of the negligent mother.'"

"Are you a teacher?"

"In a way, son, in a way I have to admit I am. But my degree is in accounting. Retired, these days I'm retired." Jarbas stopped talking and observed the policemen's preparations for forcible entry, after they rang the bell and banged on the door. Then he returned to the charge.

"Dona Renata seems like a good woman. It's a shame. So nice. We quarrel now and then because of that little terrorist she has in her place, but I've come to like her. I take a liking to people. I'm from another age. Besides, as you get older your heart gets softer."

One cop looked at the other as he rang the doorbell of 202 again. They thought, both of them, about making some kind of joke, but they felt that Jarbas might not take a jest as being in the spirit of fair play.

"Are you two from the 2nd Battalion?"

The cops ignored the question. One of them asked about the other residents on the floor. Jarbas offered an improvised roll call.

"In 202 is Dona Doris, a friend of Renata's and the mother of a son the age of Dona Renata's son. The boys study and play together. The difference between them is that Doris is widowed, not divorced. In 204 is an elderly lady. Dona Laura is deaf as a post. You could knock down the walls of the building without waking her up. Number 201 is empty, ever since the resident died. His sons don't get along. The apartment is being inventoried. That business of inventory . . . That's why I've already written my will. As soon as I became a widower I wrote it."

Doris opened the door, wearing a beach robe.

"What's all this fuss? What do you want? Mr. Jarbas, what's going on?"

"Dona Renata is a drug dealer and the police are going to search the apartment."

"What?"

One of the policemen completed the information given by the super. "We need two witnesses."

"Renata? Renata, a drug dealer? That's absurd! Mr. Jarbas, don't you see that it's absurd? It's slander. It has to be a false accusation. How can Renata be a drug dealer, Mr. Jarbas? Imagine! Living here, in a two-bedroom apartment in the rear, in Flamengo . . . If she were a dealer, she'd have a higher standard of living, don't you think?"

"Dona Doris, in these cases we shouldn't think anything at all. We should keep quiet and let the police find what has to be found."

"I'll bet it was you who denounced her. I bet it was revenge because Pedrinho sassed you and Renata laughed."

"My dear, bad behavior is cured by fines, not by a police raid. You must be convinced by now that I'm a legalist. The fine was already ordered by the condominium."

Doris addressed the policemen, who had broken down the door of 203.

"The resident's not in? Dona Renata isn't at home? How do you know—" Doris protested.

The cops entered Renata's small living room and looked for the switch to turn on the light. They called the witnesses and headed toward the dark interior of the apartment. While Jarbas and Doris argued, the two cops emerged from the bedroom carrying a bag.

"There you go. Mission accomplished. Here it is. Cocaine

and marijuana. Must be a couple of kilos of each. Let's see if she also keeps guns in the house."

Doris was unable to contain her perplexity, now intensi-fied. "Guns?"

The cop was experienced in search and seizure. "I want the two witnesses to come see where the bag was found."

OFFICE OF THE SECRETARY, SEPTEMBER 30, 2:59 A.M.

"How did you settle on Santiago?" asked the secretary.

"Because of Renata, Mr. Secretary," said Vaz.

"We've been following Moisés's moves," said Amílcar. "*Moves* is a figure of speech, because the man's in prison. You understand . . . We've been keeping tabs on the guy. He changes cell phones all the time. As far as possible, we've tried to monitor the traffickers in Mineira, Providência, Maré, Alemão, Jacarezinho, Borel, and Coréia, all the Command people closest to Moisés. It's difficult, because nowadays it's hard to find anyone willing to cooperate. Nobody wants to be a snitch and end up roasting in the microwave. In addi-tion, the bosses, the managers, and those who serve as bridges to Bangu are careful. They use prepaids, Nextel, radio, they switch all the time and avoid talking for long. In one of the conversations we managed to tap, the name Renata came up. It seems she made friends with one of the inmates and has been helping by bringing and taking away information. Small things of no importance, family photos, stuff like that. But it was enough to gain the guy's trust. We took advantage of it and shifted the focus to the girl, which is a whole lot easier. We gambled and won. We knew that sooner or later she'd lead us to a gold mine."

Vaz chimed in. "We found out that Santiago is a very problematic character. He got into some trouble in the corps. Colonel Fraga will be able to help us learn more from his dossier. He began in the interior, got into some kind of dustup right at the start of his career, came to the capital, was a totally straight policeman, a guy respected and even feared, that's how rigorous he was. Even the problem he had in the interior appears not to have been his fault. He got married, had a child, everything as it should be. An excellent professional. Little by little, it seems he began changing and the talk going around about him isn't much to his credit. We're investigating, but we've already come up with some rather incriminating signs of outside wealth. An imported car, a boat, a home in the Alto da Tijuca, a house in the lake region, vacation trips to Las Vegas, lots of beautiful women . . ."

Vitor Graça became uneasy. "Please, Vaz. I'm not MP, but now it's my turn to squawk. For the love of God, that's why I wonder if our intelligence isn't off base, foundering around. This strikes me as a witch hunt. A professional can't travel, have his women, buy the car he wants and is able to buy? If he makes a lot of money, who's to say he doesn't earn it honestly, at part-time jobs? I'll bet he's doing well in private initiatives. Let him who has nothing to do with private security throw the first stone . . ."

The secretary jumped up from his chair. "Hey! Hold your horses there. Watch what you say, Vitor. I'll have you know I don't have, never have had, nor ever plan to have anything to do with that. If you take care of supermarkets, shopping centers, and drugstore chains, that's your problem. Giving you a hard time about those things isn't a political priority of the administration or of the secretariat, by express order of the governor. We already have enough to worry about. Besides that, if we nose around in that story, where does it stop? Are we going to fire all the higher officers and precinct chiefs? Are we going to turn our fire on ourselves? Who's going to pay for the lost salaries? We'll have to face strikes demanding pay hikes . . . That's all I need. Therefore, infractions and such petty illegalities don't interest me. We're not going to talk about it. But let one thing be very clear: I'm clean on that score."

"I had no intention to offend, Mr. Secretary. Everyone knows you don't get involved in that sort of thing. My intent was to point out that we have to be careful with precipitous accusations. This Captain Santiago may be the victim of envious colleagues . . . We know the most common source of denunciations against colleagues: somebody envies them . . . And furthermore, I disagree with the line of investigation the Intelligence personnel are pursuing."

"How so, Vitor? Explain," the secretary demanded.

Vitor went on. "It doesn't seem correct to me to follow the lead on that Renata woman. A very fragile lead. There's no evidence. None. The work has feet of clay. A child overheard his father's conversation, we don't know with whom, where, when, in what terms. A conversation that may well have been a joke. Or that may have purposely had a double meaning, because the other person could have been another policeman and the two could've been talking about some kidnapping that had happened or that they were trying to solve, not about their having kidnapped anyone. How can an entire line of investigation be mounted on the basis of a conversation among friends about a different conversation overheard by a ten-year-old child? This Renata woman could very well be mistaken and have given Moisés wrong information. And the entire reaction of the RC, all that savagery that rained down on the city, the vandalism and terrorism, may all be the result of a tremendous mistake. I feel we should hand the case over to the constituted authorities, who are us. Investigation comes under our jurisdiction. That's in the constitution, Mr. Secretary. If you'll authorize it, I'll convoke the anti-kidnapping squad right now. Let's analyze which criminals could have an interest in kidnapping Moisés's wife. It must be some kind of fight between them. If you'll authorize—"

"Tell me something, Vaz," said the secretary. "What interest could Santiago have in this business?"

"That's unclear, Mr. Secretary. At the moment I don't have the answer. This is precisely the point about which no theory seems to make sense. I've discussed this question with Amílcar, and nothing we come up with holds water, no hypothesis stands up."

"There I disagree, Mr. Secretary," said Vitor Graça. "To me, there's no evidence that the police are behind the kidnapping. But in case it's true, if the party responsible turns out to be this Santiago, I'd have no reservations at all in stating that the interest is financial, Mr. Secretary: money. Why wouldn't it be money? Of course it's money."

"Why wouldn't it be money, Vaz?" asked the secretary.

Amílcar interjected. "Because anyone who receives the money from a kidnapping like this doesn't live a week, and any experienced policeman in Rio knows that, Mr. Secretary."

The secretary thought for a moment. "Okay. So, why would any policeman who's aware of that kidnap the guy's wife? After all, whether for money or some other reason, if you're right, the kidnapper's signed his own death warrant. Why would he take the risk?"

"Santiago might risk everything he has—and his very life—for some extremely powerful motive," Vaz speculated, "especially if he could protect himself with a very strong alibi. Santiago can always get more money from the source he feeds off."

"I disagree," said Vitor. "Really, I don't agree. Mr. Secretary, I repeat my request. I'd like to take on the case. The civil police would like to take on the case."

The secretary got up from his chair. "I'll think about it. Now I'm going to lie down on that sofa and try to get some sleep, if you'll allow me. When I wake up, I'll decide. The meeting is over, gentlemen."

THE LIVING ROOM IN LUIZÃO FRANÇA'S APARTMENT, THE LAGOA NEIGHBORHOOD, SEPTEMBER 30, 3:40 A.M.

Luizão was in his undershorts. He turned on the air-conditioning before sitting down. He stuck his arms into a short-sleeved pajama top that fell like a curtain over his prodigious belly. Vitor Graça was seated in the leather armchair in the corner.

"Shit, Vitor, it must be serious as hell. I hope it's very serious. I'm exhausted, partner. My body's chewed up. It was after 1 a.m. when I got to bed."

"Yeah. The worst part is that it's serious as shit."

"Fuck, then spit it out. You want to give me a heart attack? Look at this vein in my neck. It's swelling and throbbing. I've been having that lately. Hypertension. It's bullshit. A policeman's life is shit. Don't fucking drag it out. Tell me now."

"We have to move fast to eliminate Santiago. Him and his people."

"You're crazy, man. Are you out of your head?"

"I'm serious. We have to act fast. It's got to be now. We can't wait a minute longer."

"'*We* have to act'—I know what that means, goddammit. That means *I* have to act. Isn't that what you mean? You came here to ask me to take out Santiago? And his men too?"

"Luizão, you think I'd ask you for something like that if it wasn't necessary? If it wasn't absolutely necessary?"

"But what was the shit that came down?"

"That fucker Santiago has an ex-wife, and the fucking bitch shot off her mouth because she heard from their small son the story that daddy kidnapped Michele. Just that, for chrissake."

"But how'd the boy find out?"

"The kid overheard his father's conversation."

"And how did the whore spill the beans?"

"She works in Bangu, she's a social worker."

"Those little whores are always social workers."

"Intelligence was monitoring her because it unearthed a promiscuous relationship with the lowlifes."

"I get it. The woman had the bright idea of telling her best friend what her offspring heard from daddy . . . And she did it by telephone . . ."

"More or less."

"Son of a bitch."

"The worst part is that the story found its way to Moisés."

"The woman told him."

"Yeah."

"The bitch. But this Santiago, that's fucking bullshit. How fucking incompetent, how irresponsible. You can't trust anybody anymore. There's nothing but pieces of shit in the MP."

"Here's what I've done, Luizão: In the first place, I've bought some time. I called up the meeting with the secretary. I laid claim to the case, cited the constitution, all that shit. I said I didn't believe the guys' theory and that to me it didn't smack of a police thing. Second, I pushed the investigation toward the line of money. I blew smoke up their asses. I tried to argue that something like that's only done for money. But it didn't fly."

"What do you mean, it didn't fly?"

"Those two clowns Amílcar and Vaz, those cretins don't think it's about money, that the kidnapping has to do with something else."

"What, for shitsake?"

"They don't know."

"You want me to have a heart attack? Why the fuck didn't you say right away that the fuckers are clueless? Thank God."

"They are. But I think not for long. They're after Santiago

and I think he doesn't even suspect it. If we don't get to him before they do, we're fucked."

"Before who does? The two clowns or the people from the RC?"

"The clowns, of course."

"Right. The thing to do, then, is to wipe out Santiago, along with his team, by lending Moisés's group a hand so they can do the dirty work for us."

"Good. All that's left is to set it up with the enemies. If that were easy, everything'd already be resolved. Except I don't know where that piece of shit took off to with Michele. I don't have any direct contact with Moisés's gang. I'd have to find Índio."

"No. Better for you not to meddle in this. Better not to get involved."

"But I'm already involved in this shit up to my ears."

"That's exactly why. Let me do it. From here on, I'll take over. Go get some sleep."

"But wait a minute, Luizão. Think. Let's rethink this. Let's say you locate Santiago and Michele, make immediate contact with the Red Command people, and that they get there ahead of the clowns. Fine and good. Now, imagine that Santiago decides to spill his guts to keep from dying. What if he spills everything, the entire plot from beginning to end? What the fuck's going to happen to us? Think, Luizão. Think, man. We can't outsource this job. We're the ones who have to resolve this business."

"'*We're* the ones' is a figure of speech, isn't it, Vitor? Actually, you want me to resolve this business."

Vitor attempted a smile, which came out crooked.

A MOTEL ROOM ON AVENIDA BRASIL, SEPTEMBER 30, 4 A.M.

Renata awoke, soaked in sweat. She had trouble locating herself in the penumbra of the Arabian setting. If she had
awoken on a samba school float, the sensation wouldn't have
been that different. Using the motel telephone, she dialed her
own cell phone number. Because the device was turned off,
she had access to the voice mail. She had been checking
hourly. Her worry about her son was greater than her fatigue.
This time, there was a message.

"Renata, it's Doris. Look, sorry about the hour, but I had
to talk to you. They went into your apartment. The police.
They said they'd received a tip. I resisted as long as I could. I
said it was slander. They found something there. It seems it
was four kilos of cocaine and marijuana. I mean, two kilos of
each product. Uh, I mean, product? I don't even know what
to call it. When you can, call me. Don't worry about Tabatha.
She's here with me and is behaving beautifully. She's so sweet.
She only pees on newspaper. She's adapted very well. You'll
have to have them repair the door tomorrow morning. If you
like, I can—" The message time ran out.

Renata redialed. She got the number wrong several times.
Her fingers wouldn't obey. "Baby?" she said when she heard
someone pick up.

"Who?"

"Is Carlos Augusto there?"

Silence.

"Hello? Who is it?" asked another man's voice.

"Baby, it's me, Baby."

"At this time of night, Renata? You woke up Érico. That job of yours is making you hysterical."

"Baby, don't say that."

A pause. Renata was beside herself. Her fortress was crumbling. She couldn't speak. At the other end of the line, Carlos Augusto became desperate. There was a moment of agony. Then Renata regained her composure. "They went into the apartment. They planted drugs. Pedro's father's doing. Now he's going to get custody of Pedro and on top of that discredit any accusation I make, Baby, any accusation. You understand, Baby? Look, don't let Pedrinho go to school. Make up some excuse. Stay with him. Skip work. Don't leave the house. Don't leave him for a minute."

"Leave it to me. You can rest easy. I'll work something out. But where are you, woman?"

"I can't tell you, Baby. Better you don't know. I'm going to make my plans and I'll keep you informed. Better that I call you. Don't call me. You never know. A kiss, and thanks for everything. I won't forget what you're doing for me and Pedro."

"Don't mention it, Natinha. Take care."

THE GATE OUTSIDE BANGU-I, SEPTEMBER 30, 6:30 A.M.

Eight women kneeled among bags open on the ground. Reporters' cars were setting up equipment for live transmission, beside the twelve police vehicles. Two women unfurled a banner: Carandiru II. Another held a poster that read: They Are Killing Our Husbands. The remaining five unrolled a larger banner: Cowardly Government! Unlawful Police! Some members of the community council and of NGOs arrived in the same Volkswagen minibus that carried several penitentiary workers.

KITCHEN OF CARLOS AUGUSTO'S HOME, SEPTEMBER 30, 7:20 A.M.

The table was set for breakfast. Papaya, jelly, sandwich bread, cottage cheese, and yogurt. Baby took care of the final details. Érico had left early. It was best for Pedrinho to sleep late. Maybe Baby wouldn't even need to use the lie he'd come up with, that the alarm hadn't gone off, and that it was too late now to go to school. For Pedro to wake up really late would be the best solution.

Baby heard a low, distant sound. It appeared to be a female voice. The stereo? Could he have forgotten to turn it off the evening before? That wouldn't be impossible: he'd had a bit to drink, with Érico, after putting the boy to sleep. They'd listened to some music, in the living room. It could have happened. He took the first steps toward the living room, and a chill ran down his spine. He moved forward. At the entrance to the living room, on the side opposite the kitchen, was Pedro, huddled over the coffee table, talking on the phone.

A BRIGHT AND SPACIOUS KITCHEN IN A PENTHOUSE IN THE BARRA DA TIJUCA, WHERE SANTIAGO IS HIDING OUT, SEPTEMBER 30, 8 A.M.

He had just made two eggs with bacon. He addressed a tall, muscular man wearing the uniform of an armored-car company. "Sure you don't want any?"

The man shook his head. "Can't. Cholesterol."

Santiago transferred the bacon and eggs to his own plate, left the pan in the sink, and sat down at the table. "You understand everything?"

"Yes, Captain. It's not to kill, just to scare, to teach a lesson and transmit your message. I don't have to say anything. The person's going to understand all right. I'm supposed to follow the person, choose a public place, in Copacabana, do the job and walk away calmly. The patrol in the area is your people. I don't have to worry. Just walk away. Miranda's going to get in touch to give me the address of the residence, right?"

"Absolutely right. Professionals are something else. Take a seat, at least have some coffee."

"I can't, Captain. I have to rush off to get everything organized. If I don't run, there won't be enough time. There's a lot of things. I'm going to set up the surveillance immediately. As soon as the mission's completed, I'll let you know with that commercial message from the firm, by cellular like always."

"Right. Good work. Afterward, Miranda will look you up to settle accounts."

"No problem. Whenever it's best for you. Your credit's good."

OFFICE OF THE SECRETARY, SEPTEMBER 30, 8:06 A.M.

"I'm whipped, Marquinho."

"I feel like I've been run over by an eighteen-wheeler, myself. I can just imagine how you feel, Mr. Secretary."

"What's that supposed to mean?"

"I mean, if I'm like I am, I can imagine how you're feeling, since you're a little—you're further along in years than me."

"Don't bother me. Any recent report?"

"Negative. Everything as before. Peace reigns in the city, on Avenida Brasil, in the Baixada, Niterói, and São Gonçalo, in the favelas, in the entire state."

"Not so bad."

"Congratulations."

"Why?"

"Everything's calm. The city is peaceful. A victory for Public Safety."

"Don't talk stupid, Marquinho. The worst thing in the world is having an ass-kissing assistant. It leaves you totally unprotected. You lose contact with reality. You know I detest it."

"Fine, Mr. Secretary, you're right."

"There you go again."

"Sorry. You can be sure that I'll work hard at it from now on."

"Work hard at what?"

"At speaking the truth. Don't you want maximum sincerity? Isn't that what you want?"

The secretary said nothing.

"May I really be sincere with you, sir?"

"To a point, Marquinho. To a point."

NORTH GALLERY OF BANGU-I. SILENCE. SEPTEMBER 30, 8:09 A.M.

The prisoners were sleeping. They'd received towels and cloths to dry the cells. Those who were coughing the most had been sent to the infirmary.

THE GATE OUTSIDE BANGU-I, SEPTEMBER 30, 8:10 A.M.

Close to thirty women were sitting on the curb, in the shade of a leafy tree. They talked and rested. They drank the maté tea they'd brought from home and ate sandwiches. The banners and posters were stacked on the ground. One reporter's car remained at the site. Four police vehicles were still parked in front of the main gate. Barking dogs could be heard in the distance. The characters relaxed; the setting was one of repose.

CARLOS AUGUSTO'S BEDROOM, SEPTEMBER 30, 8:11 A.M.

"Natinha, it's me, Baby. My heart's leaping out of my mouth. I'm going to talk fast to have time for the whole message to record. Look, everything's all right. I'm all right. Pedrinho's all right. But his father knows he's here. I screwed up, Natinha. I forgot to disconnect the landline. Completely forgot. I never imagined that Pedrinho would wake up before me. When I woke up, he was on the phone, talking softly to his father. I couldn't hear exactly what he said. But he had that expression of somebody who's hiding something. Know when he's cooking up something? Yeah, that expression. I don't know what he might've said. Érico slept here, but we were superdiscreet. You know how discreet Érico is. And I did everything I could to hold back, angel, everything. But you know how it is. And you know what a child's little head is like. He keeps asking me what happened, why you didn't let him know where you are, why he's at my house. I said you and I had agreed on it. But he's very sharp. He's a very sharp boy. Now I don't know what to do anymore. I'll wait for your phone call, okay, love? Call right away, please, before my heart jumps out of my body. Call me on the cellular, because I disconnected the landline. I'm not going to let Pedrinho out or open the door to anybody. I'm not going to work. I've already let the office know, told them I'll get ahead of the work from home. It won't be a problem, because I'm on good terms. That's one advantage of keeping my nose to the grindstone. Except I have to dash out to the bank, but Suely will stay with Pedrinho. For ten minutes. You know she's totally reliable. She stopped being just a day worker long ago and became my friend, a real friend. Rest easy. But call as soon as you can. A kiss."

A ROOM ON THE 15TH FLOOR OF A DOWNTOWN COMMERCIAL BUILDING, SEPTEMBER 30, 8:12 A.M.

Luizão França told everybody to shut up and listen to him. He leaned against the air vent that faced the interior of the building, both hands behind him. He stared at the group, now silent.

"Since five this morning I've been here with Otacílio, chasing you. Shit, this won't work. I've said that everybody has the right to some rest. Even me. But nobody can turn off his radio. What kind of shit is that, for chrissake? Are we in the middle of a war or just fucking around? Maybe somebody would rather fuck around, go to nightclubs, to dance, huh, Sander? Huh, Bernardinho? Don't laugh, damn it, it's no laughing matter. I'm speaking seriously . . . Isn't that how you talk, just like fags, 'I'm hitting the night, I'm going to get down'? Or maybe somebody prefers going to a club, to screw his favorite whore in a motel in São Conrado and get drunk on Campari, huh, Adriano? It's nothing to laugh about. If anybody would prefer to screw around, go, and Godspeed. But for those who stay—I've already said this, pay fucking attention, I've already said this shit—for whoever stays, it's the real deal. It's standing up and being counted like a man, goddammit. Anyone who turns off his radio is out; from now on, he's out. I don't even want to know about it. 'Oh! The battery gave out.' Fuck it. That won't work. You can't let it give out. I'd like to see how funny that'd be if you were in Iraq. Or in Israel. Félix was over there, he saw how the Mossad does things. Did you or didn't you, Félix? Was there anybody pulling stupid stunts there? In a civilized place, you hesitate and you get waxed. That's what I ought to do, but I don't, because it's not my style. I'm just saying that I'll fire the son of a bitch in our group, and I mean it. The radio's turned off? Then adios to the little faggot. I'm not going to wax him; I'm going to let the asshole go. But he's through. Anybody not understand? Anybody got any questions?"

Luizão went to the desk, sat down with his legs apart, facing the back of the chair, his ample belly rubbing against the crossrails, and gazed slowly at the men under his command. He drank a glass of water in one gulp, then proceeded. "Here's the story. Lincoln will go with Otacílio after Anderson, the informant that Deputy Amarildo Horta rammed down Vitor's throat and who's attached to the Botafogo precinct. Anderson is wiretapping everybody who's an actor, the wife of a secretary, son of some authority, football player, to see if he can pan out something that'll bring him a little dough, and more important, that'll provide Amarildo with a strong move on the political chessboard. To say Amarildo is to say the governor, because they're joined at the hip. Look, I'm not going to try to teach fishes how to swim. Everybody here knows that when you tap phone lines you hear both what you want and what you don't want, you find what you're looking for and what you aren't looking for. I have information that Anderson found what he didn't want. It seems he has interesting recordings of the wife of Nuno Cedro, that magnate who finances the governor's campaigns."

"The guy from the bingo parlors?" asked Otacílio.

"No, the bingo guy's somebody else. Nuno's a serious businessman. It seems there are some conversations between the guy's wife and a trafficker, something really hot. Pure dynamite. In the hands of the government, it's a sure thing, because it can stay on file, in case it becomes of interest in the future. But today, if it fell into the hands of the press, everything would blow up, it would destroy the governor's plans, kill on the runway his most ambitious flights . . . All of you know . . . It would pit Nuno against the governor. After all, how can the governor's police do such a thing to an ally? So then, boys, task number one: find Anderson and get hold of Mrs. Nuno Cedro's compromising tapes. Objective: to keep the governor on a short leash; breathe down his neck so he'll know Vitor is untouchable. It's just covering your ass. A policy of prevention."

Luizão was sweating more and more, even at that time of morning and with the air-conditioning running full blast. He wiped his broad forehead with his handkerchief and continued. "Félix, you'll go look for Índio. Pay a visit to the Mineira favela. Talk to the boss there, sound them out. Find out what their thinking is. We have a good relationship with them over there, don't we? Go there. Ask around like somebody who's after information on what could've led Santiago to kidnap the guy's wife. But the main objective is to give Índio the impression that you, and therefore me, us, Vitor's crew, aren't involved in this mess. The mission is to transmit to the RC, through Índio, the message that we don't have anything to do with the kidnapping of Moisés's wife. Understood?"

After another full glass of water down the hatch, Luizão França was ready for the third play. "Bernardinho and Adriano, you two will shadow the anti-kidnapping personnel. The objective is to discover everything they know and pass along to me whatever they find out about all this shit. First, you're going to call the tip hotline, an hour apart, and tell them similar stories. I said similar, not identical. It's a kind of vaccine. It may become necessary to immobilize Mauro Pedreira or even something worse. And we've got to be prepared for anything. Here's the story: Mauro, the senior precinct chief of anti-kidnapping, is involved in a scheme with the Third Command that aims at discrediting the leadership of the Red Command by kidnapping Michele, Moisés's wife. She'll be killed and no ransom demanded. The proof of interest in discrediting the RC is the leaking of the kidnap to the press, which the precinct chief promoted, using some of his henchmen who're sources for the newspapers. Understand?"

"But the story is so airtight," said Adriano, "how are we

going to make up differences so it won't be all the same, like you ordered?"

"Use your head, dummy. Bernardinho will call first and won't use the verb *discredit*, won't mention the RC, or talk about the senior chief. He'll say that Mauro Pedreira wants to fuck Moisés, period. And you're going to repeat what I just said, without adding or subtracting a thing. Understand now? Do you understand, Bernardinho?"

Luizão stood up to give his final order. "The others will come with me. We're going after Miranda. The objective is to eliminate Santiago. It doesn't matter where or how. He mustn't survive the next twenty-four hours. Let's split up: Criciúma will go after our people in the MP, carefully, because there's a lot of double agents there. Juremir will go after our contacts in Intelligence. I have a few hunches and a working hypothesis, which I won't disclose to avoid getting in your way. Sander and Sales, you stay with me."

THE RECEPTION AREA OF GUANABARA PALACE, SEPTEMBER 30, 8:59 A.M.

Corporal Maria do Carmo put down the telephone, pushed back her chair, and stood up, saluting. "Colonel Fraga, Mr. Secretary, Dr. Vitor . . . I'll advise that you've arrived. You may go into the waiting room." She pushed a button on the desk and the door separating the reception area from the governor's waiting room unlocked with a strident hiss, followed by a sharp sound.

The waiting room was vast, full of mirrors, paintings, tables, and armchairs. The wide windows opened onto the greenery and light of the gardens.

"Mr. Secretary, did the governor say what the agenda is?" Fraga inquired as they waited.

"Fraga, when the governor calls you in, he doesn't announce what the agenda is, and he's not limited to the agenda. But it's obvious that in the present circumstances the subject is that one-note samba."

"I ask, Mr. Secretary, because, as you know, the governor is a politician, and like every politician he sees things somewhat differently than we do."

"What are you trying to say, Fraga?"

"Well, I don't mean to be inopportune or impertinent, but considering that the kidnapping of Michele is a very serious fact with enormous explosive potential, I'd be tempted to admit it might be better for it not to be disclosed in the media."

"Of course it can't be. No way, Fraga. Unthinkable. If something like that gets leaked, the guys we've managed to hold off may find themselves forced to take action."

"That's exactly what I was thinking. They've got their own code of honor and their own policy. If the kidnapping goes public, the RC will be discredited if it does nothing. In the meantime, they raised hell yesterday, but the message was intended only for those in the know. The population as a whole didn't understand. As long as the kidnapping doesn't become public knowledge, they can draw back. If it does, who knows what might happen."

"Of course. You're right, Fraga. Do you agree, Vitor?"

The civil police official nodded. The secretary then turned to the commander of the MP.

"Fraga, I don't understand what you're driving at."

"It's that the governor, being political, may evaluate the situation only from the political angle. And who can say in that case what the outcome of that evaluation might be? The governor might consider it politically convenient to release word of the kidnapping."

"Are you suggesting I lie to the governor?"

"Not at all, Mr. Secretary. That would be very irresponsible. And unethical as well."

"Ah, good."

"You could just not make mention of the fact."

"Fraga, that's out of the question."

"Whatever you decide, Mr. Secretary. I was just thinking aloud."

"Better to keep your thoughts to yourself from now on."

"Yes, sir."

The two joined Vitor in silence. The secretary stretched twice and complained about the air-conditioning. In his opinion, the governor lived in a refrigerator.

"Coming into this cold-storage plant and then going out into Rio's Senegalese heat plays hob with my lungs," said the secretary.

No one said anything. Vitor essayed a smile.

Time tautened and stretched out like the strap of a slingshot, and the secretary began to feel like a glass window—he, of all people, who was always critical of everything, who always played the role of the stone in the sling. He started to imagine who would now fill the role of the projectile. It was always like that when one sat in that waiting room. He had the feeling that at any moment orderlies would come looking for him, to shave his head and saw into his skull.

"Does anyone have something for a headache?"

Neither of the police chiefs had anything. Vitor offered a sugar-free cough drop.

From the rear of the room, more than twenty yards away, her voice nearly inaudible, smooth and gentle, the governor's private secretary invited them to enter. The governor was ready to receive them.

The secretary rose more quickly than his auxiliaries and issued orders to them through his teeth. "Fraga, Vitor, we're not going to mention the kidnapping. Let me do the talking. You two just follow my lead." They headed toward the office.

The governor waved them in. He was speaking with his chief of staff, at his work desk. He pointed to the wide table used for meetings, and the three collaborators sat down, as they had many times before. The place at the head of the table belonged to the governor. The secretary sat on his right. To the secretary's right sat the commander-general of the military police, across from whom, in the second available chair to the left of the governor, was the chief of the civil police. They waited for long minutes.

Finally, the governor crossed the office with short, quick steps, initiating the meeting with the first question. "Well, Mr. Secretary? What's this story about Moisés's wife being kidnapped? Michele, isn't it? Have you been able to prove that Captain Santiago is behind it?"

Luizão, sitting in the rear seat, answered his radio. "Talk to me, Félix."

"I wasn't able to speak to Índio, but Jonas confirms that they're on Santiago's tail."

"I'm going to end up having a confrontation with them. Do you know what leads they have?"

"Negative."

"Did the guy refer to any neighborhood, any location? Did he say what group was handling the mission? Whether it's personnel from the South Zone, the West Zone?"

"Nothing."

"But are they after Santiago or trying to find where Michele's being held?"

"Both. According to what I understood, both."

"Do they think Santiago is managing the captivity personally?"

"I doubt it, they're not that naïve. They know Santiago's a professional."

"Any lead then about where he's holding her?"

"Nothing."

"Besides Santiago, did they mention anyone else?"

"You mean—"

"Just that. Do they think Santiago was acting alone in this crap? Did they mention Vitor?"

"No. I don't know what they think about that, but Jonas only talked about Santiago."

"My name didn't come up?"

"No, not at all."

"Good. Go on trying to get something. Stay there. Try to talk directly to the Man."

"Copy that. Out."

EDITORIAL ROOM OF THE CITY'S HIGHEST-CIRCULATION NEWSPAPER, SEPTEMBER 30, 10:22 A.M.

"Somebody turn up the volume on the TV," said a reporter.

In a special broadcast, the Globo newscast *Top of the Hour* breaks the story about Michele's kidnapping. The secretary of public safety appears as he descends the steps of the governmental palace and declines comment. The heads of the two police forces accompany him, silently.

STONE SLAB FROM WHICH CAN BE SEEN THE IMMENSE PLANET THAT IS THE ALEMÃO COMPLEX, SEPTEMBER 30, 11:25 A.M.

The owner of the drug site looked at the horizon while waiting for an answer, under a sun at its zenith.

"Nothing, Cezinha. Nobody knows nothing. Nobody could make contact with Bangu. Nothing. I talked to Noca, to Nereu, Jonas, Rivaldo, everybody. Nobody's got any news.

Noca thinks it's turned bad for us too. The news is all over the place. He thinks we're going to have to respond, even if it's—hold on, I've got a radio call."

Urubu hunched over the radio, which was a bit heavier than a normal cell phone, said something, and then handed it to Cezinha. "Talk to him, bro. Talk to him. It's for you."

"Cezinha speaking, over. Talk. Come on, come on!" He talked and listened, mostly listened, inclining his head to improve the sound, moving away from Urubu, who was leaning against a metal post, good for resting but terrible for the radio signal.

"Was it really him? Speak up, Cezinha. What happened? Anybody die? Did the pigs kill any brother?" Urubu asked.

"No, but nearly. And there's two missing. They went to the infirmary and nobody knows nothing about them. Moisés almost ended up in the drawer. He barely got out of it."

"What else?"

"Call the people together. We're going to hold the meeting right now. We got urgent business ahead of us."

A GAS STATION ON AYRTON SENNA HIGHWAY, SEPTEMBER 30, 11:26 A.M.

Luizão had a soft drink in a small room at the rear of the convenience store. He interrupted his conversation with his old partner Lúcio Pé-de-Valsa Moraes to answer his radio.

"Go ahead."

"It's Adriano."

"Yes."

"Anti-kidnapping is taking it slow. They don't know and don't want to know about the Michele case. They got other things to do. Vitor ordered them to stay away from it."

"What about the tip hotline?"

"We haven't done that."

"Why not?"

"If anti-kidnapping's off the case, why would we need—?"

"Fuck it, Adriano. You guys are real shit, aren't you? You haven't understood a fucking thing, have you? That's why it's a waste of time explaining anything to you. The MP's got it right. Order given, order obeyed, and fuck everything else. Didn't I say it was preventive? Didn't I say we had to be ready for anything, goddammit? That we may have to immobilize Mauro Pedreira, or even worse? Didn't I? Didn't I use those words?"

"Correct."

"Not fucking correct. Wrong. Now go and do what I ordered, goddammit. With an hour between the two calls, you hear? I want you on the tail of the anti-kidnapping people. You can't trust what those fuckers told you. They could be trying to throw you off the scent. Keep on digging there. Copy?"

SECRETARIAT OF PUBLIC SAFETY BUILDING, OFFICE OF THE SECRETARY, SEPTEMBER 30, 11:27 A.M.

The secretary was standing at the head of the table and had just pounded on it, knocking over water, coffee, and sugar. Marquinho slipped past the arms of the secretary to place a wad of napkins over the mess to contain its spread.

"Leave that shit, Marquinho. Goddammit. Goddammit. I want to know. I don't care how you find out or what you're going to do. I want to know today. Either I find out or I resign. But before I resign, I insist on having the pleasure of firing you two. You understand? Do I need to make it any clearer? Today, this very day, at this piece of shit table, I want the explanation: Who's taking classified information to the governor? Who does Intelligence answer to, Amílcar? Can you tell me? Is it to me or isn't it, goddammit? Who's its boss, Vaz? Is it me or isn't it? Now, there's one thing I know: Fraga has nothing to do with this. I have my reasons for that conclusion. He didn't know that the governor knew about the kidnapping. And he didn't want him to know. Of course it also won't hurt to check. With all the sons of bitches in Public Safety, anything is possible. We've got to be paranoid, mentally ill, to imagine the fantastic collection of perverts—even so, even in the most pathological fantasy, we'll never be able to conceive the degree of degradation, underhandedness, and backstabbing among that gang. I wish our enemies were the outlaws. Don't I wish. That'd be paradise. So it might be Fraga after all. Investigate Fraga too. Anything's possible. Where those fucking police are concerned, anything is possible. In any case, to me the principal suspect, after the two of you, is Vitor, who was very quiet today."

The secretary went to the window, leaned his head against the glass, and observed Avenida Presidente Vargas.

"Turn down that goddamn air-conditioning, Marquinho. Tell them to lower the fucking thing. Have we got nothing but perverts in this place? Doesn't anybody feel cold in this shithole?"

He returned to his desk, loosened his tie, and sat down. "Do you understand? I want to know the connections of everyone involved in this investigation with the military office of Guanabara Palace and with other possible agents of the governor. I want this room swept, my telephones swept. I want to know who's the real secretary of public safety; the son of a bitch who's on my ass, out to get me, hidden behind these walls, under my chair, inside my pillow. Who that power is, that thing, what the fuck it is. I want to know what I am, when all is said and done; what my role is in this farce. If I'm the clown, I'm out of here, but first I'll settle accounts with you two. Now please be kind enough to leave me alone."

Amílcar, Vaz, and Marquinho left the office silently. The secretary felt dizzy and collapsed onto the sofa.

SARAMAGO'S PORCH, SURROUNDED BY VENERABLE MANGO TREES, IN JACAREPAGUÁ, SEPTEMBER 30, NOON

The housekeeper placed white linen tablecloths on the small round wicker-and-glass tables, amid lounge chairs, ferns, and her master's wheelchair. She served appetizers on a silver tray and juice from tropical fruits in crystal glasses. Among the many cages made of worked wood, one drew special attention because of the delicacy of its ornaments, its size, and the exotic pheasant that occupied it. The birds provided the sound track for the bucolic dialogue.

"You're very well set up here," said Luizão. "What a beautiful yard you have. This veranda is beautiful."

"Very kind of you," the host replied modestly.

"I'm serious. When I grow up, I want to have a house like this one. I want to live in a place like this."

"Ah, Dr. França, please. You don't live in a house because you choose not to. I know you're very well off."

"Not so much. You know how it is, Saramago, one day business is good, the next day not so good. This country of ours isn't serious. It lacks stability, balance, predictability."

"That's true. It's difficult to invest in a situation of uncertainty."

"Right. I was reading an article by an economist the other day. It said exactly that. Without juridical security, expectations don't stabilize and investments decline."

"Of course, it's natural."

"It's a fact, isn't it?"

"Doubtlessly. But politics don't help, Dr. França, they don't help."

"A pack of scoundrels, opportunists."

"You can't trust anyone anymore. Especially in my field, which in fact isn't going very well. I sense a certain weariness in the old animal game, my dear Dr. França. However much I've taken precautions and diversified my investments into bingo parlors, slot machines, the transport sector, and waste management . . . the fact is that we're no longer living in that exuberant moment. But, okay. I'm not one to complain. I'm not ungrateful to fate. After all, I built my life; my children are well on their way . . ."

"It's like I always say: we have to thank God, my friend. Despite everything . . . Did you say you'd invited Brito to our chat?"

"Yes. He must be about to arrive. He lives near here. It won't be long."

"Great. I owe you an apology, because, after all, you don't do that, do you? Set up a meeting like this on such short notice?"

"How can you say that, França? There can't be any awkwardness between us. One hand washes the other."

"Thank you, Saramago. You're always very gracious. And you receive us with this prodigious abundance, this generosity."

"Those turnovers really are delicious, eh?"

"Wonderful."

"To me, they're torture, because I can't eat them . . ."

"You can't?"

"No, some minor health problems. Natural at my age. I'm over seventy, França. I passed seventy some time ago."

"You're in very good shape. No one would guess your age."

The housekeeper returned to the veranda to introduce the third character.

"It's Brito," said Saramago, addressing Luizão França.

After the ritual greetings, Saramago asked Luizão to explain the reasons for the unexpected visit. At that moment, Luizão's radio vibrated in his pocket and he excused himself to answer it. He got up and walked toward the far end of the veranda. "Speak, Otacílio," said França. "Say it fast, because I can't talk now."

"The mission is aborted, chief."

"How so?"

"Anderson has disappeared. Lincoln and I spent all morning looking for the guy, but he's vanished. Disappeared. Nobody knows anything about him."

"At the precinct—"

"Nobody knows."

"Since when?"

"Since last night. It's now been about twelve hours without anybody knowing his whereabouts."

"And his family?"

"He's from the interior. He came to Rio when that deputy got elected."

"But did you try to contact the family?"

"Of course. No sign of life."

"What about the deputy's office?"

"We tried that too."

"Nothing?"

"Nothing."

"Well, then it's better not to waste any more time. Somebody thought the same thing we thought before we did."

"Santiago?"

"Isn't it obvious? Call Sander or Sales. They're having lunch near here. Set it up with them. I want you and Lincoln with us. We need to strengthen our team. Our mission is a lemon too."

"All right, sir. Out."

Luizão returned to his chair and resumed the conversation. "Sorry. A policeman's life—"

"Is like a doctor's," said Brito.

"Are you a doctor?" asked Luizão.

"Brito was one of the best in his specialty," replied Sara-mago.

"Was. Today I'm retired. Actually, I left the profession back in the '70s."

"Other businesses became more attractive," said Saramago, smiling and patting his friend's left leg with his right hand.

"But I requested this meeting, my friends," Luizão re-claimed the floor, "because I need the help of you both. I urgently need to locate a person you know, a person that you have good relations with."

"Go on, we'll see what we can do," said Saramago. "Who is it?"

"Santiago."

AVENIDA NOSSA SENHORA DE COPACABANA, SEPTEMBER 30, 2:20 P.M.

Carlos Augusto left the branch of the Bank of Brazil. He was wearing khaki cargo pants and a white cotton shirt, almost a smock. His leather sandals were bought on a vacation trip to Caruaru. He carried a moss green backpack on his right shoulder. He walked toward the corner and lifted his dark glasses to look at his wristwatch, but he didn't see either the dial or his wrist. He saw the geometric pattern of the sidewalk and faces that swirled around the walls of the buildings and the brilliant blue of the sky that melted in the water puddle and in the colorful can of roasted peanuts, which scattered and slid to his leg and shattered the display window and broke the black thread of steel. Hands, arms, fists spun. Baby felt the warm, viscous taste of blood as he blacked out.

When he recovered consciousness, stretched out on the sidewalk, Carlos Augusto was surrounded by people and heard voices recounting the assault. He learned that three men attacked him; that by their build and the skill with which they struck, they appeared to be private security professionals. He discovered that they didn't flee; they walked calmly to the corner and turned left, toward Avenida Atlântica, like any other pedestrians. The torn backpack was tossed beside him, his belongings scattered. Some of the items had been stomped on, such as the cellular, the comb, and the photos.

Baby refused the ambulance. He accepted a taxi. He asked them to call his doctor, but he didn't remember the phone number. He would be eternally grateful to those kind and dedicated people, worried about him and attentive. He was moved and thanked them, insisting, thanking them again. In the cab, en route to the hospital, he laughed when he realized that he wasn't crying from pain but because he was flooded with gratitude. He had never felt himself so immersed in a sea of brotherhood. And he thought how odd it was to be invaded by warm waves of love while spitting fragments of teeth.

A broad and deserted yard with overgrown grass, two orange trees, a few chickens scratching in litter near an old brickfront house, September 30, 2:40 P.M.

A middle-aged man peeked out through the blinds of the living room. "Easy. It's them," he said.

An unshaven youth hid his pistol under a cushion.

Santiago and Miranda knocked at the door.

The older man greeted them with a complaint. "You took so long to get here that we were—"

Miranda said in an almost inaudible voice, "Where is she?"

The youth pointed to the corridor. His partner said, "In the rear bedroom."

Miranda said, still in a low voice, "Is everything okay? Is she all right?"

"Everything's okay," said the first man.

The young man added, "She's half hysterical, but we gave her a small dose of Valium to calm her down."

Santiago spoke for the first time. "Let's see then. Let's see the woman."

The youth headed for the corridor, fumbling in his pocket. Santiago went with him, and interrupted, "Can you get me a glass of water?"

The youth went to the right, followed by Santiago. The kitchen was long. The refrigerator was behind the sink, to the right. The youth took a key from his pocket, deposited it on the edge of the sink, opened the refrigerator door and crouched down to get the water bottle from the lower shelf in the door. He collapsed with three bullets in the head. The shots were sharp and silent. Santiago didn't even need to check. The job was done. He left the body kneeling beside the open refrigerator, picked up the key, and returned to the living room.

Miranda pressed his thumb against the old man's neck to feel the carotid. Like a professional, he wore gloves. He looked at Santiago, showing his typical expression of mission accomplished. The body on the floor was inert.

They walked together to the room in the rear.

They opened the door slowly. Michele was asleep, clutching two pillows, sitting on a thin mattress stuck in the junction of two walls. The room was empty and dark; the window was boarded shut.

"Wake up, Michele. You're free. We liquidated the kidnappers, but there are still risks. You'll understand later. For now, you need to trust us. We're going to give you some coffee and get you out of here."

MINEIRA FAVELA, COURTYARD OF THE SMALL LOCAL SAMBA SCHOOL, SEPTEMBER 30, 4 P.M.

Jonas gathered the drug-traffic soldiers. Almost all of them were sitting on the small side wall, protected from the sun by the tin roof of the court. He ordered complete attention. He informed them that the time for war was approaching.

From the small room of the school's administration, Índio watched the meeting of his subordinates. He had called his friends in Bangu-I and asked permission for a personal consultation with Moisés. He was waiting for a reply.

Jonas shouted, inflaming the passion of the combatants. He gave the floor to the recruit Juvenal, the professor who traded the history department for the army, to serve his community by bringing culture and practical knowledge to the movement in Mineira. This was what Jonas said in his introduction. Juvenal explained the difference between a band and a platoon, a company, a battalion, a unit of war, an intelligence agency. He hammered home the importance of organization, hierarchy, and discipline. Juvenal spoke of the power of the anti-kidnapping squad in Rio de Janeiro and its dispute with the antidrug squad.

"Anti-kidnapping has been greatly strengthened, but antidrug has grown again thanks to the business of importing Colombian cocaine paste via Angra dos Reis, which has the largest concentration of private boats in the country, where the Brazilian GDP spends its holidays and which maintains connections with the rich interior of São Paulo via clandestine landing strips."

"Professor, it's best to explain what GDP is, where Angra dos Reis is, and speak a little slower, because people here ain't very used to this kind of thing," said Jonas.

Índio couldn't hear very well what they were saying down below. In any case, even if he had been able to hear, he wouldn't have paid attention. His mind was far away. His heart was leaping in his chest. The telephone rang. He quickly grabbed it. "Talk to me, brother."

"Índio?"

"Yes, it's me."

"How ya doing, friend? How's the family? Rodriguinho? Marcinha? Dona Rita?"

"Solid, brother. Everything's beautiful."

"You really needed to talk to me. It hadda be with me. That right?"

"Right. Here's the word, boss: that pig Santiago made contact."

"He speak to you?"

"No, he ain't dumb. He sent a message."

"And?"

"He wants a meeting with me. Him and me, just the two of us."

"What for?"

"He says he's got Michele. And she's okay. He says he rescued her."

"How much does he want?"

"He says he don't wanna talk about dough."

"He wants it in drugs?"

"No, he don't want nothing."

"Guns?"

"Negative. He says he didn't have nothing to do with the kidnap. He knows you think it was him, 'cause his ex-wife ratted him out. But that was because she wants to keep their son. It's all a shitfight over child custody. He says she wants to see him dead or in prison, or on the run and discredited."

"He said that?"

"Yeah. And he said he risked his life to save Michele, and even had to kill the two kidnappers, 'cause it was the only way to save his life too."

"She's with him, safe and sound?"

"That's what he says."

"Praise God!"

"Amen, boss."

"Did he denounce anybody?"

"He knows, don't he? He's gotta know. If he don't, how'd he rescue Michele?"

"True. You think he's willing to hand over them cowardly pigs? He did at least confirm it's the pigs, didn't he?"

"I don't know, boss. That, I don't know. But it sure as hell looks like the police. Gotta be. How else could Santiago work that fast if it wasn't some scheme he knows from the inside? However much negotiating he does with guys from the Third Command and the FOF, Santiago couldn't deal with them that easy."

"Yeah. Makes sense. He talks to our enemies the way he talks to us. It's business."

"That's what I thought."

"It must've been the pigs all right."

"Had to be."

"And what's he want now, for returning Michele? Just to meet with you?"

"Yeah."

"Why?"

"He didn't say. I don't know, boss, could it maybe be some kind of move? A trap? What should I do?"

"Did he set up a time and place?"

"No. He said he's gonna call me. He asked for the number of my radio. He's gonna call at four thirty."

"Ten minutes from now."

"Yeah."

"Then you're gonna say you talked to me and I authorized it. What matters is Michele's life, and that everything's okay."

"Nothing else?"

"Nothing. When you find out when and how the meeting's gonna be, prepare the best personnel available to go with you.

Ask Rivaldo to pick out some of his boys . . . He's educating and training a tough bunch. The plan's gonna be like this: our people'll form a 360. Just like the BOPE does when it invades a favela. Except in this case the circle of protection's gotta be fucking large so that from the center nobody can be seen, besides you, of course, 'cause you're gonna be in the center, which is the spot where you meet with the pig. It's obvious the circle is gonna lose that pretty shape, all nice and neat, because it's gonna have to hug up against the things in the area, the streets, the buildings, all that. And it's obvious too that the objective won't be to defend your life but to capture Santiago when he lets Michele go, or to rescue Michele if he's got other intentions and betrays you. Anyway, whatever happens, I want Santiago alive. Copy that?"

"Copy. There's just one thing."

"What?"

"There won't be time to talk to Rivaldo, ask for his help, wait for the personnel to arrive . . . Santiago may want a meet an hour from now. What then?"

"Then forget Rivaldo. Make do with the everyday silverware."

"Sorry, boss. I don't understand. What silverware?"

"Nothing, forget it. I was trying to tell you to use your own personnel."

"Ah! Right, boss. But there ain't nothing to worry about. I've got very good people here with me. Now I even got an army professor here, giving instructions to my boys."

"Careful about infiltration, Índio."

"We're doing the infiltrating, boss."

"You never know, Índio. Keep a close watch on it."

"No problem, boss. I'll give it loving care. And I'm gonna start organizing the personnel immediately. The plan's gonna work. We'll have Michele here today, celebrating, boss."

"Keep me informed. Is the other plan already under way?"

"Everything's under control, boss."

"Is Cezinha in on it?"

"Cezinha, Urubu, and their team."

"Very good."

Índio waited for Moisés to say good-bye, but the RC leader, imprisoned in Bangu-I, broke off the connection without a word. The boss of Mineira opened the window and summoned Jonas with a shout. Pupils and professor looked up, shielding their eyes from the sun with their hands. Juvenal couldn't disguise his smile when he realized that the scene seemed to demonstrate the efficiency of his teachings. Anyone seeing that image in a photo would conclude that the followers were saluting their commander. The young recruit and historian resumed his lecture, while Jonas dashed toward the stairs. In the small room, Índio was drawing something.

"I want the maps that the pilot from the civil police prepared for us," said Índio. "I want everything here, fast. War footing. It's an emergency, Jonas. Choose eighteen of our best soldiers. Guns for short-, mid-, and long range. We're gonna need six drivers and six cars."

"Can I replace some cars with vans, to reduce the number?"

"No. We're gonna need six cars, six mobile units, 'cause each point needs maximum maneuverability and complete independence."

"Right."

"And for backup, four more experienced men. They'll go in pairs into the buildings and orient the action from there. I want binoculars and special radios for them. I need that hidden microphone and the transmitter to keep track by GPS. Bring night visors too. I don't know yet the time of the operation. Get from the file the photos of Michele I ordered put together. Does everybody know Santiago?"

"I can't answer that."

"I want photos of Santiago too."

"We don't have any of Santiago."

"Tell Vikie to look on the Internet."

"Is that all?"

"You want more?"

"No. It's enough."

"Then run, goddammit, get moving."

HOSPITAL BEDROOM, SEPTEMBER 30, 7:25 P.M.

Carlos Augusto slowly opened his eyes, and slowly made out the outline of Renata. The cloudy silhouette of his friend took him back to earlier days and the memory of the last hours. Little by little, he understood that it must not be Renata, it couldn't be. He shut his eyes, then reopened them. It *was* Renata. She greeted his return to consciousness.

"Everything's all right, Baby. The worst is past," she said, squeezing his hand.

"What—" A sharp pain interrupted the question.

"Don't talk now, Baby. It's better not to talk. It was terrible and it's going to hurt a bit, but the worst is over. You lost two teeth and broke your nose, your left forearm, and two ribs. You have abrasions on your back and legs. But you're going to be all right, Baby."

"My teeth . . . Am I going to be toothless? In the front?"

"Don't talk now, Baby. Everything's going to be all right. These days prostheses are even better than the originals."

"But they're"—he garbled the words, because his tongue was swollen and his mouth numb—"artificial . . . I'm going to be like my father, who's had dentures since he was thirty-five . . ."

"No dentures. That was in Pernambuco, back in the '60s. Forget about that, Baby. Relax. Go to sleep. Everything's going to be all right."

"What about you? And Pedrinho? How did you—" Pain overcame curiosity.

"Everything's all right. Suely called me. Since you didn't return and she had to leave, she called me. Remember that I had given her my cell number once when she stayed with Pedrinho? Luckily, I heard the message a short time later."

"But didn't they call her? I gave them the number at home. I remember I gave it to somebody as I was entering the hospital . . ."

"I'll bet they tried and didn't get anyone. Remember you disconnected the landline so Pedrinho couldn't talk to his father?"

"Pedrinho's father—"

"Yes."

"Natinha . . ." Baby started to cry.

"Don't, Baby. I know, I know. But you're safe now. I've called Itamar and Júlio. They're there outside. I felt you wouldn't want to involve Érico in the story. I think it's too early for him to dive headfirst into the cauldron—"

"Baby's cauldron," he smiled without his front teeth, and Renata concealed her shock. He continued: "Natinha, wasn't it a mugging?"

"Look, Baby. The money's in your wallet, your checkbook, credit cards, everything's there. It wasn't a mugging."

"Did you call the police?"

"They told me in the hospital admitting area that you had expressly forbidden getting the police involved."

"I did?"

"But it's better that way. Just imagine getting the police involved in this. That's all we need. Pedro's father could've shown up here with his gang . . . to protect you . . ."

"God in heaven! Rosemary's baby! Oh, for the love of God don't scare me like that, Renata."

"That's not going to happen. Nobody called the police. Stay calm. Relax."

"It was Pedro's father, wasn't it? It was him, wasn't it? What does the man want? My God in heaven."

"He doesn't want anything from you, Baby. You were beaten up, but I was the target. It was a message, a threat. It had nothing to do with you."

"And how did you locate me?"

"The hospital staff found a paper in your pocket with my mother's number."

"Yeah, I remember that. Your number and Suely's cell-phone number I know by heart, but I didn't know your mother's, and with that business with Pedrinho I thought I might need it."

"Mother left me a message with the address of the hospital. She was very worried, poor thing. She adores you. I'll bet if it weren't for her osteoporosis and the trauma from that fall, she'd be here at your bedside right now. Look, Baby, I have to go. Don't worry about me or Pedro. We'll be all right. We're going somewhere very safe. I promise to send word. For your safety, it's best you stay far away from me. I'll call the boys. They'll take turns, and as long as you're in the hospital one of them will stay with you. You won't be alone."

Renata leaned over and kissed Baby on the forehead.

HOSPITAL RECEPTION AREA, SEPTEMBER 30, 8 P.M.

Renata checked her address book and dialed from a pay phone.

"Alice? It's Renata. Good, good, everything's fine. What about you? Can you talk? Yes, it's been a long time. This life of being constantly on the go . . . But are you okay? Great. That's great. And the PUC, when are you done? Already? Really? This year? Wonderful. Are you going to have a graduation party? Of course, you can count on me. I'll be waiting for the invitation. Yes, the same address as always. The same address and the same old life as always. Nothing, no boyfriend. You think some interesting and free man wants to get involved with a social worker at the maximum-security penitentiary of the state of Rio de Janeiro? I go out now and then, just to brush away the cobwebs, my friend. Only that. Nothing of the sort. Nice of you to say that. I wish it were true. Life's not like that, Licinha. It's not. I wish it were. No, not bitter. You can be sure I'm not giving up what's good. But I promise you I'll be in the front row at your graduation. Pedrinho is good, he's fine, growing up so quickly. You won't even recognize him. How long has it been, six months, since you were at our place? Longer? That long? Gee. Then you really won't recognize him. Mom is so-so. She fell and broke her femur, a bad situation. Yes. That's right. Poor thing. It's not an easy age. Women live longer than men, but literally by fits and starts, falls and fractures. It's obvious, isn't it? It's on our shoulders. But Mom deserves to be treated well. I was a lot of trouble. Yeah, me too, despite being alone, everything's all right, everything's calm, I mean, actually, Licinha, more or less. No, it's not anything bad, but I think I'm going to need your help. It'd be great if we could talk in person. Are you still going out with that nice good-looking young man? Yeah, the policeman? How great, how cool. I'm so happy for you. Maybe after the graduation there'll be another ceremony coming up. Hey, girl, who knows? I'll bet there is. Let's hope. Well, what matters is that it's still cool, right? So then, can we talk for a bit? Whenever you can, I mean, if it could be to-day—that'd be the greatest. It is, you swear? Well, for me, to be frank, perfectly frank, ideally it'd be right now, if it's possible for you. Are you sure? Could you call your boyfriend? No, I'll explain later. If it's doable, that'd be fantastic. It'd be marvelous. Then I'm on my way, before he leaves. A kiss."

Luizão chewed his beef jerky with cowpeas and melted butter. Criciúma, Sander, and Sales vigorously attacked the cassava. They sipped mangaba juice with acerola. Luizão's radio vibrated along with the silverware, while he repeated the mantra, "Too bad this bar doesn't have air-conditioning."

"Talk to me, Félix."

"It's not Félix."

"Who is it?"

"Félix can't talk right now. He's occupied with something else. Him and the snitch you put here are very busy right now. And from the looks of things, they're not gonna be able to talk to you anytime soon. Only in the next incarnation. If you like barbecue, you're invited. There's gonna be a barbecue tonight."

The line went dead. Luizão's carotid throbbed, pumping blood to his ears, his nose, his forehead, his cheeks, everywhere but his brain, which was stunned by what he'd heard.

Living room of Alice de Andrade Melo's apartment, September 30, 8:10 p.m.

Actually, it was the living room of Alice's parents' apartment. More specifically, Alice's mother, as the proud owner liked to point out so as to leave no doubts about the slice that had come to her in the bitter divorce settlement with Alice's father.

At the moment, however, the apartment was Alice's. Her mother was away evaluating, on-site, the extent of her holdings in the Iberian Peninsula.

"You won't be sorry, love. It's just a little longer. Don't be such a bookworm. You're off tomorrow. You can perfectly well study for the test tomorrow. You can stay a little longer without a problem, okay? In fact, now that I think about it, to be frank, you could, if you like, if you value certain things, perfectly well spend the night here."

"Licinha, I've already explained it to you. It's not because I don't want to."

"We're not talking about wanting to, baby."

"Okay, it's not for lack of horniness, if you must know. It's just that I'm a serious guy, a responsible guy and all that old-fashioned stuff."

"Cool, that's cool, okay. But you don't need to overdo it."

"It must be hard for you to understand, because—I mean, Licinha, life is difficult for everybody, for one reason or another. But for me it's difficult in every sense, and if I don't grab time with both hands, with all my strength, and bite off a piece of it, I'm screwed. That's all."

"Okay, we won't talk about it again."

"I didn't want to. You provoked it."

"Is that provoking it? To you, that's provoking it?"

"No, I didn't mean it that way. What I meant was that you brought it up."

"Ah! That's better. Changing the subject, how about Juju's party on Friday? Are we on? Don't leave me in the lurch again. C'mon, baby. You promised."

"I'll do what I can."

"What you can, no. What you can isn't enough. I want you to swear. Put your hand on my leg and swear."

"So your leg's a bible now, huh?"

"Isn't it?"

"Jeez, don't do that to me. That's unfair. It's hitting below the belt. Literally. How am I supposed to concentrate later? You know I have to leave. I have to study hard or I'll do badly. I can't do badly. If I do badly I'll lose my scholarship. Haven't you realized yet how much it means to me to study at PUC? It was a dream. To me, it was a dream."

"To me it's a nightmare. Especially at final exam time. If you, the big bookworm, with one of the best grade-point averages in the school of law, say you have to study hard, just imagine me. What's going to become of me, baby? Do one thing: stay here and study with me."

"You know that doesn't work. It doesn't."

"It doesn't?"

"Yes, it does, that way. You understood, you little vixen. It leads to something else."

"Something that apparently doesn't interest you."

"For heaven's sake, Alice. You're like a child."

"All right. So talk to Renata and then go. But don't try coming on to her. I'll be watching, you hear?"

"Is she pretty?"

"What, you don't remember her? We've been together several times."

"I think so, vaguely, but I'm not very sure."

"Yes, she's pretty. In her own way. I don't know if she's

pretty, but she's attractive. She's a really cool person. That's why I'm asking you to talk to her."

"Okay. Here I am, waiting."

"She's on her way."

"Turn up the television. The newscast's starting."

The sound from the TV flooded the room with the same theme music that was entering living rooms throughout Leblon. The lead story was alarming: "The warden at Bangu-I has been killed. Anacleto Chaves de Melo, 54, was shot to death early tonight at the entrance to his home in the Penha neighborhood. He had dismissed the bodyguards who had accompanied him since March, when he survived an attack on his life."

The anchorman called on a reporter: "Saul Noodles is at the scene of the crime. Are there any clues yet, Saul? Do the police have a suspect?"

"Good evening. For now, there are no leads as to the identity of the killers. The secretary of public safety advises that as yet it is not possible to establish any connection between the crime and the acts of vandalism that rocked the city yesterday. But he states that investigations are being carried out by a team specially selected by the civil police and that those responsible will be punished to the full extent of the law."

There was a cut to a close-up of the secretary of public safety who was commenting. "There may or may not be a connection between this brutal homicide and the skirmishes with traffickers, those savages who yesterday turned the city into a branch of hell. No hypothesis can be discounted. But

it would be precipitous and irresponsible to jump to any conclusion. What I want to say to the people of Rio de Janeiro
is that investigations will continue to the end, whoever gets
hurt. The society of the state of Rio de Janeiro can continue
to have confidence in its police."

"Back to you, Fatima," said Saul Noodles.

The anchorwoman added, "Before the end of this broadcast,
more information on the murder of the warden of Bangu-I, in
Rio de Janeiro, Anacleto Chaves de Melo."

Alice's boyfriend went over to the TV.

"Is he any relation to you?"

"Was, don't you mean?"

"Was he?"

"No."

"What a scare."

"What? You only care if he's a relative of mine. Is that how
a hero of public safety behaves?"

The interphone announced the arrival of Renata.

THE ALCAPARRA RESTAURANT, FLAMENGO BEACH, SEPTEMBER 30, 8:38 P.M.

The secretary of public safety was having dinner with Marquinho.

"I won't repeat that I'm exhausted because, besides being
tired, it'd look like I'm getting senile."

"I'm very tired myself, Mr. Secretary."

"Waiter, come here, son."

"Yes, sir, Mr. Secretary."

"Listen, son, can you turn down the air-conditioning a little? It's right on top of me. This restaurant's an icebox. Tell the manager we're not Eskimos. Have him come here."

"I'll do something about it, Mr. Secretary. Leave it to me. You're the boss here."

"Thank you, my boy, thank you."

The waiter moved away.

"I hate those things, Marquinho. Did you hear what he said?"

"Yeah."

"Yeah what, Marquinho. Did you hear or didn't you?"

"I did."

"Then talk straight, man. Never saw anything like it. Did you notice how he treated me?"

"He was polite, Mr. Secretary. I thought he was polite."

"Polite, no, Marquinho. You think I can't tell a polite person from an ass-kisser?"

The cell phone the secretary used exclusively to speak with the governor vibrated in his pocket.

"Oh, for God's sake. Can't I even have dinner in peace? The guy won't let me rest . . ." He pushed a button on the device and answered. "Governor . . . Speak, sir. Oh, it's you, Paulinho? I'm having dinner, but it doesn't matter. You can speak. No, go ahead, you can speak."

The secretary turned to Marquinho, covered the mouthpiece, and whispered, "It's that idiot the communications secretary."

He resumed the conversation with Paulinho. "I know. Oh, really? The newscast? Ah! I know. Yes, I had already reported

to the governor. Yes, I know. Very bad. Horrible. Yes, that's the
worst part. Exactly. The coincidence . . . Of course, it may not
be a coincidence. Probably isn't, in fact. I meant this series of
unpleasant facts. Horrible, Paulinho, really horrible. Good
lord, it's terrible for our image. How awful. The foreign press
only publishes bad news, just like our press. They're all the
same. A bunch of vultures. Is the governor going to the funeral? Well, I don't know; it's true that if he goes he'll call attention to the fact, which is a negative. You're right about that.
But if he doesn't go, wouldn't he be showing a certain, shall
we say, indifference? That's true. I know, I know. I understand.
All right, I'll go and represent the governor. Better that way.
That's right. Ah! About the interview . . . I don't know . . . I
understand. I know. What I meant to say is that—no, it wasn't
exactly that. I didn't say hell, I said that Rio seemed like a
branch of hell, which is different, Paulinho, very different. But
it was, wasn't it? Of course, it's our job to calm things down,
to show confidence. Of course, that's the idea I've always defended. I even called on society to continue having confidence
in the police, did you see that part? What did you think of that
part? But I—there I disagree with you, because I don't think
it's an exaggeration when you merely recognize reality. It's the
reality, Paulinho. If we don't say something resembling the
truth, how can we expect them to have confidence in us? If we
send that message, they're going to lose confidence. Right, I
know, okay, I admit that hell was a bit strong. I understand.
No, not that. Now you're going too far, Paulinho. Let's not de-
lude ourselves. No, hold on, it wasn't city hall that provoked
the chaos. No. Closing the schools was a hindrance, of course,

it helped spread fear, I know, it's true, but that wasn't what caused all the tumult. Of course, of course the mayor played dirty. He took advantage to gnaw away at us. It's fucking underhandedness, but to say because of it that—okay, okay. All right. No, me too. Naturally, we agree. Naturally. Oh! Did he see it? Did he think so too? Tell the governor I had the same impression he did when I saw the result on TV. I didn't like it either. He's right. I'm going to, no doubt at all, I'm going to try to be more careful. Tell him he's got nothing to worry about. Excellent. Excellent. Same to you."

The secretary hung up the phone. He turned to Marquinho. "I've had it up to here with that guy. Who does he think he is to criticize me, to correct me, to give me lessons? He's going to get fucked. I'll bet the bastard is this very moment calling Ancelmo Gois to plant a highly friendly item, full of love and loyalty: 'The secretary of public safety denies he has placed his position in the hands of the governor. He swears that the rumor is groundless because, as President Geisel used to say, the position always was in the hands of the governor.' What are you having to eat, Marquinho? Let's order right away, before I lose my appetite. We've got an hour to eat. The meeting's at ten. I can't wait to see the platter Intelligence is going to serve me. I can't wait to see what those two fuckers are going to say to me."

The secretary's radio for contact with the police chiefs rang, inside Marquinho's briefcase, with the sound of a rave dance.

"What the hell is that?" asks the secretary.

"Your cellular. In my briefcase. Let me look for it."

"Did you choose that ringtone?"

"Yes."

"It's horrible, Marquinho. Change it. Just imagine if I were next to some authority, or a journalist . . . Imagine me answering that thing beside the governor . . ."

While he listened to the sermon, Marquinho answered the phone. Covering the mouthpiece, he whispered, "It's Dr. Vitor Graça. I told him you were having dinner, but he said it's urgent."

The secretary grimaced and answered, "Dr. Vitor."

"Mr. Secretary. Bad news."

"And when have you ever called to give me good news, Vitor?"

"But this is really terrible. Inspector Félix Coutinho, a man who has the confidence of Chief Luizão França, was brutally assassinated in the Mineira favela."

"By the traffickers?"

"The lowlifes linked to Índio."

"Is it related in any way to the kidnapping?"

"No, not at all."

"What was he doing there?"

"He went to meet a collaborator of ours, an infiltrator."

"By himself?"

"For meetings of that type it's safer to go alone. It draws less attention."

"But how is it the collaborator can collaborate in the area where he acts as infiltrator?"

"When the guy has no way of getting out, it's what you have to do, Mr. Secretary. That's why our job is so dangerous, in spite of being held in such low esteem by the authorities."

"This is no time for whining, Vitor. Did the snitch go down too?"

"Him too. And the bodies are there. All indications are that they were microwaved."*

"What a horror, Vitor. We have to retrieve the corpses."

"That's exactly what I was going to suggest to you. I thought about sending in the COSR, from the civil police, in order to avoid involving the MP, which is concentrated there in Rocinha on that mission you consider higher priority, but—I had second thoughts and concluded that perhaps you could recommend a more thorough shock treatment, one with greater impact, which only the BOPE could do."

"Priorities change, Vitor, according to circumstances. Yesterday it was Rocinha; today it's Mineira. I'm going to redeploy the BOPE immediately."

"But this may take time, Mr. Secretary. It may demand an extended occupation. The traffickers are going to resist, they're going to call in reinforcements from other areas. This could last a month . . ."

"So be it, Vitor. The COSR isn't right for this. I'm going to call Fraga right now. From this moment forward, the BOPE has a different priority. Send some backup for the conventionals there in Rocinha. The civil police is going to be useful in Rocinha. Anything new, call me."

Turning off the radio, the secretary vented: "I wasn't born yesterday, Marquinho. Those people treat me as if I were a greenhorn. Apparently they take me for a perfect idiot. Vi-

---

*Burned alive in a cage of rubber tires.—Ed.

tor's playing a shrewd game with me. The crook. Well, to catch a thief, Marquinho . . . He proposed that the BOPE take over responsibility in Mineira. So generous, so helpful . . . shifting functions to the MP, handing over important responsibilities to the MP on a silver platter, honoring the BOPE, of all things the BOPE, his archrival. Deep down, he'd like for me to consider his attitude praiseworthy and generous but still refuse the offer and order COSR to take Mineira. That's what he wanted, the bastard. That way he'd kill two birds. He'd get what he wanted, at the same time that he'd project an image of grandeur . . . Vitor, the statesman . . . That cretin . . . But I'm nobody's fool, you hear me, Marquinho? He fell flat on his face. Get Fraga on the line. I want the BOPE in Mineira, right now."

An air taxi flying over the clandestine landing strip of Angra dos Reis. Scattered lights punctuate the irregular topography of the thousand islands. September 30, 10:05 P.M.

Santiago didn't see the necklace of marine stars. He was sound asleep, his head resting against the back of the neighboring seat, which was empty. In his inside coat pocket were the scapular and the tape with the compromising conversations of Mrs. Nuno Cedro. The unconscious abyss dragged his spirit onto profound and steep precipices. Later he would relate this nightmare to the friend waiting for him.

Down below, at the foot of an extremely high metallic structure, the group jeered, yelling his name, whistling, throwing empty cans. The clowns of the team waved handkerchiefs and screamed "Look down here, Santiago. Yeeeehaaaa. Do it; here he comes . . . Yeeehaa." At his side, at the corner of the elevated structure, some twenty yards above the ground, the instructor read the sentence: "Student Zero Six will have to walk the narrow steel bar suspended in the air, six inches wide." Less than twenty yards separated success from failure. If he flunked this, his third attempt to enter the BOPE, he would have to dig his own grave, lie down in it, and submit to the collective scorn. The supreme humiliation would be marked by the candidate's irreversible return to the conventional police.

Both fear and shame loosened his hands from the post they were clutching and propelled him onto the narrow bar over the void. He looked upward at the higher void; then looked ahead; the strip of steel narrowed until it reduced itself to an imperceptible and impassable thread proclaiming the impossibility of crossing it. He looked down; his colleagues were bellowing, hissing, in the void. He felt his legs go out from under him. He plummeted.

He landed gently on the dragon chair*, where his body was tied by his colleagues, supervised by the same instructor, who informed him: "Charlie-Charlie, Student Zero Six, Concentration Camp. You passed the heights test. You overcame dizziness. Now all that's left is to defeat pain." He found what he was being told strange, because he knew he was already dead. His colleagues in black drank beer, sang in chorus the songs

---

*A torture device used during the military dictatorship that ruled Brazil for two decades beginning in 1964. The apparatus consisted of a metal chair, kept wet with water, onto which the subject was tied while electrodes were attached to the ears, tongue, toes, and genitals; electric shocks were then administered.—Ed.

of the BOPE, and raised their fists. The instructor pulled the switch and the electric current fried his brain. His nostrils exhaled the sweet perfume of a cadaver wrapped in roses.

He awoke with a start when the copilot touched his arm. It was necessary to prepare for landing. He tightened his seat belt and breathed in the air he had to have.

Living room of Alice's apartment, September 30, 10:09 P.M.

Renata resisted the invitation to spend the night with her friend. "I don't want to expose you. Get you involved."

"We're already involved," insisted Alice's boyfriend. "What did you want? First of all, we're human beings, not machines. Next, Licinha's your friend. Indirectly, so am I. Besides that, hey, have you forgotten what I am? What I do in life, besides studying at PUC? I'm a policeman. How could a policeman sleep with something like this going on? You think I could listen to the story you just told and then say, okay, good night, see you tomorrow, I've got my own life to look after, I'm going home to sleep?"

"There are policemen who can not only sleep knowing something like this but also do something like that. My ex-husband . . . Don't forget—"

"You were unlucky, Natinha," said Alice.

"You're the lucky one, Alice."

The boyfriend resumed his reasoning. "It won't work, Renata. I'm not going to let you leave here until we've come up with a solution. Are you sure your son's going to be all right with your mother?"

"I tried as hard as I could not to get my mother involved in this mess, but what could I do? She has a good support system, at least, and Pedrinho will be watched and protected twenty-four hours a day. I don't know if his father would be crazy enough to go there or send someone. I don't think so. I think now that he's put me in such a huge jam, he must believe the court fight over custody of Pedro is a foregone conclusion. Why should he provoke a situation that could lead to denunciation by my mother and complicate things?"

Alice's boyfriend agreed. "I think you're right, Renata. So let's deal with you. Let's forget Pedrinho for a few minutes. Licinha, how about if I sleep here tonight?"

"Fine. That'll be better," Alice agreed.

"Look, I don't want to cause problems for you two, change your plans . . ." said Renata.

"Don't give us a hard time, Nati. You'd think we weren't friends," replied Alice.

"All right, agreed. I'll come back and sleep here," concluded the boyfriend.

"What?" asked Alice. "You're leaving?"

"Yes. The case is going to get worse if I don't take measures. But I'll be back."

Office of the secretary of public safety, September 30, 10:12 P.M.

The secretary removed his tie and his coat, ordered the air-conditioning turned off, sat down in his chair, checked that the supply of fresh coffee was sufficient, ordered the signal turned on that blocked entrance, extended his arms over the desk, pulled a pile of blank paper toward himself, and declared the meeting open. "Amílcar, Vaz, you have the floor."

Amílcar sat up in his chair, fiddled with the pen and notebook in front of him, looked at the secretary and again lowered his gaze. Vaz kept his head down and stared fixedly at the table in front of him.

"I'm not going to send Marquinho out. I have more faith in him than in the two of you. You may begin," the secretary ordered.

"For starters," said Amílcar, "a brief report of what we've done, if you have no objection, Mr. Secretary."

"I do object. Go directly to the conclusions."

"Absolutely, Mr. Secretary. If you think it best, we'll go directly to the conclusions: your cell phones are tapped. The landlines also, both here and in your home. We found five listening devices here in the office, and one in the private elevator. The four drivers who alternate as your chauffeurs work for P2 and present daily reports to the general command of the MP."

"A good start, Amílcar. I like it. I like it a lot. You may continue."

"Chief Vitor Graça sent an investigator in strictest confidence to the state of Paraná to look into your businesses there."

"My businesses in Paraná? What businesses?"

"I don't know, Mr. Secretary, all I know is that an investigator is there looking into something and that he's been talking to a lot of your former partners."

"My wife's family are the ones from Paraná."

"I don't know, Mr. Secretary, but there's a guy nosing around, ferreting out information, that I'm sure of."

"What a son of a bitch . . . Could it have anything to do with my landholdings there? My wife is heir to some properties, along with her brothers."

"I don't know, Mr. Secretary. But something interests Vitor, otherwise he wouldn't have sent the guy there."

"It could be something connected to the land struggle. They've been having some problems with the landless."

"Who knows? It's probably that, Mr. Secretary. Can you imagine? They paint you as a large landowner, a land grabber, an exploiter of slave labor, an accomplice in violence against the landless?"

"Son of a bitch. That's all I need."

"But that's just the beginning, Mr. Secretary. Unfortunately, there's more."

"Let's hear it."

"Marquinho's telephones are also tapped. His cellular, the one in his room here next to the office, and his home phone."

"You see, Marquinho? You thought it was just with me? You were relaxed, having fun with my suffering . . . You see? We laugh at other people's troubles . . . You see, boy, you're important too. What else, Amílcar? Is Marquinho's girlfriend heir to lands in Paraná too?"

"No, but his boyfriend sells Ecstasy at the Le Boy nightclub."

"What? Slow down, slow down. Repeat what you just said."

"No need, Mr. Secretary, I can explain," Marquinho interrupted. "Leonardo isn't my boyfriend. It's not that. We're just good friends. I don't have a boyfriend. That's slander, Mr. Secretary. In the police, you have to display virility all the time. Nobody trusts anyone. It's a horrible thing. That's insecurity on the part of the accuser."

"Marquinho, I'm not the least bit worried about who you copulate with . . . Is that what gays say?"

"I've never heard it," replied Marquinho.

"Then let me put it another way: I don't care whether you're homosexual or heterosexual, whether you're active or passive, whether you like fat women or skinny women, tall men or short men, if you've got a thing for pregnant women or dwarfs. I want you to explain to me your involvement with the narcotic traffic."

"Ecstasy isn't a narcotic, Mr. Secretary."

"That doesn't matter, Marquinho. The opiate traffic."

"Ecstasy isn't an opiate."

"Barbiturate, then, it doesn't matter, goddammit."

"It's not that either."

"Fuck you, Marquinho. It doesn't matter. I want you to explain your involvement with the traffic. What a scandal! That's all I needed. You, of all people, recommended by Cibele, the son of my favorite goddaughter. What a disappointment."

"Mr. Secretary, please, Amílcar didn't speak about trafficking," argued Marquinho.

"A gang. What's the difference?"

"What gang, Mr. Secretary? Amílcar referred to one individual."

"An individual that you happen to know . . ."

"That's true, I do know him."

"With whom, by chance, you have a degree of interaction that's, shall we say, intimate . . ."

"Close, Mr. Secretary. I have close interaction. Nothing more than that."

"And close doesn't represent any problem for you? Close is okay? Close is cool? Close to an outlaw who traffics in Ecstasy?"

"No. What I meant was that I'm just a—"

"A partner, a pal, a buddy, a bosom friend of the trafficker."

"Not even that, Mr. Secretary. Much less. I'm just someone the young man likes to talk to, among many others, probably. And I never knew, or even suspected, that he sold Ecstasy. The investigators from Intelligence are very prejudiced. They're unqualified professionals. I'm not talking about Vaz and Amílcar. But they themselves will recognize that their subordinates leave much to be desired. I'll bet they saw me talking at the beach or on the sidewalk there with Leonardo and deduced right off that we were having an affair. Because he frequents a gay nightclub, he's immediately judged as being gay. I don't know whether he is or isn't. It'd be a surprise to me. Whether he deals or not, how am I supposed to know?"

Now it was Amílcar who interrupted. "The problem is the phone conversations between the two of you."

"There's that too, Marquinho," said the secretary, tightening the encirclement. "You were hasty. You should've waited a bit more before defending yourself. Youthful imprudence, my boy. What's in the conversations, Amílcar?"

"The two of them talked about the raid on Le Boy by the men from the 13 Precinct."

"Why don't the police of the state of Rio de Janeiro ever use the ordinal number? Is it some kind of vow? An oath they swear to be admitted to the profession? You were referring to your colleagues at the 13th Precinct, which is located there in Copacabana."

"Yes, Mr. Secretary. One of two there in Copacabana."

"And so . . ."

"In the recorded conversation, Leonardo tells his interlocutor—"

"Tells Marquinho," said the secretary.

"Tells Marquinho that there was a raid the night before. He, that citizen, Leonardo, whose full name is—Let's see . . ."

Vaz came to his colleague's aid. "Queiroz. Leonardo Queiroz."

"Exactly. That citizen mentioned the fact of having been caught in flagrante delicto selling Ecstasy to frequenters of that establishment, including minors, complaining that his freedom had cost him the supply of drugs that he kept at home."

Vaz interrupted. "If you'll permit me, Mr. Secretary, I'd like to add a truly significant element to what Colonel Amílcar has already brought to light."

"Vaz," said the secretary, "after our meeting this morning I've observed a change in your style. You can relax, hear? What I said was a momentary explosion. It wasn't my intention to attack you, or Amílcar, who are my best men. Now, go ahead."

"The new element that helps clarify the episode, Mr. Secretary, is the explicit reference the citizen makes to the drug, a reference that elicits no sign of surprise or reprimand from the other end of the line."

"You mean, the end of the line where Marquinho is," said the secretary, turning to the son of his favorite goddaughter.

Marquinho lowered his head and remained silent.

Vaz proceeded. "In addition, Mr. Secretary, the aforementioned citizen—"

"Marquinho?"

"No, Leonardo. This citizen jokes about how the detectives went to his house to get his supply of Ecstasy, asking Marquinho what would have happened if he'd been there at that moment."

The secretary lowered his head. Vaz continued. "At this point in the phone call, Mr. Secretary, they both laugh."

"Vaz, listen here. How many people have heard this tape? Who tapped Marquinho? Was it court authorized?"

Amílcar replied, "In this specific case, yes, Mr. Secretary, because this Leonardo was being watched by the antidrug squad. They already had a lot on him."

"But didn't you say the detectives who arrested him were from the 13th Precinct, not the AD?"

"That's true. Someone from the specialized branch must've passed information to their buddies in the precinct, precisely with extortion in mind, with the loot to be shared. The AD personnel are really quite complicated. That sector over there functions more like a consortium of private interests. Small groups break into the database and feed operators at the other end, in the precincts, because it's the precincts where you have much more autonomy of movement, without any control."

"I know," said the secretary, sighing. "Look, if this wiretap was done legally and it's formally registered, there's nothing we can do."

Marquinho started to sob. The silence accentuated the weeping, which little by little became convulsive.

"But there's a way around everything, Mr. Secretary," said Colonel Amílcar.

The secretary looked at Amílcar with a depressed expression. Vaz added, "Only death is irreparable. With goodwill, there's always a way out, that's what my colleague meant to say. We know the boy comes from a good family. His mother is even your goddaughter, and not just any goddaughter, but a beloved goddaughter, as you pointed out. On the other hand, there's no clue, much less any evidence, that proves active complicity by Marcos in the business of his acquaintance. If he had a position with the police or in the secretariat that gave him repressive powers, in the face of irregularities he could be accused of malfeasance in a situation like this. At the very least he'd be a malefactor. But his function here is as subaltern. He plays a role that's—"

"Secondary, supporting," injected Amílcar.

"That being the case, malfeasance can't be imputed to him. Therefore, Mr. Secretary, by removing that tape from the AD files, which has already been done, the compromising conversation ceases to exist."

"That repulses me, Vaz. It saddens and shames me. But

seeing that boy cry and imagining the weeping of his mother is what really breaks my heart . . ."

"We're going to eliminate the tape. There, it no longer exists." Vaz handed it to the secretary, dramatically. With difficulty, the secretary took it and put it in his pocket. Marquinho ran for the door covering his face, but was intercepted by the voice of the secretary.

"What's this, boy? Leaving like that? I never saw such a thing. Impulses are what ruin you, Marquinho. Have you thought of the consequences of being seen leaving the office like that? Sit down and get a grip on yourself like a man. The past is erased. There. It's forgotten. I want to see you straighten yourself out from now on. Let's look ahead."

The tension gave the silence an air of nobility.

"End of the Marcos Paiva de Souza Carneiro chapter, Dr. Vaz. Let's move on," said the secretary.

Marquinho composed himself and threw into the wastebasket, behind the secretary's chair, the pile of used tissues that he had kept in his pockets.

"Of course, Mr. Secretary. If you have no objection, I'll take the liberty of turning the floor over to Colonel Amílcar."

The secretary consented with a broad, slow gesture, turning his palms upward as if handing over a package, a child, or a bomb to the colonel, who took out his glasses and put them on, read his notes, and took his glasses off again, until finally he stood up straight, deposited the glasses on the table, and resumed the explanation.

"The primary question you asked us this morning concerned the information leak to the governor. The case in point was the kidnapping, but certainly it is of interest for you to know if the channel remains open and whether it was open before this morning's episode."

"That's the point, Colonel. That's precisely the point."

"We don't know, Mr. Secretary."

"Don't you have a hypothesis? Nothing? No lead?"

"Well, we do have a lead. Vaz and I would like you to take a look at a video that came to us in a very odd and suspicious manner. It's therefore not to be trusted. It may be faked, I can't say. We've checked its material, its physical authenticity. The tape hasn't been edited. That is to say, what you're going to see isn't film editing. But it may be a theatrical production—we can't be sure that it wasn't just acting. But, if it's not asking too much, Vaz and I consider that the contents perhaps demand additional caution, which in this case—I mean, given the context, Mr. Secretary, of the problems we're facing, which are serious, even in order to protect the person in question from any unfounded future suspicion as to the possible leak, it might be best, if you have no objection . . ."

"Excuse us, Marquinho. Dr. Vaz and the colonel and I need to be alone. We need some privacy."

"You want me to leave, Mr. Secretary?"

"Do I need to make it any clearer, Marquinho? Really . . ."

Marquinho gathered his materials—his briefcase, folders, books, documents, laptop—and began to leave, saying, "Excuse me. Good night."

"Not good night, Marquinho. You're not through. I still want to talk with you. And pay close attention: you're forbidden to speak on the phone about any matter that's not absolutely trivial. Don't answer, and don't call anyone who's not a person of maximum confidence. I don't want you chatting with anyone in your room. Until proven otherwise, they're all suspect. Including you, understand?"

Marquinho nodded as he left.

The secretary barely waited for the door to close. "You can run the video."

Vaz got up and went to the TV. He inserted a videocassette. He was preparing to turn on the TV when the office door flew open and Marquinho rushed noisily in, reading sheets of paper with news from the Internet.

"Forgive me, Mr. Secretary, but it's urgent. The personnel were in the waiting room dying for you to authorize contact. Just look: 'Michele was freed.' 'The RC favelas are celebrating.' 'Free drinks for the people.' 'Early Carnaval in some parts of the city.' 'Bangu-I jubilant.' 'Obscene graffiti at the headquarters of Ebony, the security service belonging to the widow of Anacleto, the Bangu-I warden who was assassinated earlier tonight, in Penha.' Ah! There's one more, kind of unpleasant: 'No word from the police, and the secretary is the last to know.'"

BOPE general headquarters, September 30, 11 P.M.

Alice's boyfriend tried to get in touch with Ramirez, the friend in the BOPE whom he considered the most mature, correct, balanced, and intelligent, and who had the vice of being an inveterate legalist; he was the guy who was always resisting the same things that turned the PUC law student's stomach.

Alice's boyfriend had in fact found himself, day by day, to be more a law student and less a Skull, less a blind Skull. A Skull policeman in general believes he achieves justice through his own hands and tends to separate justice from laws. At PUC and in the world of law, the viewpoint is different, very different. The student had therefore been drawing closer and closer to Ramirez, whom he had previously looked on with a certain disdain, complacent but critical, if not sarcastic. The student, still a BOPE officer, no longer recognized himself in the mirror of the war diary that he had written two years earlier. He hesitated a long time before authorizing its publication as the first part of this book. He only became convinced to authorize it when, plunged into the story of Renata and Santiago, he saw how naïve he and his BOPE comrades had been. However tough and violent they might be, they had no idea of the world of Public Safety in Rio de Janeiro. They didn't have the slightest notion of how Rio politics worked, of how it penetrated into the police forces and into crime. They didn't know that crime had spilled over the limits and debased institutions. He and his BOPE partners had never imagined themselves as pieces in a game, in many games.

Alice's boyfriend, the BOPE officer and law student at PUC, the narrator of the war diary, now involved up to his scalp in Renata's drama, insisted once again, with growing anxiety, on establishing contact with Ramirez. He persisted. He called again, unsuccessfully. He then tried to contact the commander of the Special Operations Battalion to tell him Renata's version of events. To ask him to help and to intervene. To loose the dogs of war on the heels of the sons of bitches. To save Alice's friend, or perhaps to save himself from that fucking terrifying situation that with Renata's account had come crashing down on his head.

When he managed to speak to the commander's adjutant, he learned he was being sought. All BOPE officers—even those on leave—were being called in, for a "possible emergency mission to be launched at any moment."

Meeting room of the Residents Association of the Mineira favela, September 30, 11:05 P.M.

Jonas handed the radio to Índio, who found a path among the legs of his companions and knocked over two bottles of beer en route.

"We're here, brother, we're here," said Índio.

"I spoke to Michele. She doesn't seem all right."

"She's okay, boss. She's okay. It's just that they gave her a lot of medicine. But she's fine."

"Did you get the pig?"

"No, boss. It wasn't possible. He didn't show up. He said he was coming but he didn't."

"Did you get the person he sent in his place?"

"I didn't think it was worth the trouble, boss. It was a little old lady from the church in Alto da Tijuca, where Santiago lives. She agreed to bring Michele as an act of charity."

"And the old lady came by herself with Michele? Why didn't Michele run away?"

"Santiago's crew took both of them to the location and told them to stay there, waiting for them. A little later, we arrived."

"You didn't run into them?"

"No."

"Nobody from our group identified Santiago's team?"

"No."

"What was the location?"

"A spiritualist center. I talked to the president, a medium there, an elderly man. But the guy didn't have nothing to do with anything. There was so many people in the waiting room . . . I talked to him and wrote down his information, but—"

"Okay. We'll get the pig yet, one of these days."

"What if he ain't lying?"

"We'll see. In the interrogation we'll find out if he's lying or not. We're going to apply the methods he taught us."

Office of the secretary, September 30, 11:59 P.M.

After the frenzy engendered by Marquinho's untimely entrance, the dust began to settle. The secretary was on the line with Colonel Fraga, having spoken with the governor on the red phone.

"Colonel, news of the celebrations in Mineira and several other favelas is appearing on the Internet. I had ordered immediate redeployment of the BOPE maximum force from Rocinha to Mineira. I don't understand. Was the news wrong? Or wasn't my order carried out?"

"Mr. Secretary, with all due respect, your orders aren't

questioned, but for the time being I can't withdraw the BOPE from Rocinha."

"What? I don't accept that, Fraga. I don't accept it. That's insubordination."

"It's not a question of that, Mr. Secretary. There are some problems that need to be worked out . . . I even called in all the off-duty BOPE officers. They're all here at our HQ. Except that I didn't pass along your order, Mr. Secretary, because of what I told you."

"What problems? And why didn't you tell me this when I gave you the order? You mean we have the body of a brutally murdered policeman and a celebration by traffickers who are going to arrogate to themselves the heroic liberation of a kidnapped woman, while the police passively watch it all?"

"No, Mr. Secretary. Absolutely not. I've already given the battalion in the Mineira area the order to invade, which will be taking place at any moment, Mr. Secretary."

"And what the hell is the problem that needs to be 'worked out'?"

"I can't say over the phone, Mr. Secretary."

"Then come here at once."

Marquinho interrupted, "Begging your pardon, Mr. Secretary. I know that you want to resume the meeting, but since the red light still isn't on, I thought it'd be all right to bring you an urgent message."

"What is it?"

"The editor who spoke with you earlier says he has a bomb in his hands and doesn't want to detonate it without talking to you."

"Oh, Jesus! Another bomb? Is there room for any more shit? Is he on the line? Put him on, you can put him on. Hello, yes, of course, how are you? No, everything's all right. We're working, aren't we? You there, me here. Different fronts in the same war, my friend. Go ahead."

The secretary pulled up his chair and sat down. His gaze wandered. He listened, mute, for a long time. Amílcar and Vaz glanced at each other, concerned and curious. Then the secretary rose again, saying, "I understand. I understand your position. Publish it, man. What can I do? I know you didn't ask for, nor do you need, my authorization, but if you want to know what I think, as a citizen, as secretary, I'll tell you: put it in the street, publish it. I don't have anything that refutes, *in limine*, the accusations you've gathered. It's a shame. Of course it's a shame, because I've always held Fraga to be a man of the greatest integrity. But that's life. Especially public life. It's not enough to be honest, my friend, you have to appear honest as well. It's like the case of Caesar's wife. All right. Of course, I understand. It's I who should thank you. Same to you."

The secretary hung up the phone. He told Marquinho by interphone to turn on the red light and to not dare interrupt him. He ordered him to have the commander wait when he arrived. He turned to Amílcar and Vaz. "This is a volcano here. A volcano that spews shit everywhere. It's impossible to survive sitting on top of a volcano. I don't know how I'm still hanging on. You must've heard the phone call. They're going to blow Fraga to pieces. Tomorrow, with banner headlines, an apocryphal dossier is coming out with serious denouncements. Extremely serious ones. It seems that Fraga hired his sister-in-law in the entity that manages the pension fund for the retired military police, something like that."

"But the fund isn't overseen by the commander-general," reasoned Amílcar.

"Beats me. Go explain that after the accusation hits the streets. Anyone who has to explain is always on the defensive. Anyone who doesn't explain is admitting guilt. Damned if you do, damned if you don't."

"That's terrible, Mr. Secretary," agreed Amílcar. "By defending himself, the guy becomes guilty. Then come the editorials. Where there's smoke there's fire. That type of nonsense."

"There's more," the secretary continued. "Fraga is said to have awarded a no-bid contract for mechanical maintenance of their vehicles. And it's been discovered that the firm that provides that service belongs to a neighbor of his, at his beach home. It seems they're on intimate terms and treat each other like very close friends. This business of an apocryphal dossier is a piece of shit. Pure fascism. How I suffered from those things in the time of the dictatorship. It must be part of the free-for-all in the MP's internal dispute. They eat each other alive. They'll end up destroying the institution. Just take a look at the condition of our military police."

"But, Mr. Secretary," Amílcar insisted, "in the face of heavy sources of corruption, like the traffic in drugs and guns, smuggling, counterfeiting, diluted fuel, hijacked cargo, clandestine security services, illegal transport, slot machines, the animal game, in the face of Sodom and Gomorrah, that's all they've got on Colonel Fraga? That's all? Isn't that kind of ridiculous?"

"It is, but it looks like there are other things: favoritism toward colleagues who end up retiring for reasons of health, falsely claiming deafness or severe hearing loss—"

"If you'll forgive the jest, Mr. Secretary," Vaz interrupted, "it might not be a bad thing if the wiretap team were retired for deafness."

"In that case, where would that leave you two?" asked the secretary, smiling for the first time. "Anyway," he went on, "I must confess to you that I'm not saddened by this. Fraga hasn't played straight with me. He hasn't, either as a comrade or as a subordinate. That business of planting a driver on me . . . And you still haven't told me to whom I owe the taps on my phones and the listening devices in my office. And you haven't told me who leaked the story of Michele's kidnapping to the governor." He stopped for an instant and looked at both men, who lowered their heads. Then he proceeded.

"The drivers and his having the audacity to delay my orders are enough by themselves. As far as I'm concerned, he's out. I'm going to have to let the governor know that the bomb goes off tomorrow. I'm going to suggest to him that he publish Fraga's removal from the general command in the *Official Register* tomorrow, I mean today, the first of October. It's already the first, isn't it? That way, when the press thinks it's zigging, the government is already zagging. It would be a tremendous demonstration of political and administrative agility, competence in management, efficiency, efficacy, effectiveness, all that shit that the governor's so fond of. The entire process is going to end up strengthening me, because I'm going to leak it that the initiative came from here, from this office."

Both Amílcar and Vaz spoke at the same time. They asked the secretary to think about it some more and watch the video before deciding what to do. As they spoke, the red phone rang. The secretary rose, went to his desk, and picked it up.

"Do you prefer that we leave?" asked Colonel Amílcar.

The secretary made a broad and emphatic negative gesture with his arm as he waited for the governor's private secretary to transfer the call.

While he waited, he addressed the pair. "There's only one thing worse than being the secretary of public safety of the state of Rio de Janeiro: being the governor. Greetings, Governor, no, no. I was just making a comment here . . . I know, perfectly. I know. I know. He called, did he? Ah! Then you already know. That's what I—yes indeed, very sad. Of course, that's not done, not done. A horror. Totally, totally undemocratic. Trifles, trifles. Right. That's it. You're right there, governor. Ah! You've already decided? Well, you're the boss. It's not my place to say anything, governor. I'm here to follow orders. As for the political side, you're the one with all the experience. Who am I, Governor, to judge a decision of yours? Yes, yes, in full agreement. I think so too. Yes, exactly. It's brilliant, a brilliant move. Fast. It was very fast. Extremely fast. Yes, it does show that. Precisely. It shows a lot of capability. When it comes to administration, you're the champ. As a leader and as a manager. Exactly that.

"Congratulations, Governor. There's no shortage of good

replacements, of course. There's a lot of very good people among the MP colonels. You've already decided? That's right. Very early. Leave it to me. Good night."

He replaced the red phone on its hook and turned to Amíl-car and Vaz. "He already knew and had decided to publish the removal in the *Official Register*. See how he is? Quicker on the trigger than we are. He caught me by surprise, even though I agree . . . He's a jet plane, the governor. Later I want to go over with you, from the point of view of Intelligence, the names for Fraga's replacement in the MP. But, friends, let's get to the video finally."

Faded images of a commercial building appeared. The focus was shaky. The entrance to the building could be seen. In the upper left-hand corner was the date, September 30, and the time was running, including the rapidly changing seconds: 5:02:57 a.m. It was dark. From the left of the frame came two figures walking together. They gestured to the building's watchman, who opened the gate for them. Cut. A new scene: bright daylight, 8 a.m. Clear image. Heavy movement of cars and pedestrians. The date was the same. Several people entered and left the building. Then the sequence was interrupted. The camera zoomed in on a man entering the building. Cut. The time was 8:02. The scene appeared the same. A new zoom, this time onto two people. The process was repeated. All told, nine people were the object of special attention by the person doing the filming.

At that moment, Vaz rose to his feet and asked permission to explain and said, "Mr. Secretary, what you've just seen was done this morning. The Intelligence team is staking out the front of that building because about a month ago we discovered that one of our suspects regularly frequents a room on the fifteenth floor of the building, which is located in downtown Rio. The room was originally rented three and a half years ago by an entity known as 'the Vitor Graça Movement for Security and Social Justice.'"

"What's that?" asked the secretary.

Amílcar was the one to answer. "It's the trade name of the entity that financed Vitor's campaign for state legislator in the last election."

With the secretary's permission, Vaz resumed the explanation. "The two men who appear first are Luizão França and Otacílio Malta. Chief Luizão and his faithful squire Inspector Otacílio. The others are detectives and inspectors from the civil police. Later I'll read you their names. Félix Coutinho is the next to arrive. The one who went in by himself. We assume they were there to attend a meeting, because some of the group were seen entering the building when Félix was there. Besides which, they all leave more or less at the same time. In pairs or in groups. Félix is the only one who comes out alone."

"Why have you been following that guy?" the secretary inquired.

"It's a long story, Mr. Secretary. I think it'll be easier to understand once I've told you everything, but for now I can tell you that the guy has, shall we say, close ties to Índio, the owner of the drug site in Mineira."

"All right, Vaz. You may continue. Wait, hold on. Isn't this Félix guy the one who was killed by the traffickers today, right there in Mineira?"

"Yes and no, Mr. Secretary."

"How can it be yes and no? It's either yes or it's no."

"You'll understand."

"All right. Move along."

"Now take a look, Mr. Secretary, at these other images."

The scene appeared to be the same. The angle was unchanged. Eight fifty-five and ten, eleven, twelve seconds. People came and went from the building. One of them was circled with a halo when the image froze.

"Félix leaving, Mr. Secretary."

The sequence resumed. The seconds in the right-hand corner flew past. Félix could hardly be distinguished from the passing crowd. The images had been taken from a relatively low angle, probably from the facing building's ground floor or mezzanine, no higher than that. The character walked among the people, crossed two streets, always in a straight line, crossed the avenue where the building was located, and walked to the side where the camera watching him was installed. He headed toward a pay phone. He stopped, looked around, and used the phone. Cut.

"Strange," said the secretary. "A policeman on duty without a cell phone? Or a radio?"

"That's the question, Mr. Secretary," said Vaz. "Why would he call from a public phone? And why would he walk all that distance to do so, if there were a couple of pay phones right in front of the building he came out of? Did you notice the detail that appears in the very first shots? Could our subject have only remembered to make the call after he'd gone three hundred yards? That hypothesis doesn't stand up because, after speaking on the phone, he returned. His car was in the parking lot a hundred yards from the building, in the opposite direction from the public phone he used. He deliberately walked three hundred yards. Which means there was something that couldn't wait."

"And that couldn't be said over the radio he uses," added Amílcar. "He had his radio, Mr. Secretary—they use them all the time. I'm as sure he had his radio as I am that he was armed. We've discovered that the frequenters of Room 1509 use a closed radio system with voice encryption. Only they have the code. There's no way to tap into it. Go on, Vaz."

"That means the following, Mr. Secretary: Félix didn't fear wiretapping, but he couldn't allow his own group to know he was calling or to hear what he was saying. And perhaps even more important, *to whom* he said it—"

The secretary didn't even let Vaz catch his breath. "Who did he call?"

"That's what we set out to learn, as soon as our man in the field told us what he'd seen. Félix called Vitor Graça."

"Then that group is Vitro's enemy and Félix is Vitor's agent, an infiltrator? But how can Vitor's enemies be meeting in his room?"

"Good question, Mr. Secretary. The policemen who frequent Vitor's room aren't his enemies. Just the opposite. Everyone knows that Luizão França is Vitor's main ally in the civil police. That's why we found Félix's movement very odd. But he didn't just call Vitor. He then called the 10, I mean the 10th, Precinct, in Botafogo, asking for Anderson, as we found out later when we interrogated the detective who took his call. He didn't identify himself to the detective as a policeman."

"Anderson . . ."

"That's right, Mr. Secretary. Anderson's a typical Rio police figure. He's an informer, brought from the interior to the capital by Amarildo Horta, that state deputy with ties to the governor. He practically lives at the precinct, he acts like a policeman, he uses and abuses all the prerogatives of a police officer, and he resorts to dubious expedients to carry out other missions of a nonpolice nature. For example, tapping phone lines. Especially of celebrities."

"In Vitor's service? Was he the one who tapped my lines?"

"No, Mr. Secretary. The thing is much more complicated. Vitor did everything he could to keep from having Anderson put into the 10th. He knew the risk he'd be running with that guy planted in a precinct, with protection from higher-ups, operating in the background, behind the scenes, blackmailing, manipulating, extorting. On the other hand, he knew Amarildo was the governor's man and that he couldn't go head-to-head with him. He came to suspect the hand of the governor in the ploy, aiming to control the police. But that doesn't seem to be exactly the case, because—according to the rumor, and we didn't even have to investigate, because the rumor's spreading through the hallways—Anderson recorded compromising conversations by an upper-class lady, the wife of an industrialist, a heavyweight in the economy and personal friend of the governor's."

"And? Félix telephones Vitor and the precinct, asks for Anderson, and—"

"And right afterward, Mr. Secretary, while one of our men was investigating the call to the precinct, Inspector Otacílio and Detective Lincoln, who were also at the meeting earlier, showed up. Otacílio is Luizão's right-hand man. He's the one who arrived first, at five in the morning, at the building in the video. And what do they want at that precinct? To speak to Anderson."

Amílcar interrupted. "Isn't that interesting, Mr. Secretary? They were all together. Presumably they discussed something important or they wouldn't be there, at that time, on a weekday, in a workplace."

"I call that a conspiracy."

"Conspiracy. That's just what it is, Mr. Secretary," said Amílcar. "There was a meeting with tangible effects, decisions were made. The group splits up. It's deduced that they're going to implement decisions. Why then is it that a member of the group gets in touch with the precinct ahead of his partners and does so in a suspicious manner? Just look at it, Mr. Secretary, Félix fails to identify himself to the colleague who answers his call at the precinct; he walks three hundred yards to avoid using his radio, which could identify his calls to his own group. Take it from there, Vaz."

"Our man surveilling the building received our order to follow Félix. You can imagine, Mr. Secretary, where he went. Anderson's apartment, in Catumbi. He entered empty-handed and came out an hour later carrying a supermarket bag. From there he went to a delicatessen in Botafogo. He gave the supermarket bag to the cashier and left. The deli is owned by Vitor. It's registered in his wife's name. We sent an investigator to Anderson's apartment. He didn't answer the interphone, but he hadn't left home, according to the doorman. The building doesn't have security cameras. His telephone didn't answer. He hadn't shown up at the precinct. Our man on the scene confirmed it: Anderson was killed with a bullet in the mouth."

"I had already imagined something like that," the secretary said.

"We continued to follow Félix. From the deli he went to Tijuca. He parked his car near Saenz Peña Square, walked less than a hundred yards and got into another car, with a false license plate. He didn't break in. He used his own key. From there he went to Avenida Brasil and headed toward Via Dutra. He didn't get very far. He was stopped at a roadblock by the federal highway police. He was taken to an FHP station wagon and disappeared. The roadblock held up traffic long enough for the station wagon to vanish. A man, perhaps a policeman in civilian clothes, took over Félix's car, followed the station wagon, and disappeared when it did. There's no record of its plates in the Rio police."

"And what does the FHP say?"

"Officially, nothing," Amílcar answered.

"What do you mean, officially nothing?"

"They deny setting up the roadblock or the operation."

"And your investigator doesn't have the data on the FHP vehicles involved?"

"Of course, but the FHP says they don't exist."

"But weren't there other cars, witnessing everything?"

"There were more than twenty cars. We have the plates of six and we're trying to contact them."

"Don't we have images of the operation?"

"Unfortunately, no. Our service is still quite deficient, Mr. Secretary."

"But that means the FHP is involved in something. What?"

"We're going to show you another very interesting video, recorded about a month ago," said Vaz. "But first allow me to call your attention, Mr. Secretary, to another highly significant question. At around 10:15, Vitor called from the office of the head of the civil police to the office of the MP general command. He asked to speak to Colonel Fraga and told him that Félix Coutinho had been assassinated by traffickers in Mineira and his body was being burned in a bonfire of tires, something the outlaws call microwaving. He told Fraga it was urgent that the BOPE occupy Mineira."

"But . . . Deep down didn't he want the COSR to take action in Mineira? Why—" The secretary was perplexed. "And why did he take so long to talk to me? Why didn't he talk to me first?"

"Here's our hypothesis," said Vaz. "Vitor was informed that Félix had handed the FHP a copy of the most valuable tape, the one with the recording of that upper-crust woman, which would probably bring Vitor down if it became public. He could have given them the tape for either of two reasons: money or coercion."

"First, Vaz, you should explain to the secretary why Félix made a copy of the tape before removing it from Anderson's apartment and taking it to Vitor," said Amílcar.

"Right. Amílcar and I believe it's plausible, Mr. Secretary, that Inspector Félix made the copy to have a trump card, an ace up his sleeve, for any eventuality. He knew the risk he was taking as a double agent, because he was helping Luizão, as a member of his clandestine group, but also serving Vitor—after all, Mr. Secretary, the fact of Luizão and Vitor being allies doesn't eliminate the need for caution and watchfulness. That's true in both directions. Félix knew he could end up squeezed like a sandwich, as actually happened."

"But he could be interested in playing one off against the other, for some reason," said the secretary.

"He could, though personally I don't believe he had the green light at his own risk, to beard the lion," said Vaz.

"Maybe he was working for still another person," the secretary insisted.

"It doesn't seem reasonable, Mr. Secretary. We don't see anything on the horizon to support that."

"But he could have been after money, looking to do business with the tape," said the secretary, refusing to give up.

"No doubt, Mr. Secretary, even though we don't consider it likely. For the same reason: he wasn't an individualist; he wasn't a guy who followed his own path. The most probable thing is that Félix was not only in our sights but also in someone else's. Some other . . . organism, let's put it that way. This is our hypothesis: at the meeting with Luizão, Félix saw two companions in the group being given the task of finding Anderson, probably seeking some kind of agreement or deal for the group, even though Luizão may have represented the operation as a service on Vitor's behalf, because he always makes a point of emphasizing his loyalty to Vitor. Meanwhile, Félix had been having secret and confidential meetings with Vitor, probably as a precaution on the part of the chief of police, who lacked sufficient trust in Luizão's loyalty . . ."

"Vitor distrusts anyone who might compete with him," Amílcar opined.

"So, Félix, who worked for Vitor, infiltrated Luizão's group—" Vaz continued.

"And Luizão's group defended Vitor." The secretary's discomfort was evident.

"Yes, Mr. Secretary, but in that setting—you yourself called it a volcano . . ."

"Worse, Vaz. I was putting it mildly. It's a napalmed jungle."

"Indeed. The fact is that when Félix saw that the group was going to get hold of the tape, which would give Luizão life-and-death power over Vitor, he rushed to inform the chief. Vitor, uncertain, ordered Félix to act first, with all the risks that implied for his career, because a confrontation with Anderson is a confrontation with Amarildo, and therefore with the governor. But he had no choice. He probably gave the order for Félix to eliminate Anderson, get the tape, leave it like some ordinary package at the delicatessen, and withdraw to a safe location they had set up some time before."

Amílcar gestured to Vaz and interrupted. "It's at this point that the . . . other organism comes in that's also been following the steps of all these people. They must've seen what we saw. They thought Félix might have kept a copy for himself; they kidnapped him, got their hands on the tape, and then eliminated Félix. They probably killed him."

"But, Amílcar, how did Vitor find out about the killing of Félix?" asked the secretary.

"He answered a call from Luizão, using the phone in the office of the chief of police."

"And?"

"He knows we tap that telephone. We discovered that he knows and that he lets it stay that way, to try to manipulate us. He only says on that phone what he wants us to hear. The recording we made last night, around eight o'clock, is here." Amílcar pushed a button on the small device. Voices were heard:

UNIDENTIFIED VOICE: "Dr. Vitor, Chief Luizão on line two."

VITOR: "Hello."

LUIZÃO: "Shit, why'd you turn off your radio?"

VITOR: "You can talk, Luizão. What happened?"

LUIZÃO: "What happened is that they killed Félix."

VITOR: "What?"

LUIZÃO: "Just what you heard."

VITOR: "Who?"

LUIZÃO: "The Mineira traffickers. Índio's people."

VITOR: "What a tragedy. How cowardly. How did you find out?"

LUIZÃO: "They called me on the radio. They took his radio and used it to piss in my face."

VITOR: "My God!"

LUIZÃO: "They said they were going to cook him in the microwave."

VITOR: "There in Mineira?"

LUIZÃO: "Affirmative."

VITOR: "Stand your ground, my friend. We're going to
    answer this humiliation. I'm going to take measures
    and get back to you."
LUIZÃO: "And the—?"
VITOR: "I'll call you back."

Amílcar resumed his account. "Mr. Secretary, two and two
makes four. Whether Félix really died, we can't be absolutely
sure, but we can be sure that he didn't die in Mineira. If the conversation you just heard isn't staged, isn't great playacting—"

"I doubt it. Luizão would have to be a tremendous actor,"
said the secretary.

"I doubt it too. If it's not theater, Luizão really was informed of Félix's murder by Félix's own radio, and he'd have
a way of verifying it through his radio's two-way. Therefore,
probably someone from the FHP called Luizão, posing as a
trafficker from Mineira."

"But why? Who in the FHP would be interested in incriminating the Mineira traffickers?"

Vaz continued with his careful argument. "If Vitor insisted
on turning off his radio and forcing Luizão to talk over our
tapped line, it's because for some reason it's in his interest for
you, and us, to hear that conversation. What was said in that
conversation? That a person died. That a person died at a certain location and at the hand of traffickers."

"Everybody would find all that out anyway, for chrissake,"
said the secretary.

"Really? Where's the body? Microwaving destroys the
body. Yes, a DNA analysis is possible, but how long might it

take to find the ashes? There are so many clandestine cemeteries in the favelas and so many more in the Baixada Fluminense. But maybe the focus of attention isn't the death and the body, but the location and the circumstances. Maybe that's the big issue."

"They want to incriminate the favela and certain traffickers? Is all this related to Michele's kidnapping?"

"Yes, of course. Look, Mr. Secretary, the kidnapping was thwarted. Santiago set it up and probably had to dismantle it in order to survive. If the purpose of the kidnap wasn't dough—"

"Wasn't it? I'm still not convinced," said the secretary.

"Let's say, for the sake of argument, merely for the sake of argument, that it wasn't for money. Then what else could it have been? Let's go back to Félix. Vitor called Colonel Fraga, requesting the BOPE. Then he called you. What did he want?"

"I'm certain he didn't want the BOPE, he wanted the COSR in Mineira," replied the secretary.

"But what did he get as a result of your decision? The BOPE in Mineira, right?"

"Yes, but I don't think it was what he really wanted . . ."

"But it was what ended up happening, wasn't it? And your decision, resulting from the conversation with him, coincides with what he asked Colonel Fraga to do."

"So what? What does that decision have to do with the two crimes, the kidnapping and the possible murder?" asked the secretary.

"Both crimes point to the same place," said Vaz.

"The BOPE," concluded Amílcar.

"The BOPE?"

"Of course, Mr. Secretary."

"What do you mean, of course? Are you trying to incriminate the BOPE?"

"No, just the opposite." Vaz resumed the explanation: "Colonel Fraga doesn't seem very inclined to relinquish control of Rocinha, where the BOPE is fully tasked, right? An apocryphal dossier against Fraga explodes like a bombshell, by chance, by coincidence, in the editorial room of the most important newspaper in the state. The kidnapping fails, right? So another death is ordered. A death that relocated the BOPE to Mineira. In what direction did the Michele case intend to nudge the BOPE? Maybe toward the need for redeployment of the BOPE."

"Toward Mineira?" asked the secretary.

"I don't know, but probably somewhere far away from Rocinha."

"I admit to being a bit confused."

"That's natural, Mr. Secretary," said Amílcar. "We would be too, if we hadn't seen the images we're going to show you now."

Vaz got up, changed the tape in the machine, and said, "These are pictures of your car, taken on August 29. Notice: behind your car is another car with your security team. Observe the car that's behind the security car, staying at a certain distance. It's a white Passat, with phony plates, and two men inside. That car tailed you for a month. Watch carefully now, Mr. Secretary."

The image froze in a close-up. In the halo was the face of the driver's companion, in the white Passat.

Vaz continued. "Do you see that man, Mr. Secretary? We followed him and discovered who he is. He's Jaime Correia, known as Jaiminho Onça, right-hand man for matters less savory and more unofficial for the superintendent of the Federal Highway Police in the state of Rio de Janeiro, Polinices Vieira da Silva. Silva to his friends."

Amílcar went to the television, fast-forwarded the tape, and said, "Now look at these images, Mr. Secretary. A quiet, peaceful, pleasant, and innocuous supermarket. Notice that cart in the corner. It's just been left there by the same man who was in the white Passat. I'm going to rewind the tape a little for you to see. I went back too far. Here. Now, yes. Notice, Mr. Secretary: Jaiminho Onça making his frugal purchases, calmly, like a good head of the family helping his wife with the domestic chores. He moves away. Observe that at this moment another man enters the field of view. There, he took over the cart. But neither of the two will make any purchase. The cart will be abandoned in some corner. These people are such believers in their impunity that they don't even sweat making the handoff in the middle of the supermarket, where there are cameras everywhere."

"They don't give a damn," emphasized Vaz.

"Mr. Secretary, we started following that Jaiminho guy after we identified him in the car that was tailing you. We came upon this handoff: one takes the package, leaves it in the cart, another picks up the package and leaves the cart."

"If they don't fear punishment, why not trade packages without all that playacting?"

"Because the ones who exchange the package don't know

each other, Mr. Secretary, they're not always the same ones and mustn't see each other. It's not forbidden to look at each other, but they should avoid it for their own safety. One day we put a woman on Jaiminho, and as soon as he left the cart, she left hers with a package and picked up his. As the players don't look at each other, check the packages, or look back, it wasn't hard. Take a look at the operation."

Amílcar rose again and fast-forwarded the tape to show the secretary what he had described to him.

"And you have the package?"

"Of course, Mr. Secretary. Here it is," Amílcar replied, as Vaz opened a small suitcase, removed a large envelope, and handed it to the secretary, who tried and failed to open it.

"Is it glued shut? Didn't you open it?"

"We did, Mr. Secretary. Pull the blue tape there at the edge. Here, let me open it for you."

Photos and photocopies of bank documents in English were deposited on the table.

"My God!"

"The worst isn't the photos, Mr. Secretary. Take a look at the bank documents."

"What is this, Amílcar, money laundering? Where is this bank? In some offshore financial haven? And these codes, do they belong to this account? Could this account be the governor's? Vaz, this is impressive. Those guys have the governor in the palm of their hands. The photos alone would be enough to finish him. And I thought that everything came to him, without my knowledge, because he was superpowerful. It's time to put the pieces of the puzzle together. What do you say? How does all this relate to the taps on my phone and the eavesdropping devices in my office? Who made the exchange of packages with Jaiminho? Is the FHP with Vitor or against him? If it's with him, why did it kill or negotiate with Félix? If it's against him, why did they call Luizão on Félix's radio, telling Luizão what Vitor wanted said, in other words, that Félix had been killed in Mineira?"

Vaz pulled the portable blackboard close to the table, turning it toward the secretary. Marker in hand, he presented his hypothesis. "My conviction and Amílcar's, Mr. Secretary, is as follows. For some reason, Vitor doesn't want the BOPE in Rocinha. If he doesn't, it's because the BOPE is hindering something that interests him. We know the BOPE is violent, undergoes tough training for operations of war, doesn't spare anybody, treats the favelas like enemy territories and their communities like enemy populations. On the other hand, it neither corrupts nor allows itself to be corrupted. It doesn't permit 'grease,' those transactions with the traffickers that are destroying the MP. Today, Mr. Secretary, you can't think about crime in Rio without thinking about the drug traffic. And you can't think about the drug traffic without thinking about the police forces. One doesn't exist without the other. Not just the MP—the other divisions are involved too. The exception is the BOPE. How long it'll continue to be the exception, we don't know. It seems inevitable that it'll be contaminated too. It's impossible to maintain it as an island, surrounded by corruption on all sides. But for now the BOPE is still an island. Fraga isn't corrupt. He makes deals here and there with this one and that one, because he knows he wouldn't survive politically if he confronted the focal points inside the police on all fronts. Anyone who tries to do that, Mr. Secretary, is either removed from office or killed."

"Fraga's image is too golden for my taste, Vaz. You think having a driver keep watch on the secretary is an acceptable norm, part of the work program of a commander-general, correct?"

"No, Mr. Secretary. It's not acceptable. It's just that in this war each one hangs on to power however he can. If he had to rid himself of you, and could, he'd do so, calmly. Without it weighing on his conscience. What he did with Amílcar was no different. He tried every way possible to burn and remove Colonel Amílcar, because he always feared our closeness to you. He can't touch me, because I'm not MP. If he could, he'd go after me as well."

"Go on with your reasoning, Vaz. You set up the board and picked up the marker. You looked like a professor. Return to the classroom. Let's leave the speculation aside."

"Exactly. The point is this: the presence of the BOPE in Rocinha isn't in Vitor's interest."

"Is he after my position? Is that what Vitor wants? To be secretary of public safety?"

"I don't believe so, Mr. Secretary. Your job isn't all that coveted, because it's a high-risk position. The job gives you maximum visibility and therefore confers on you tremendous political potential. On the other hand, it's a position that exposes you to a lot of wear and tear. It's very difficult to assume the post without paying a very high price. You're getting knocked around every day. The personal and political toll is immense. It's more comfortable and more useful to remain as head of the civil police, as long as the secretary doesn't interfere much. It's there that the distribution of precinct chiefdoms is decided, and that's the key operation, because each precinct is worth a certain amount on the police black market. Every month, one senior precinct chief and his team pay tribute into the coffers of the leadership, coffers that aren't only the head man's; he pays off the group in power. The payment's a kind of tax on the profit that each precinct provides. In the MP, it's quite different. The scheme is much more diverse, much more fragmented, precisely because the hierarchy organizes the institution much better than its civilian counterpart, which, strictly speaking, has neither discipline nor hierarchy."

"Which means the following, Mr. Secretary," said Amílcar, adding to Vaz's lesson: "The more organized the institution, the more retail-level the corruption; the less organized the institution, the more centralized and organized the corruption."

"Makes sense, makes sense," agreed the secretary.

"Sorry, Vaz. You can continue. It's just that you started to get balled up a bit."

"Okay. I'll be more direct. I think it's easier to begin with what we don't know for sure. We don't know whether Santiago is or isn't linked to Vitor." Vaz wrote the number 1 and summarized his declaration. "We're unsure whether Michele's kidnapping had noneconomic motives." He wrote the number 2 and summarized the statement. "We don't know if Vitor is or isn't involved in the Michele case." He wrote the number 3 and abbreviated the item. "We also don't know whether or not the FHP acted on behalf of Vitor in the disappearance or in the strange negotiation with Félix." He wrote the number 4 and divided the declaration into two parts, which he labeled A and B.

"And what is it that you *do* know?" asked the secretary.

"We know the FHP and Vitor came to an understanding, whether or not they're part of the same scheme; and we know that the lie that Félix was killed in Mineira is in Vitor's interest."

"I don't get it," the secretary admitted. "Why are you so sure that Vitor and the FHP came to an understanding?"

Vaz himself replied, picking up the argument. "Because the false news of Félix's murder in Mineira came over his own radio, after he was captured or after his encounter with the FHP. If that lie benefits Vitor, as we've seen—do you remember that Vitor made a point of answering Luizão on his office phone, which he knew we were monitoring? So then, if the lie benefits Vitor and was transmitted to Luizão by the FHP, it's because they came to an agreement, either before or after Félix disappeared and before any participation by Vitor in that disappearance, if there was any participation."

"That makes it clearer. It's clear to me now. And what about the organization you two spoke of? Is that the entity that swapped packages with the FHP? Is that exchange tied to Vitor and the taps on my telephones? And what about the leak of the kidnapping to the governor?"

"Relax, Mr. Secretary." Vaz resumed command of the presentation. "We're getting there slowly. Step by step."

Alice arranged the sheet, folded over the edge, fluffed the soft and generous pillow, and pulled the lamp nearer the headboard. Bath and face towels lay folded at the foot of the bed. Renata was sitting on the arm of the easy chair with Pedrinho's photo in her hands, letting her bare feet enjoy the shag rug. The friends had dedicated the past forty minutes to talking about children, about how Pedrinho was growing and how charming he was, and about a prerequisite for motherhood that complicated the project: fatherhood. They also talked about mutual friends and Renata's dog Tabatha, a basset temporarily sheltered through the kindness of her neighbor Doris. Now they were ready to get to sleep. The next day was approaching with its myriad of problems and tasks. A pity that the reunion of the two girlfriends couldn't have taken place under more auspicious circumstances. Renata's pain constituted a permanent obstacle. And it spilled over to Alice, affecting even the most lighthearted topics.

"Gee, Licinha. I'm embarrassed. So much attention and affection. I'm causing you so much trouble."

"Don't say that, girl. See if this nightgown fits you. Look here, pay attention: here's where you control the air-conditioning. It's central, but you can adjust the temperature to your liking. You can even turn it off if you want to."

Alice was doing everything she could to push back the darkness of Renata's drama, as if talking about practical things and trivialities would be enough to exorcise the demons.

"I think I will prefer that. I like to sleep with the window open. Air-conditioning dries me out. It doesn't agree with me."

"I used to be that way, before I started going out again. But I got used to it."

"We get used to anything."

"Nowadays I turn it on even when I'm by myself. Isn't that incredible?"

"Is it to feel closer to him?"

"No, I've actually just come to feel the heat much more than I used to. It seems a person's sensitivity adjusts, adapts. Even physical sensitivity. Isn't that incredible?"

"Yes, it is."

"My aesthetics professor says that couples grow more alike. Really alike. Physically. I think it was Bergman who originated that thesis."

"Who?"

"Ingmar Bergman."

"I don't know who that is."

"Wow, Natinha. Bergman. You don't know Bergman? The great Swedish director."

"I don't recall the name, no."

"He did so many things: *Wild Strawberries, Cries and Whispers, The Hour of the Wolf, Scenes from a Marriage* . . ."

"I haven't been to the movies in a long time, Licinha . . . When you talk that way, it makes me really depressed. I suddenly realize I'm falling behind. Life is passing me by and I'm dragging my feet. I feel so ignorant. Kind of empty, you know? People talk about cinema, theater, literature, politics. Even when it comes to politics I'm out of it. Me of all people, who used to be tuned in to it."

"I know. You think I don't know? I met you in the leadership committee. You belonged to the student movement."

"Now I'm so far removed from all that. It's as if I were in
exile. I feel like I'm in another world. Distant from the world
I used to frequent, from my friends, from my things. It seems
that the ship sailed without me."

"Hey, Natinha, that's silly. You've just shown me a photo
of your beautiful and wonderful child and now you tell me
the ship sailed without you, that you feel empty?"

"That's true. There's Pedrinho. If it weren't for him—"

"Except that he's not a detail. He's an entire world. You
have no idea, not the slightest idea, of how I would love to
have a child like Pedrinho . . ."

"As long as his father wasn't part of the package . . ."

The two friends laughed, took each other's hands and em-
braced. Renata cried copious tears, washing away the fear of
recent days, of recent years. The embrace became stronger.
Renata sobbed. Little by little, she recovered her composure.
Alice offered her a mild sedative that she usually took when
she was nervous, just to relax. Renata refused.

"How about some tea? Chamomile tea?"

"Tea? That sounds good."

The two went to the kitchen together. As they passed
through the hallway, discreet indirect lights went on automatically.

"Wow," said Renata. "That's the greatest. How chic can
you get, Licinha? Isn't your place the greatest? I've never seen
that before."

"That's my mother's crazy idea. She's got a nouveau-riche
complex."

"I'm different from her. I think I'm *nouveau-pauvre*."

They both laughed and Alice put water to heat on the electric range. Renata said, "Licinha, it's time I started rethinking my life, you know? I believe this horrible confusion is at least going to force me to stop a bit, look back, and look ahead. Rethink everything."

"That's so important, isn't it? I think so. I think we should always do that."

"Are you still in analysis?"

"Of course. How do you think I can put up with my mother's craziness and my father's insanity?"

"I'd love to go into analysis. I don't know, some kind of therapy."

"Are you still going to Ravi?"

"Who?"

"Our tarot reader. You introduced me to him."

"Never since then."

"I go there whenever I can. At least once every three months."

"Analysis and tarot reading?"

"Not to mention the spiritualist center I attend, there on the Rio-Manilha Highway."

"I don't believe it. You?"

"Yes, ma'am."

"I don't believe it, Licinha. You cross the Rio-Niterói Bridge, get on the Rio-Manilha—that's some trip, eh?"

"A longer trip's the one I take in another sphere, Natinha. The spiritual sphere."

"Fine. I'm not against it. Who am I to—huh. I think it's the coolest thing. It's just that I never thought you would . . . In fact, to tell the truth, maybe it's prejudice on my part. On some level I thought that rich people didn't need those things."

"'Umbanda* is just for poor people . . .'"

"Yeah, I know that's stupid, I know it's prejudice. But I admit that deep down—I hate prejudice, you know that. Prejudice of any kind. Even so, now and then I catch myself clinging to it."

"It happens to everybody. Even open-minded people. I myself admit that I don't understand how a person like you can spend her days, for years, in the middle of criminals in a penitentiary. It must be prejudice on my part, beats me."

"No, I understand. I used to think the same thing. When I passed the entrance exam, three years ago, I almost didn't take the job. I had just gotten my degree at PUC and you were finishing your freshman year. You'd finished the basic courses and were beginning your communications classes, remember? I was dying to find a job. I was already separated, and Pedrinho was big. I couldn't take living with my mother anymore, not having a place to call my own. On the other hand, I couldn't imagine having to go to Bangu every day. That's where it begins, doesn't it? A real martyrdom. Bouncing up and down in a bus. I mean, in several buses. Or driving the miserable car my salary would allow me to buy and keep running. Then the plunge into hell."

"But you've got some fucking courage. Seeing a woman

---

*Umbanda is a syncretic religion that arose in the early twentieth century in Rio de Janeiro and has spread to other parts of Brazil and to Uruguay and Argentina. It blends elements of Afro-Brazilian, Catholic, and Spiritist beliefs.—Ed.

like you I feel even more disgust when I think of those asshole macho types who give us a hard time, who see us as arm
candy, as scared airheads."

"It's not really a matter of courage. I don't know."

"Actually, Renata, you've always suffered from a Mother
Teresa complex. At least a little . . . Admit it. You changed
from psych and I thought you were going to go into communications, because you always had the greatest talent for jour-
nalism, that kind of thing, but what did you do? You went
into social work. Look here, Mother Teresa. The tea is ready."

"Thanks, Licinha. It's true. I do have a little of that.
Maybe it has to do with my family. I lost my father at an early
age. My mother always worked. Nothing was easy for us."

"But you're keeping things on an even keel, there in Bangu,
despite everything."

"More or less. I've learned to look on all of it with different eyes. Not that it isn't hell, but when you only see that side,
you tend to put one more brick in the wall and that wall will
make your life there hell. I can't explain it very well. Pity and
disgust aren't the best sentiments. They don't help change anything at all. They only reinforce everything that's bad. They
only serve to keep detractors well protected, a long way from
that filth, that garbage, that hell. Those feelings only serve to
expiate our guilt, Licinha. In practice, disgust and pity end up
shoving that reality down to the bottom of the well where it's
out of sight. So that it's a long way off and the stench it em-
anates doesn't contaminate our life, Licinha, or our values, our
superiority. Maybe someday I'll write about it."

"Have you thought about getting a master's? With your
brains you shouldn't stop studying."

"I know. I think about it a lot. Know what my dream is? To find a wonderful partner and leave Brazil for a little while. Study abroad, whatever. Go away for a time. Escape this suffocating day-to-day routine. To look at all this from a certain distance. To think about everything I've experienced. Did you know I've gathered a lot of interesting documentation over the years?"

"Maybe have another child . . ."

"Maybe so. Pedrinho needs a brother."

"And get far away from the outlaws."

"More or less. I wouldn't put it just that way. I don't like to talk like that, calling them outlaws, closing the lid and flushing."

"That's not what I'm saying, Renata."

"In a certain sense, it is. But never mind. Why sugarcoat the pill? That's what people really think. That's how society thinks. I thought and felt that way too, at the beginning. But over time I changed."

Renata pulled toward her a tin of cookies that Alice had offered her earlier, when she refused dinner. Alice fell silent and made random designs with her fingers on the kitchen table while her friend chewed hungrily. The hostess broke the silence.

"Gradually, you came to see them as human beings . . ."

"Yeah, but . . . That's not saying a lot, is it? It's our obligation to see people as human beings. That holds for everyone and everything. It ends up not meaning much. I don't know. I'm sort of intolerant with politically correct talk about human rights, about religion. To tell the truth, I consider it a pretty disgusting demagogic bore."

"But you were a militant in Viva Rio, that NGO on

human rights. Wasn't it Viva Rio? I remember you, up there on the quad, rallying people to the peace demonstration."

"Yes, it was. I remember too. And fondly. In fact, I owe a lot to Rubem Cesar* and Viva Rio. If it weren't for them, you think I'd have gotten the scholarship to PUC? Merely because of my lovely eyes? I owe them a lot of other things too. That was a great time. But I got fed up with speeches, symbols, pretty palaver, everybody all dressed up in white. 'The day of caring.' It doesn't work, Licinha. It doesn't work anymore. It's become ridiculous. My heart's somewhere else. Sometimes I even feel angry about it all. Hell is paved with good intentions. Everything's a long way off from reality, Licinha. In Brazil, reality is different, my friend. You want to know? Reality is fucking tough. Fucking tough. It's gunshots, blood, crap, brains scattered on the ground, mixed with fetuses in an open sewer. The state, politics, the police, justice, it's all one big fiction, Licinha. A fairy tale. It's right to call the prisoners criminals, of course; but it also isn't. I can accept calling them that as long as we agree to call the state a criminal too. And the justice system, the police, politics, all that crap. If it's not the same for all of them, then I disagree, because the outlaws in Bangu-I are no worse than the outlaws who arrested them. The society they grew up in made them what they are. This shitty society we live in, Licinha."

"Then there's no such thing as free will? Nobody chooses

---

*Rubem Cesar Fernandes, anthropologist, human rights activist, and director of the Viva Rio NGO based in Rio de Janeiro. He received a Ph.D. from Columbia University and has been a leader in efforts to control the proliferation of firearms in the hands of the public.—Ed.

anything? It's all society's fault? If it were like that, every poor person would be a criminal."

"It's beyond me. All I know is that those men who're caged up in maximum security and tortured and humiliated there, in that cage, are no worse than Pedro's father."

"That's it, Natinha. You put your finger on it. That's exactly what I thought: that you were talking about yourself. Not about society or institutions, but yourself. You had a horrible experience with a policeman, traumatic, but not every cop is like your ex-husband."

"Only every one I've met so far . . ."

"All of them?"

"All of them."

"My boyfriend too?"

"No. Of course not, Licinha. He's different."

"So then, it's not all of them."

"You're right. But he's an exception."

"Natinha, when he leaves in the morning, he sometimes says he may not return. Because he thinks he's going to die. Natinha, there are days when he leaves thinking about death. He takes three buses every day to go and return. He spends his nights at war and his mornings at the university. He supports his retired stepfather, who has heart problems and can't work, and his mother. He pays the rent, the condo fees, the food bills. There's almost nothing left over for him. He doesn't buy clothes, nothing. He doesn't drink or smoke. And not because of religion. He thinks it's his duty. He won't let me pay for anything. He avoids coming here, eating here, sleeping here. He doesn't even like to ride in my car. We only go out in his Fiat 1000. It's his car, but he doesn't have money for gas, so he only takes it out of the garage on weekends, for us to drive around in, Nati. You can't imagine how it pains him, and me, when we hear our classmates and professors talk about the police as if they were a gang of outlaws, the scum of society."

Alice paused, went to the refrigerator, and opened two beers. They drank, and she continued. "I don't know if you're aware of what they go through to get into the BOPE. Do you have any idea?"

"More or less."

"They suffer every kind of challenge. Mind and body are pushed to the limit. You can't calculate the suffering. There are people who have vertigo, fear of heights, but they don't spare anyone. To be accepted, you have to balance yourself on a kind of bar ten yards in the air, with no safety net. Did you know the candidates go through torture sessions?"

"No, but it doesn't surprise me."

"They're tortured: the parrot's perch,* the dragon chair, drowning, beatings. Even so, nothing's worse than the pain of being disdained by the others. They call that part of the test Charlie-Charlie."

"Charlie-Charlie?"

"It's the police way of saying CC."

"What's CC?"

"Concentration camp."

"God forbid. And you find that healthy?"

---

*The parrot's perch (*pau-de-arara*) was a torture device commonly used during the military dictatorship. The victim, usually naked, is suspended by the backs of his knees from a metal bar and his hands tied to his ankles. Electric shocks and beatings are then administered, often accompanied by waterboarding.—Ed.

"No, of course not."

"Do you find it healthy that your boyfriend was subjected to that? You think it's good for him to be a member of a group that's formed by such methods? Have you ever asked yourself how people who are trained by terror act? Won't they act by applying the same methods?"

"Renata, I don't know if there exists any other way of preparing a person to face what those men face. You can't forget that the insanity of training has another side: the better trained a policeman, the less likely he's going to risk his life and the lives of other people; the more responsible and efficient he's going to be. It does no good to demonize the training. It's done all over the world, independent of the political regime. I know it's insane. But we live in an insane world."

"I don't accept that, I can't accept it. I don't know what kind of efficiency we're talking about."

"Renata, I'm sure of one thing: they hate corruption. They risk their lives to do their duty and reject corruption in any form, under any circumstances."

"And you believe an island can withstand the force of the ocean?"

"How so?"

"You think the BOPE is going to remain immune to corruption for long, as part of a corps that's so profoundly degraded?"

"But it's not just the BOPE, Natinha. There are some very good people in the police. I hear beautiful stories every day."

"And what about police violence, Alice? The problem with the police isn't only corruption. It's also brutality. How do you feel about extermination? About torture?"

"You yourself criticized your former human rights comrades and now you're talking just like them. What about the extermination of policemen, Renata? And the traffickers' cruelty? It's okay for them to do it, because they're poor?"

"Alice, look what time it is. I have to get up before seven tomorrow. How do I go about leaving without waking you up?"

"Renata, you promised you wouldn't leave this apartment until this case was settled."

"For the case to be solved, I have to help. I can't stay here, waiting. Relax. You know I can watch out for myself."

"Promise to send word? At least that?"

"I promise."

OFFICE OF THE SECRETARY, OCTOBER 1, 1:45 A.M.

Amílcar took the floor and went over to the television as Vaz returned to his seat. He turned on the video and rewound the tape to the image of the handoff in the supermarket. He froze the sequence when, after Jaiminho rested his cart against a display case, an older man with a full head of gray hair appeared in the right-hand side of the frame.

"Watch carefully the face of that man, Mr. Secretary."

Amílcar went to the table, opened a yellow cardboard folder, and handed the secretary a small black-and-white photo.

"The man in the photo, Mr. Secretary, is the same one who appears in the video. His name is Carlos Meireles, a former National Intelligence agent and a retired army officer. No known current position. He was in the Brazilian Intelligence Agency some years ago. He returned to Rio, supposedly to take advantage of retirement. He frequently meets with some of his ex-colleagues. Colleagues with the same background, but not all are of the same age and not all of them were involved in the repression under the military regime. They don't mix with people from the police. That's an important point, Mr. Secretary. Another important piece of information: our sources in the police, who have proved to be quite reliable, swear that P2 and the intelligence service of the civil police have nothing to do with the wiretaps or the listening devices in your office or in the private elevator. In reality, the civil police intelligence service doesn't warrant that name. It's extremely precarious and has been kept on short rations, because it's not in the interest of any chief to reinforce a unit that can act independently and cause him headaches, one way or another, by blocking his actions or creating problems. The MP won its dispute with the civil police because of the privilege of driving your car and offering you personal security. For them, that was sufficient control over your movements and your relationships. They wouldn't dare do more than that, nor would they have operational conditions to go further."

"Did either of the police forces attempt to co-opt one or both of you? I must confess that I'm impressed with the competence of the two of you. The impression I had was different. I'll speak frankly: I thought you two were a couple of clowns."

"Think about it, Mr. Secretary," Vaz replied. "In the police, you have to be careful. No one shows his hand and everyone's very jealous of the hierarchies. We only display the level of competence that the situation demands. Being too shrewd backfires. In the police, it's even more so. As hard as it is to believe, the guy's ability can be fatal to his career. Better to look like an idiot than risk being considered a threat to your superiors. And as for co-optation, Mr. Secretary, the answer is no. Our story, mine and Amílcar's, is well known. We've already caused enough confusion in the two corps for someone to risk an approach that could—and would—signify a shot in the foot. Amílcar has been commander of the BOPE. He's commanded P2. He's done counterintelligence. He knows everything that goes on in the MP. He's had every opportunity in the world and has never wavered. Everyone knows he's serious. Even the politicians know it and don't mess with him. But everyone also knows he's prudent and doesn't bite if they don't provoke him. The risk he runs isn't that they'll try to co-opt him; it's that they'll kill him. But he's careful."

Vaz smiled and was interrupted by Amílcar. "What he just said about me, Mr. Secretary, I have to say about him."

"Let's put an end to this mutual admiration society and move on," said the secretary.

Amílcar resumed his explanation. "I was saying that neither the MP nor the civil police would have conditions for eavesdropping, nor would they take such a risk. And according to the reports from our informants, no one in either force is doing it. Just as no one in the police would have access to the governor. Now let's examine the hypothesis that the taps may have originated in the military office. The military office, Mr. Secretary, lacks the proper structure for such action and its ties to the corps are mainly institutional. Naturally, any head of the military office does everything possible to have the ability to replace the commander-general of the MP or the secretary of public safety. He uses personal contacts and does what he can to obtain classified information. But in our case it would be hard for anything to be done without

Colonel Fraga's knowledge, because he and Colonel Elpídio have a long-standing and deep relationship. They're old comrades from the academy days."

"Elpídio really doesn't seem like the kind of person who would do that," said the secretary. "By chance, I met Elpídio on a mission outside Brazil some time ago. We've always had an excellent relationship."

"Therefore, Mr. Secretary, excluding the two police forces and the military office, we're left with the hypothesis that the tap and maybe the leak are the work of that group, that—what'd we say?—clandestine organism."

"And what's this Santiago's role in the whole story?"

"We don't know where Santiago is now," said Vaz quietly. "We know we're not the only ones looking for him. But we don't have the slightest idea about his fate. Remember, Mr. Secretary, that if our hypothesis is correct, the hypothesis about Vitor's curious interest in Rocinha, he and Santiago would be partners."

"Vitor, Santiago, Luizão . . ." the secretary calculated.

"Not necessarily. It's not always tactically advisable to work with cohesive groups whose members know one another and share strategic information," said Vaz. "In general, Mr. Secretary, it's better to deal with a network, as leftist organizations normally did during the authoritarian regime."

"During the dictatorship, Vaz. Let's not mince words."

"In networks, Mr. Secretary, only one member of each segment establishes a connection with an element of the other segment. Networks aren't made up of agents who know one another. Knowledge is restricted to the confines of each segment."

"I know, Vaz. I'm familiar with that."

"Of course you are, Mr. Secretary, I'm just reiterating it for you to understand our analysis of the case. In networks, not even the leaders know everyone they're leading. It's safer that way. Networks are efficient, flexible, and secure, precisely because they're opaque on their horizontal and vertical axes—as you know very well. Therefore, we can't know whether Luizão knows that Santiago is connected to Vitor in this kidnapping story. He might, and he might not. Just as we don't know whether Santiago knows anything about the involvement of the FHP or even whether Santiago or Vitor knows about that organism's scheme."

"What about the governor, Vaz? How much does he know about all this?"

"That's something else we don't know, Mr. Secretary."

"Could he have seen the dossier they're putting together against him?"

"Probably," said Amílcar. "A blackmailer only has power to the extent that the one being blackmailed is aware of what the blackmailer has."

"But given the photos and the bank data, the tape of the impresario's wife is secondary," mused the secretary.

"Naturally."

"It's all precious ammunition," suggested Vaz.

"Who is this organism working for? If they exchange so much with the FHP, would that mean they're maintaining contact with the intelligence agency or with the federal government in some way?" asked the secretary.

"It doesn't appear that the personnel of that club, whatever it is, had contact with the intelligence agency, or at least, it's not linked to the agency. And I say this not *in spite of* the group's contacts with the FHP, but precisely *because* of those contacts," said Amílcar

"I don't understand," the secretary admitted.

"The FHP is completely beyond the federal government's control. In keeping with a political agreement signed some time back, its supervision was given to a deputy who charges dearly for his support of the federal government. A very independent and very powerful guy in the state, Ademar Caminha Viana Torres."

"Does he have ties to that group?"

"No proven ones, Mr. Secretary. But you never know."

"In any case, if the FHP has copies of those documents that compromise the governor, Deputy Viana Torres also has them," surmised the secretary.

"Probably so. I say probably because in this atmosphere of coups and traps, it's impossible to be sure, but Viana Torres likely needs some big card up his sleeve in order to negotiate future steps in his career or to shield himself against unpleasant future surprises."

"I know," agreed the secretary. "It's common for politicians to store up ammunition against one another and never use it. It's the logic of the Cold War. You stockpile arms to dissuade the enemy. If everybody threw shit into the fan, one against the other, no one would survive. Or almost no one."

"They have to think about collective survival, about the preservation of the species," added Vaz.

"That produces a certain equilibrium," said the secretary.

"An equilibrium under tension," added Amílcar.

"As long as the rope doesn't snap, I survive, I'm still the secretary. But, speaking frankly, after this night, one thing is very clear: What do I command? Gangs and groups of gangs and feudal barons and politicians. What kind of secretariat is that, Vaz? What kind of police are they? They're not institutions, they're battlefields. They're Persian bazaars. They're warring tribes. No one commands anything. Those police don't exist. This state isn't governable, Amílcar."

"I don't know, Mr. Secretary. I don't know. Perhaps it is, but only by someone who doesn't get caught up in blackmail."

"Someone who has nothing to hide," said the secretary. "Let's speak plainly. Is there such a person? If he exists, could such a person find his way into government? And if he did, wouldn't he have to stop being the person he is? Wouldn't he have to pay a price? Wouldn't he have to hide things? And, further, one honest person isn't enough. Things don't work that way. There'd have to be more than that."

"I don't know if there's any way out, Mr. Secretary. I hear people more experienced in politics ridiculing moralism, but they don't understand that in Rio moralism isn't a spiritual virtue, it's the minimum—and quite practical—condition for the government not to become a hostage."

"Do you think that people will one day understand that, Amílcar? What do you think, Vaz?"

"I think we've come a long way, that you've come a long way, and that now there's no way to retreat."

"But advancing would be naïve willfulness, Vaz, it'd be suicide. What support do we have for it? We're standing in quicksand."

Epilogue

I don't really know why I did it. I don't understand the impulse. But the fact is that I went to see the commander-general of the military police. I asked for an audience and he agreed to receive me. Perhaps the strangest fact wasn't my impulse but the colonel's receptivity. The MP exercises a curious attraction on its members. Even over those who've left, like me. I never stop thinking about the corps, my colleagues, the operations. Once it entered my life, the police force never left. I believe it never will. This book is proof of that. Even if it's also proof of the opposite—I mean, of my wish to free myself of the past. Maybe I still cherish the illusion that my story has become part of the history of the corps, and that I'm as embedded in the police as it is in me. Saying that, I can't help thinking about the knife embedded in the skull, the BOPE's coat of arms. I bet that type of symbiosis only happens with people who go through all the tests and become officers in the elite squad: each test a scar, or

several. The result is a kind of tattoo engraved on the body
and stuck to the soul. There's no washing it away. Just as the
guilt can't be washed away, or the pride erased.

"Is everything going well with you? Thank you for seeing
me, Colonel. I came to say a few words to you about the book
I'm writing. Yeah, the book about the police, about the BOPE.
Actually, the book's about me or about my experience in the
BOPE and in the police force in general. In any case, thanks
for your willingness to hear me. Not all of your predecessors
who've sat in that chair were willing to receive me, much less
listen to me. Even when I was on the job. As a matter of fact,
it's funny, if the others had shown that generosity, maybe I'd
still be in uniform. Anyway, Colonel, I'm going to put that sen-
timental talk aside, otherwise I'll get emotional and end up
making a scene. But you should understand. It's not easy to
come back here, come into headquarters, see the old colleagues
again, gawk at the new boys, climb those stairs in civilian
clothes, look at the old photos, the flags, smell the scent of varnished wood on the stairs. Sure, I'll get to the point. I know
you're in the middle of the workday, in a crossfire, with a million problems to solve, pressures from all sides, the governor
calling, the secretary on the line, the press on your tail, criti-
cism from every side, stray bullets, communities setting fire to
buses, outlaws burning buses. Okay, I'll get directly to the reason for my visit: I came because I don't want to hold your feet
or the institution's feet to the fire, Colonel. There's been
enough fire including friendly fire, if you get my meaning."

And I explained the sense and the intentions of the book.
I told the commander that truth sets people free. He even

smiled at that moment, probably thinking I was another convert.

"No, Colonel, I haven't become a Protestant. I really do believe that, but I'm not referring to religious or metaphysical truth, which is revealed to the faithful and demands faith. I'm speaking of that more modest truth that divides people into liars and straight shooters, the false and the sincere, the hypocritical and the authentic. Or that divides our comrades between imposture and loyalty, deceit and dignity, betrayal and fidelity."

I was going to continue, shifting my tone and speaking of the truth that separates institutions into the infamous and the legitimate, the corrupt and the lawful, but I stopped myself. I thought it would be an exaggeration, kind of bombastic, somewhat conceited. It would look like I was trying to lecture on morality or show off. Me of all people, who detests that sort of thing. The colonel doesn't like it either. He's a simple guy, like me. An intelligent guy, but simple. Besides which, if I continued down that road, I'd end up getting lost or, worse, going somewhere I didn't want to go. Because if I wound up where I didn't want to be, the thing would backfire on me.

All that effort to get an appointment, find an opening in the commander's schedule, be received, prepare the groundwork, create a favorable climate, everything would be lost. I wasn't there to open fire on the police as the lair of hypocrites, the den of the most outrageous lies. Just the opposite. I was there to put the commander's mind at ease. My intention was merely to tell the truth. Nothing more. Of course that's not a small thing. And of course the consequences could be serious. It's obvious that the truth would be shocking for someone who wasn't aware of it. But the shock would be therapeutic. After the storm, the calm.

In other words, the police have been a great lie that affects, first and foremost, the police themselves. Rip back the curtains and tear away the masks: there's nothing like the truth. A blessed remedy. And don't come to me with that line about how the wrong dose can kill the patient. If it does, so be it. Lots of people have already died in this game. What I can't accept is that we continue to play along with this farce in silence, pretending that nothing is going on.

Naturally I didn't say that. I mean, I did say it, but carefully, without the colonel realizing the explosive charge of what I was saying. Everything is a matter of approach. I feel I carried out my mission. So much so that I left there reinvigorated, with my soul cleansed, with a sensation of relief. He thanked me for the attention and asked me to take care with each word of what I was going to relate. He mentioned the responsibilities, the public image of the institution, and all the rest.

"Very well, my friend. So then, use your judgment, and good luck."

I thanked him again for the opportunity to meet with him and touched my forehead with the back of my right hand, automatically. Some things that were of the police are still mine, to this day. I turned on my heels and retreated.

In the waiting room of the office, I was closing the door behind me when Laerte saw me and spread his arms. Major Laerte was an old comrade from years ago. He was in the

BOPE more or less at the same time as me. Not too long ago I heard he'd been promoted to legal counsel of the general command. I was impressed.

"Man, you're looking good . . . When's your next promotion? I want to see you make light colonel by the end of the year, you hear?"

I was speaking sincerely. I always liked Laerte. He was a very decent guy.

"Ah! It's great to see you here. What brings you to the commander-general's office? You're not going to tell me you plan to unretire?"

"No, Laerte, I wouldn't do anything like that even if it were possible. The best decision I ever made was to leave the MP."

"Shit, don't tell me you're here to spit in the plate you ate out of? You were always the most gung-ho of the group. Nobody took the police as seriously as you. And now you tell me leaving was the best thing?"

"That's it exactly, Laerte. What can I do? I won't lie to you."

"Fine, okay. I understand you don't want to come back. I was just kidding around to rattle your cage. But, speaking of which, now that I've run into you, I'd like to have a little chat with you. Something quick. Got a few minutes?"

"Shit, Laerte, just tell me. It's like you don't even know me. Just because I left the MP doesn't mean I stopped being who I am, man. Since when have you ever had to make an appointment to talk to me?"

"Cool. Then let's sit on that sofa there. With any luck, the commander's adjutant or the chief of staff will bring us some coffee."

I followed Laerte to the sofa, unbuttoned my coat and sat down beside him. The waiting room was in penumbra, a pleasant temperature—the privileges of command. At the moment it was empty, which was in fact really unusual. My friend put it in second gear and began his petition.

"Shit, man, what I wanted to tell you is this: they've been saying you're writing a book about the police." He stopped and looked at me. I went on looking at him, silently.

"Yeah," he continued. "That's what I heard."

He looked at me and I looked back, in silence.

"Is it true, man?"

"Yeah, Laerte, it's true."

"They say you're going to throw shit into the fan . . ."

Silence here, silence there. Eye to eye.

"Is it true?"

I remained silent, looking my friend in the eye.

"Say it, Laerte, c'mon. Don't beat around the bush, man. Say what you came to say. Or maybe you think I think our meeting was accidental, that you just happened to be passing through the waiting room just as I was leaving . . . Jesus, Laerte, I'm not a child. I hung up the uniform, not my brain. So, what's the word?"

"Okay, man. I have nothing to do with your life. Who am I to tell you what to do? Besides that, you're a big boy now. But it can't hurt to share a few concerns with you. Will it bother you if I lay out some considerations about it?"

"Say right now what you want to say, Laerte. Stop pissing around. You're going to talk in any case. You think I don't know you?"

"Fine. Here's what it is, man: think hard about it. Shit, man, think long and hard. Understand what I'm saying? I'm asking you to give a lot of thought to what you're going to do."

He was looking at me and at the entrance door. At any moment someone could come in. Evidently he didn't want to be interrupted. Maybe that's why he was speaking in a low voice, as if we were conspiring. I was hoping someone would come in soon. The conversation was making me nervous.

"I understand you resigned in a complicated way; I know the police force didn't do right by you; of course I know what you went through in here, man. But shit, think about it. What good is revenge going to do? Why write out of bitterness? You're only going to reinforce your image of resentment and give ammunition to those who're out to get you. They're going to say 'See? He deserved it all. He wasn't worth a damn. This proves it.' You're only going to confirm that those sons of bitches were right when they persecuted you on the force."

I went on listening, my eyes fixed on the small table in front of us. I was making an effort not to get irritated and to understand that, after all, maybe Laerte really was speaking as a concerned friend. It was funny. I'd gone to the general command precisely to talk about my theme, to speak my piece. Everything had gone swimmingly with the commander-general, much to my surprise. And then, seconds before the end of the second half, when I was already on my way out, when I was least expecting it, an old friend shows up with the bullshit I thought I was already free of. Laerte seemed to be rushing ahead. He picked up momentum.

"So then, man, why write a book? You've got so many more

interesting things to do. And also, think about your friends, your old comrades. Shit, man, if you tell everything, like they're saying in the hallways, where does that leave us? How can I face my father, my wife, my son? They're going to read your book and question me. One day my son is going to ask me, 'Dad, how could you work for an institution like that?' What am I going to tell my family, my son, man? And what's going to happen to the image of the corps, which has already taken so many hits? You're going to be the end of it. You'll bring everything crashing down. What'll become of us? I'm talking about your friends, man, your comrades."

At that moment, the door opened and Colonel Ariosto, with his baritone voice, entered as if landing at Normandy. That was his style—something that had become folklore in the MP. He was like an ambulance breaking through a procession. He was accompanied by the commander-general's aide-de-camp, who asked him to wait a moment—the commander would see him shortly—and left again.

I stood up before Laerte.

"Colonel. It's been a long time," I said. Laerte and I asked how he was as a formality, without expecting a reply.

Ariosto greeted me warmly when he saw me. He was simpatico. An expansive, friendly guy. He was loved by everyone. Or almost everyone, because in the police there's no such thing as unanimity. I had worked with him during the good years. We always got along well. He had come today from the interior of the state, where he commanded a battalion, for an audience with the commander-general.

"You know I'm here laughing, joking around, but my heart

is heavy. A very unpleasant situation." He paused to wipe the sweat from his brow with his basketball player's hand, which looked more like a tennis racket. "My heart, deep down, is heavy. A truly disagreeable situation. I'm here to say hello to the commander-general. To thank him. He was always very correct with me. Always. Even now, he's done what he could . . . I've lost the command of the battalion." He tightened his lips and shook his head, confirming what he'd just said. "I've lost the command. What can you do? That's life, my friends. That's how our police are."

He placed his hand on my shoulder. I thought he was going to change the subject and ask about my life. But he was focused on his lost command. "That's right, Major"—he looked at Laerte—"Captain." He looked at me, then continued: "Day before yesterday, Colonel José Henrique came to see me. He wanted my support. He's going to run for deputy. I was frank. You know that I'm frank. I said I couldn't. I'd like to, but I couldn't. I had already promised the mayor, who got me the position as commander and who'd advised me he was running also. What could I do? I couldn't do a thing. A promise is a promise, isn't it? A debt's a debt. I thought Zé Henrique had understood. But the next day I was informed that the government—the secretariat—needs my position. They gave me a week to get out of the city and prepare the way for my replacement. A week. The commander-general did everything he could to stop it. I know he did. The possible and the impossible. It didn't do any good. You know how politics is, my friends. Politics is shit."

Ariosto squeezed my shoulder and patted me on the

back. Then he added, "I feel—I can't put it into words. You know . . ." He took a deep breath.

"I feel betrayed. After all, you're a witness, aren't you, Laerte? I was always loyal, always faithful. Every single month I brought to the office their seven thousand reais. Never missed. Did I ever miss, Laerte? I never missed. I mean, there was that problem in April. I only brought four thousand. I needed three for some work at home. But it was only that one month. I never missed. I'm a guy who honors his commitments. I'm a loyal, faithful guy. To Zé Henrique too. I personally delivered his money to him every month, religiously. It would come to me and I'd pass it along to him. Is that the truth or not, Laerte?"

Laerte kept his head lowered. He stared at the worn carpet. The aide-de-camp came back into the room and told Ariosto the commander-general was ready to see him.

"Men, it was good to see you. Good luck."

Ariosto said good-bye with handshakes and went forward in a sudden movement that seemed like an infantry thrust.

Laerte took me by the arm and pulled me to a corner opposite the door. Almost in my ear, after checking that the room was empty, he whispered, "Shit, man, write that fucking book now. Publish that piece of shit right away."

ACKNOWLEDGMENTS

I am grateful to Isa Pessoa and José Padilha, my partners since the conception of this project. I owe Domingos de Oliveira, Denise Bandeira, and Gideon Boulting for fundamental lessons. I have tried to apply what they taught me in this book.

For their unwavering solidarity I thank my family and friends, especially Candido Mendes, Eugênio Davidovich, Gildo Marçal Brandão, André Corrêa, Antônio Carlos Carballo Blanco, Carlos Alberto D'Oliveira, Carlos Furtado, Carlos Henrique de Souza, Renato Lessa, Ricardo Benzaquen, Luiz Jorge Werneck Vianna, José Eisenberg, Maria Alice Resende Carvalho, Leilah Landim, Helio R. Santos Silva, Eduardo Martins, Otavio Velho, Marcos Cavalcanti, Roberto DaMatta, and Sonia Giacomini.

To Maria Isabel Mendes de Almeida, a very special note of gratitude and affection.

To my partners Celso Athayde and M.V. Bill I owe fraternal loyalty and the example of commitment, courage, and leadership.

My recognition goes to Miriam Guindani for so many critical readings and inspiring suggestions throughout the process of writing, and for her persistent confidence, even when it wasn't reasonable to confide.

Luiz Eduardo Soares

I thank above all God for my being alive to tell this story; I thank the troop that never retreated; and my three inspirations for returning home—my mother, my wife, and my goddaughter—and all those who recognize the importance of special operations and understand their constitutional role in furthering public safety.

André Batista

My most sincere gratitude to my whole family.

Rodrigo Pimentel

ABOUT THE AUTHORS

LUIZ EDUARDO SOARES holds a Ph.D. in political science and is a professor in the Department of Social Sciences at the State University of Rio de Janeiro. He has been a visiting scholar at Harvard University, Columbia University, the University of Virginia, the University of Pittsburgh, and the Vera Institute of Justice in New York. He is the author of fifteen books and coauthor of an additional thirty. Professor Soares has been National Secretary of Public Safety (2003) of the State of Rio de Janeiro, Coordinator of Public Security, Justice, and Citizenship of the State of Rio de Janeiro (1999–2000); Undersecretary of Public Security of the State of Rio de Janeiro (1999–2000); and Municipal Secretary of Human Rights and Violence Prevention of Porto Alegre (2001). He is currently Municipal Secretary of Violence Prevention of Nova Iguaçu.

ANDRÉ BATISTA is a major in the Military Police of the State of Rio de Janeiro. He was a member of the BOPE from 1996 to 2001. He completed the course for officers of the Rio de Janeiro military police and did postgraduate work in political science and security at the Fluminense Federal University. He is a graduate of the law school of PUC, the Catholic University of Rio de Janeiro. He is currently the Municipal Undersecretary of Violence Prevention of Nova Iguaçu.

RODRIGO PIMENTEL was a member of the Military Police of the State of Rio de Janeiro from 1990 to 2001. He served as a captain in the BOPE from 1995 to 2000. He holds a postgraduate degree in urban sociology from the State University of Rio de Janeiro (UERJ). He has been a columnist for the *Jornal do Brasil,* coproducer of the documentary *Bus 174,* and co-scriptwriter for the film *Elite Squad.* He is now a security consultant.